---- ★ ----

I took one careful step sideways, and Bo slid in beside me. Sunlight flooded across the awesome array of gauges and gadgets on the dashboard, the nifty little laptop cantilevered above it and the complex gearshift box on its high console between the seats. In the brightness we could see, with merciless clarity, the gory mess of blood and tissue and bone fragments that had turned John Dietz's fancy new tractor into a slaughterhouse.

The biggest splash of blood and tissue seemed to be concentrated around the front doorpost on the passenger's side. The glass on both sides of it had been cleaned off, but blood had soaked the door padding and the seat, the floor in back and the covers on the bunk. Blood had run down the door in streaks and pooled on the doormat, and the passenger's seat was black with blood.

"Some above your head, too," Bo said. I looked up. A double track of tiny blood spatters marched across the ceiling.

"Now look at that." I twisted my neck half off to get the picture. "It looks like the blood spatters we found on the overpass."

---- ★ ----

"...an entertaining, well-researched police procedural with an interesting cast of characters and an intriguing regional setting."

—*The Mystery Review*

Elizabeth Gunn

FIVE CARD STUD

WORLDWIDE.®

TORONTO • NEW YORK • LONDON
AMSTERDAM • PARIS • SYDNEY • HAMBURG
STOCKHOLM • ATHENS • TOKYO • MILAN
MADRID • WARSAW • BUDAPEST • AUCKLAND

FIVE CARD STUD

A Worldwide Mystery/July 2001

Published by arrangement with Walker Publishing Company, Inc.

ISBN 0-373-26389-9

Printed in U.S.A.

Acknowledgments

Thanks are due to many people who contributed information to this book. Any errors are mine, not theirs.

Chief Roger Peterson of the Rochester, Minnesota, police department, gave me unstinting help in the description of gunshot wounds and autopsies. At the Bureau of Criminal Apprehension in St. Paul, I am indebted to Gary Kaldun for an overview of blood spatter analysis and DNA testing. Jim Jerylo, an investigator for the Minnesota lottery, explained Powerball to me; Dave Thomson, of Thomson Consulting, introduced me to paperless record keeping; and Mary Jo Pappas generously shared her family's comprehensive knowledge of the village of Mantorville. For insider knowledge of long-haul trucking, I have to thank Michael Killough, terminal manager for Consolidated Freightways in Tucson, Arizona; Linda Kushnieruk, controller for Southwest Peterbilt of Tucson; and Jeff McConnell of Elgin, Minnesota, who drives one of the big rigs from Minnesota to Texas and back, every week.

ONE

"LET'S SEE, NOW," Darrell said, "has everybody got three cards?"

"One, two, three," Rosie said. "Yessir, three cards."

"What a coincidence," Kevin said. "I have three cards also. How about you, Lou?"

"I have exactly three cards," Lou said, "no more, and certainly no less."

"Okay, you guys," Darrell said. "Make fun of me for being careful."

"What makes you think we're making fun of you?" Rosie said. "We're just trying to help."

"And as soon as you master this counting thing," Lou said, squinting into the wavering blue light, "we'll give you a boost with your ABCs."

"Hey, my spelling's just as good as yours is," Darrell said, "for all intensive purposes." His iron-pumper's shoulder muscles bulged under his T-shirt as he slid a card carefully off the top of the deck and laid it faceup in front of Rosie Doyle.

"Seven of clubs, now isn't that sweet?" Rosie smiled smugly at the pair of sevens lying next to her ace. Her expression plainly indicated that she had a second ace in the hole. She dropped five one-dollar chips into the pot from the fistful she was holding. Her brothers must have taught her to wear that infuriating smirk when she plays poker; I've never seen her look like that anyplace else. Her other favorite trick is holding that stack of chips in one hand, as if she can't wait to raise the bet again. Rosie likes to win.

Kevin, on Rosie's left, had a jack and a ten showing, got a five, shrugged amiably, and folded. His handsome Eagle Scout face looked oddly exotic in the flyblown funkiness of Lou's rumpus room. The table light was an unshaded seventy-five-watt bulb in a white ceramic fixture nailed to the rafters, augmented by an old beer sign hanging on a stud. It featured a voluptuous woman in filmy lingerie holding a long-neck bottle of beer, reclining above a length of blue neon tubing that spelled out *Pabst lue Ribbon*. Power arced across the missing *B* with a nervous buzz like a fly caught in flypaper.

Darrell dealt me a six of diamonds, which fit very well with the rest of my lousy hand: a four of spades and a three of hearts. I called, because my hole card was the seven of diamonds, and it amused me to stay in the game and pretend, for a few minutes, that I had the kind of luck that would ever, in this universe, fill an inside straight.

It wasn't a high rollers' game, anyway, just a monthly amusement Kevin and I had ginned up last summer to create a little camaraderie in my newly assembled investigative team. We had promised each other we would keep it simple: no sandwiches, no housecleaning. We split the cost of cards and a few boxes of dollar chips, which we agreed were worth a dime in this game. Every month we chipped in two bucks apiece for snacks that we took turns buying in a Circle K on the way to the game.

Originally we played in my apartment, which was grubby but spacious, since I owned hardly any furniture. After I moved to the country, for a couple of months we borrowed one end of the teachers' lounge at Northside High. The chairs were comfortable, but a lot of our ritual razzing was drowned out by the rhythmic thump of Sunday night basketball practice overhead. Tonight we had moved to Lou's house so he wouldn't have to take his asthma out in the winter's first blizzard. Heavy snow had been falling all day; high winds and a temperature of twenty below were forecast by midnight.

"Oh, just look at that pair of ladies," Lou crowed, as Darrell dealt him a queen. "Yes Lord, we are starting to cook now." He had a second queen showing, and a ten; he blew a kiss to his hole card and tossed five chips into the pot. "I'll see your five and—" he added five more "—raise you five. Let's get some money in this game, make it interesting." He beamed triumphantly at Ray Bailey, who sat on his left looking sad.

Ray can't help looking sad. His mournful expression is a family trait; he has a long, sallow face and tragic eyes. A tableful of Baileys can empty the rowdiest bar in town in just a few minutes. Ray looked worse, of course, as we all did, in the dim light of the basement, where Lou, in a rare attempt at home improvement, had nailed some studs to a section of the cement floor, hung pegboard on the studs, and sprayed red paint haphazardly over all. He put in an old dining room set, hung up his tacky collection of ancient flyspecked beer signs, and started calling the space "my rumpus room." It smelled like the laundry machines on the other side of the partition, and the poor light gave everybody eyestrain. Ray called it "Lou French's Last Erection."

Ray got a deuce, which gave him a pair of deuces and an ace showing. After a lot of pondering, during which Lou implored him to piss or get off the pot, Ray reluctantly pushed ten chips to the middle of the table and stayed in the game.

Darrell dealt himself a four of clubs, which he laid alongside the ten of hearts and eight of diamonds he already had showing, and said, "Now let's see, what have I got?"

"Goddamn little, unless your hole card has magical powers," Lou said.

Mamie French clattered down the bare wooden stairs into the basement, carrying a cordless phone. "Dammit, Lou!" She brought it to the table and shoved it at her husband. "You gotta remember to bring this thing down here! I was way upstairs at the quilting frame—"

Lou touched her arm, said, "Sorry, Mame," and began to cough. He whooped helplessly into his left hand, holding the phone at arm's length with his right. Mamie, instantly silenced, watched him intensely, like a scientist observing some carefully thought-out experiment. After a few seconds she took a small respirator out of her jeans and moved a step closer to him. He shook his head and began some sort of self-control exercise behind his hand. Mamie watched. When his breathing returned to its normal heavy wheeze, she laid the respirator on the table and went back upstairs without another word.

Lou punched a button and said, "French." He listened a minute and said, "Jake's right here. Just a minute," and handed the phone across the table to me.

My inner wimp wailed, Leave me alone, it's Sunday night! but I kept my voice neutral when I said, "Hines."

The muffled uproar of the dispatch desk reached out to me, compelling attention, blotting out the game. Three or four voices were issuing commands, "See the man at One-one-two-two Third—" "Neighbor reports possible burglary in progress—" "Officer needs help, there's a fight going on in the intersection at—" Each voice was quiet and civil but insistent, pouring out rapid-fire information while the computer keyboards thumped a relentless undercurrent. A desk phone rang endlessly in one of the empty offices just outside the door.

"We have a DOA," Woody said. "I got a nine-one-one call, motorist said somebody's lying in the snow by the street. I sent Hanenburger, he reports a dead male. He's yellin' for a detective to come right away, says he's freezin' his ass off by the Twenty-ninth Street overpass. Nobody left me the duty list for investigators, who'm I s'posta call?"

Seven years ago, when I first made detective, off-duty calls were rare, and assigned haphazardly, often according to who was easiest to find. Then Rutherford entered a growth spurt, crime kept pace, and dodging the phone on weekends became an art form. When the chief put me in charge of the division last summer, the first thing I did was make a schedule for after-hours calls. Investigators take nights and weekends in rotation, no excuses unless you or your loved ones are near death. I post the lists every Friday, without fail, one on the bulletin board outside my office and one at the dispatch desk. The first detective who fails to copy the list has been promised a return to uniformed duty on straight nights, split between the recycling plant and the city dump.

"C'mon, Woody," I said, "it's on the bulletin board behind you where I always put it. Somebody must have pinned something on top of it."

"I been through everything twice," Woody said.

Then I remembered: last Friday was New Year's Eve. About four-thirty, the support staff had sprung a little surprise party in the department, featuring noisemakers and double-strength eggnog. This week's list was locked in my office, still on the clipboard where I left it when Schultzy's conga line snaked through my office and gathered me up. Clever office techies. Careless Jake.

"You don't see it there anyplace, huh?" I knew he didn't. My mind groped for cover. "Well, shit, then—" I tried to sound vexed but generous "—just give it to me, I'll handle it."

"Okay, ready?" As always, Woody was anxious to download. Dispatchers guard their short-term memories like precious jewels, needing to keep them clear for the massive amounts of information they channel every shift. "Location is section fifteen, Burton Hills Drive under the Twenty-ninth Street overpass. Where the river and the drive go under Highway Fifty-two there? Victim is white male, maybe thirty, cause of death unknown but he might've froze to death because he's almost naked, I guess."

In January, in a blizzard? "Motorist called it in, Hanenburger took the call, Cooper was backup."

"You called for paramedics?"

"No. Hanenburger said, 'Fixed eyes, not breathing, and his hands and face are black.' He said, 'Believe me, this guy's dead, he's stiff as a board,' so I called you.''

"Okay. Thanks." He gave me the computer-generated Initial Crime Report number that would follow this case wherever it went. I wrote it down, punched the Off button, and looked around the table. Rosie was smiling at her cards. Darrell was rearranging his hand as if he'd just noticed some new combination. Other guys fill inside straights, I thought. It could happen to me.

"What's up?" Lou asked.

"Got a DOA out northwest." I stood the phone carefully on the end table by the bean dip, searching my memory desperately.

"Damn! Well, who's got the duty?" Lou's expression became uncomfortable as he realized he could not remember copying the list. "Who'd he say was s'posta take it?"

"Seems like those turkeys mislaid the duty roster." Once planted, my lie had taken root and now was growing unchecked.

"Aw, that's bullshit! Well, who's got a copy?" He looked around the room again. "I didn't bring mine down here, I guess." They were all sitting there, looking at each other.

"I musta left it home," Kevin said, patting his pockets. "Let's give it to Bo; he's not here to defend himself." Everybody laughed, but they all knew Bo stayed home because his wife was sick.

They looked at each other again, and then Rosie said, "You know, Jake, I don't remember seeing a duty list on Friday before we started that par—"

"Okay," I said hastily, "We'll just have to draw

for it." Everybody groaned. "Come on, one of us has to get out there, Hanenburger's freezing his balls."

"Good, they need cooling off," Rosie said, and everybody laughed again. Hanenburger must have been hitting on her while she was still on patrol.

"Here we go, low card takes the call." I put the deck in the middle of the table.

Rosie drew a queen and smiled that infuriating Mona Lisa smile.

Ray got a ten, Kevin turned over a six. Darrell drew a king, looked up at Rosie, and laughed. Lou reached toward the pack, but I pushed his hand away. "Too cold tonight, Lou." He opened his mouth to protest but closed it again. He had six months to go till full retirement and had reluctantly accepted that we were all trying to get him through his last working winter alive. I took the next card. It was a five.

"Poor Jake," Rosie said, not sorry for me at all.

"Hey," I said, "No sweat."

"For sure," Lou said. "Temp's droppin' fast out there. Better lace up your booties."

"Don't forget the pot, though," Darrell said, "You've got some money in there."

"Jake can take back what he put in," Ray Bailey said, suddenly relaxed and casual, "and the rest of us can go ahead and play this hand. Can't we? We've all still got our cards." His eyes glittered for an instant as they all agreed; then he lowered his long lashes and looked gloomy again.

Climbing the rickety stairs out of Lou's playroom, I told myself, not for the first time, that I would never make a poker player. I had been watching Rosie and Lou, waiting to see which one of them was going to take my money, and all the while Ray Bailey must have had an ace in the hole, or maybe even a third deuce, and was sitting there, looking unhappy, ready to pounce.

Unlocking my pickup in Lou's driveway, I could feel the cold already nipping at my cheeks and ears. I unplugged my head bolt heater from the eight-socket grid at the front of Lou's garage, checking carefully to be sure I hadn't knocked anybody else's plug loose. If somebody's engine froze up before the game ended, Lou might find himself hosting an impromptu sleepover, and I would hear rude adjectives attached to my name for a week.

Climbing into my frigid pickup, still mentally replaying my abandoned poker hand, I realized suddenly that the unlucky low card that had awarded me this assignment had been the five that would have filled my inside straight, and I laughed out loud. My breath froze to the windshield.

The motor started promptly, that was something. I shoved the defroster lever as high as it would go and turned on the power to the rear window heat grid. While I waited for a quarter inch of frost to melt, I pulled on a knit cap and leather gloves, wrapped my wool muffler higher on my neck, and tucked the ends inside my coat.

A peephole opened slowly above the steering wheel. When it was twice the size of a silver dollar, I backed into the street and turned west, peering out of my icy foxhole into the brilliant tube my headlights carved in the dark. Then another vehicle turned into the street at the west end of the block and came toward me. As soon as his lights hit the ice castles on my windshield, I was blind.

I pulled over to the curb, shifted into park, and left

the motor running. I found my scraper in the glove compartment and got out, clutching it grimly. A mysterious fact, well known to citizens who live north of the forty-third parallel, is that ice scrapers, once dropped into snowbanks, disappear forever. No amount of digging locates them, and somehow they're gone by spring.

It took five minutes to clear the driver's side. While I worked, the motor warmed the truck body just enough to release a couple of gallons of dirty snow from the underside of the front fender and drop it in my boot. I shook my foot several times, which packed most of the snow firmly around my ankle.

Stomping uncomfortably around the truck to clear the right side, I paused to admire the wet stripes of clear glass appearing around the wire gizmos in my rear window. It was my first winter with this pricey pickup, and I was watching for any signs of superior performance that would ease the monthly pain in my wallet. So far my list included good radio speakers, plenty of space in the back for trash, and a rear window defroster that was fast and thorough. Otherwise this vehicle was doing just what the old one had: hauling me back and forth between my house and my job.

As soon as I was rolling again, I found my phone in my briefcase and called the coroner. He answered at the end of the first ring, "Pokornoskovic." I can say his last name, too, if I concentrate, but I never quite get the Ukrainian gutturals right. Most Rutherford cops won't even try it; they just call him Pokey.

"Jake Hines. Got a treat for you."

"Aw, Crimeny Moses," he said, giving American slang his usual thirty-degree tweak, "you ain't out findin' stiffs in this weather?"

"Just one. And you said it right, he's frozen stiff. Sounds like he might have died of hypothermia; he's almost naked, according to Woody."

"Uh-huh. You ever see one before?"

"No. Read about it is all." Minnesota cops and paramedics are expected to know the stages of hypothermia, including the final one, when the victim often feels warm and takes off his clothes.

"You sure he's dead? I seen 'em come back from what looks like corpse."

"Fixed eyes," I recited. "Apnea. Hands and face are black."

Pokey sighed. "Okay. Where you want me?"

I gave him the location and punched Off, put the phone down, and turned cautiously onto Broadway, watching for lights through the fog on my side window. I didn't want to open the window and dump all the air I had been warming for ten blocks.

Usually South Broadway, even on Sunday, has a fairly raffish air after dark, but tonight, at nine-fifteen, it was almost empty. Bar signs made fuzzy clumps of color through halos of frost. The thermometer on the First National Bank flashed minus twelve degrees. I punched the speed dial for the chief's house and waited, listening to three rings over a distant, tinny conversation bouncing off the Heaviside layer from a truck driver in Texas. Then Frank yelled, "Mc-Cafferty," above a great clatter of music and voices.

"Jake Hines," I shouted into the din, and Frank said, "Wait—" and set the phone down so hard it hurt my ear. A few seconds more of loud conversation and barking dogs came over the phone before he picked up again in a quieter place, saying, "Whee.

There. Go ahead,'' and somebody crashed the first phone back into its cradle.

"If you're busy with a riot—"

"Aw, Sheila's birthday, is all. But everybody came from both sides." Frank and his wife both have huge family clans, and they're creating another one of their own. I try not to listen to his descriptions of weekends. "What's up?"

"I'm on my way to look at a DOA. It's probably just a frozen drunk, but in case something looks funny—we're gonna stick to this new rule, right, that if we call BCA for help with a homicide, we get them to do the autopsy as well as the lab work?"

"Sure. You bet. Why not?"

"Just that they're very backed up right now, and there may be quite a delay," I said. He didn't ask me where I got that information. He knew I was splitting the rent on a farmhouse with Trudy Hanson, the photographer and fingerprint analyst at the state crime lab.

"Maybe so, but if it looks like a homicide, then you know we're gonna want their lab work. And they say if they're gonna handle the evidence, they wanna start with the body. Which seems reasonable to me. I know Pokey doesn't like it, but that's just tough titty. Pokey's not a forensic pathologist, he's a dermatologist with a part-time coroner's license, and I can't justify having him handle sensitive evidence when there's better help available."

"I wasn't thinking about him," I said, although I was, a little. Pokey got pretty outraged, last summer during the Rowdy's Bar case, about "goddamn fascist bureaucrats" invading his turf. "Just wanna be sure

I know what my options are, before I get there and say the wrong thing.''

"Okay, let's go over it again. If you're pretty sure you got a homeless person who fell down drunk and froze, something like that, get Hampstead County to put him in their morgue overnight, and in the morning we'll get Pokey to confirm the cause of death. But if you got any reason to think it's homicide, call BCA.''

"Gotcha." I put the phone down on the seat and pulled my 35-millimeter camera and flash out of the glove compartment. If it turned out we were handling this DOA by ourselves, I'd want to take a few pictures. I dropped the camera in the inside pocket of my jacket, felt how cold it was, and remembered the manufacturer's admonition: warm it up too fast in very cold weather, you'll fog up the lens. So I pulled it out of there and dropped it on the seat, just as I made the wide turn onto Burton Hills Drive. A broad new express road that hopscotches on pilings across a grid of older streets to reach the new developments at the northwest edge of town, it's busy at rush hours and almost empty after dark. Four costly lanes of new concrete glittered under a glaze of ice. Snowplows had windrowed three-foot snowbanks along the curb, and now a rising wind blew them in white streamers back across the street. Occasional gusts threw whirl-winds of snow up to halo the streetlights.

I speed-dialed Milo Nilssen's home number. He answered before the first ring ended. One thing about this lousy weather, most people were staying close to the phone.

"Nilssen?" He put a funny little question mark after his name, as if he were looking for somebody to confirm his identity. Milo's self-esteem seemed to have shriveled, not grown, since his sudden jump to acting county attorney last September. His former boss had departed suddenly during a scandal, and even though nobody was blaming Milo, the sudden weight of responsibility had made him jumpy and defensive.

"Jake Hines. I'm on my way to look at a DOA out on beautiful breezy Burton Hills Drive. You wanna come out and play with me?"

"Oh, hey, that's really thoughtful of you, Jake. I mean it's only about twice as cold as a witch's tit out there tonight, right? Whaddya got? Homicide?"

"Don't know for sure. Possible. But probably hypothermia because the body's way out on the edge of town wearing hardly any clothes."

"Ah-*hah*. A clue. You haven't seen it yet, huh?"

"No. But I promise you, I'm not going to take any longer than necessary deciding what to call it. It's twelve below downtown, and out here it's starting to blow. Not a good night to stand around and speculate. So if you want somebody from your office to view the scene, you better be sending him soon."

"I hear you." He took down the address, sighed, and said, "Hell, I'll probably come myself. It's easier than chasing down my joy boys on a Sunday night." Milo had been given a staff of three newly graduated attorneys, shanghaied out of various other county offices, to help him through his transitional phase as acting CA. The county paid them peanuts and expected donkey's labor. Milo was supposed to make it work.

As I punched Off, I saw the two squads, far ahead and downslope from me, parked close to each other with their headlights blazing into the underpass. Their roof lightbars flashed a jittery message of trouble into the night. Battery-powered caution lights blinked, four ahead and four behind. Two officers were stringing crime scene tape around something on the ground.

TWO

I PULLED PAST the squads, made a U-turn on the other side of the bridge, came back, and parked just inside their caution lights, on the wrong side of the street facing the other two cars, so that I added my headlights to theirs. A dark shape bulged under the tarp they had spread by the road. I dropped the camera in an outside pocket, then decided it might get damaged there, moved it to a zippered cargo pocket on the right leg of my khakis, and dropped the flash attachment into the big outside pocket. Reluctantly, I took off my leather gloves and pulled on a pair of the surgical ones I keep in the glove compartment.

"Hey, Al," I said, getting out of the truck. "Buzz." Two red noses bobbed at me out of fur-lined caps sunk deep in turned-up collars. Al Hanenburger handed the roll of tape to Buzz Cooper and came over.

"Howsgoin', Jake?" His breath made a great plume of white against the dark sky.

"Whatcha got here?" I picked up the corner of the tarp nearest me. A young man lay on his right side, his arms flung forward on top of the snowbank, which was level with my knees. His body paralleled the roadway, facing me. He wore pants but no shirt, and one of his shoes was missing. His bare chest and shoulders looked like pale blue marble, mottled a little, and his eyes were open and fixed. His nose had turned black, his cheeks were dark purple, and his hands were frozen into grasping black claws. I touched his arms and face; he felt like stone.

"He got a wallet on him?"

"I couldn't find one," Al said. "I didn't want to mess around too much till you saw him." I searched all four of his pockets, carefully. They were empty. Cooper came over and turned on his Streamlight. The three of us stared.

"What did you do with the clothes he took off?" I asked them.

"I never saw any other clothes around here," Hannenburger said. He turned to Cooper. "Did you?"

"Nope."

"They have to be here," I said. "He wouldn't walk around in a blizzard like this."

"Look around," Hanenburger said. "We haven't moved a thing." We all swung flashlights around the area randomly till we got sick of it and went back to staring down at the body.

"I can't see any other damage," I said, "except the freezing."

"I couldn't either," Hanenburger said, "but do you notice the way his head seems to be kind of down in a hole? Lower than the rest of him?"

"Something shiny under there, too," Cooper said, "kind of orange colored."

"I don't want to mark up the snow before I take pictures," I said, "but do you think we could roll him from here?"

"Sure. He's stiff as a board," Hanenburger said. We leaned across the curb. Hanenburger grabbed the knees; I lifted a shoulder. Cooper pointed his light underneath.

"Careful," I said, "he's brittle. Oh, look at that."

The right side of his face was disfigured by a hole about the size of a baseball. A great string of fluorescent orange blood and tissue hung out of it. Fragments of bone and bits of brain glistened along the length of the strand, which was frozen to the snowbank at the lower end. Beneath it, hot blood had melted snow to make the hollow we noticed. Blood and melted snow had crystallized into orange ice that glittered where the light hit it. All the blood must have run down into the snowbank and frozen there; I couldn't see any blood in the street.

Car lights swept across us. I looked up to see Pokey's old Jeep parking behind the squads.

"Can you hold him there a minute longer," I asked Hanenburger, "till Pokey gets a look?" Cooper moved to help him. I said, "Here, I'll take your light," and Hanenburger said, "Not the arm, get the shoulder." They leaned there, hunched against the cold, while Pokey crunched up to us, jaunty in his red watch cap. He cast a long shadow across the body as he stepped across the light, then stood beside me, holding his black bag, while he stared at the gruesome string of blood and tissue hanging out of the dead man's head. He shook his head and clucked. "This looks like hypothermia to you guys?"

"Put him down," I said, and the two men laid their burden carefully back into his indentation in the snow. "See how good he looks from this side?"

"Ah," Pokey said. "Yah." He dropped his bag in the street and opened it, propped his knees against the snowbank, and began his examination. I went back to my pickup, got my phone off the seat, and started back toward the body.

"Jake?" Pokey turned, peering through the headlights. "Show you something." Buzz was standing close beside him, shining his Streamlight directly on the dead man's face. Pokey's fingers, ghostly in surgical gloves, were busy in front of the dead man's ear, spreading dark hair away from a section of temple. "See here?" He wiggled his right index finger above a small red spot, less than half the size of a dime, glistening in the light. "Is your entry wound."

"Entry wound? That little tiny hole? You mean we're looking at a gunshot victim?"

"Well—sure. Whatcha think made big hole like that? Mosquito bite?"

"I thought he got attacked with something heavy and sharp like a chisel. Looked like somebody tore a great big chunk out of him."

"Yeah, well, you just ain't used to seeing anybody shot so close up. Hardly ever happens here. Is kinda like execution style."

"Well, but Pokey, a bullet that small, to tear a hole like that on the other side? Hard to believe."

"Don't have to be so small; your own gun could make entry hole like this at close range. If gun is close to head, skin blows apart some from pressure when bullet goes in, shrinks up after."

"And you think there could be that much difference between the entry and exit wounds?"

"Sure. Bullet explodes as it goes through, maybe bounces off bone, path keeps gettin' bigger."

"Okay." I poked the speed-dial number for BCA, asking Cooper, "You guys didn't see a gun around here, I guess, huh?"

"Nope," Buzz said.

"It sure would be convenient if we found the gun that fired this bullet."

"Guess it would," Al said, peering under the bridge supports. "You want us to look around?" He had mentioned a couple of times that he was past due for his lunch break. Now he wanted to be sure I understood that he was hungry and very cold. He swung his flashlight aimlessly around beneath the underpass, while the phone at the state crime lab rang and rang and rang. Finally a woman's voice said, breathlessly, "Bureau of Criminal Apprehension."

"Jake Hines, Rutherford PD." I told her about my gunshot victim and asked to speak to the forensic specialist in charge.

"Mr. Chang is here," she said, "hold on a minute." I listened to Muzak for some time before Jimmy's voice said quietly, "Chang."

"Jake Hines," I said. "Why are you working Sunday night? You get demoted?" Jimmy is the head scientist at BCA, famous in the bureau for his workaholic tendencies.

"Oh, Christ, Jake, this place is a zoo. Christmas must have disappointed a lot of people this year; they can't kill each other fast enough. Plus a couple of staff people aren't back from Christmas leave yet, and one has the flu. And now this weather... What do you need?"

"I've got a gunshot victim frozen in a snowbank. He's damn near naked, and his clothes are nowhere in sight. Also the gun is missing. Can you send a team?"

"Well, not for at least...uh, it'll be twelve hours, minimum, before we'll have a van available. We've been backed up for days—"

"Uh-huh. Trudy told me that."

"Yes. There are four calls ahead of you, and I'm

telling all of them I don't know when we can get there because one of the vans is stuck in a snowdrift up near Thief River Falls. Trudy's in it, by the way."

"No kidding? Really stuck, huh?"

He sighed. "They got about a foot more snow up there than we did, I guess, and out in the country it's drifting badly. They slid off the road. They put chains on and tried to power their way out, and they just dug in deeper.... I guess the van is barely visible. They say they found a farmer nearby who's got a tractor with lugs on, and they hope he's going to pull them out."

"Poor poor Trudy. But listen, Jimmy, this body's outside. On a major street, right where it goes under the highway, and the wind is coming up—" I watched a fine layer of drifting snow settle over Pokey and the body in front of him. We were all turning white. "Actually I guess it's starting to snow again."

"I understand, Jake, but I can't send you what I haven't got. You know what, I think it would be best if you just get a hearse to bring the body up here, and you take as many pictures as you can of that crime scene, huh? Can you still see it?"

"Just about. It's gonna be drifted over before long."

"Yeah, well, so get as many pictures as you can right away. What else have you got there? A vehicle? Do we need to get blood samples from his car or his house?"

"No vehicle in sight, and we have no idea where he lives. How soon you think you can do this autopsy?"

"Well...I don't see how we can possibly do it tomorrow. But I'll get it on the list for Tuesday if I possibly can.''

''Really backed up, huh? Maybe we'll go ahead and fingerprint him before we send him up. See, he's got no wallet on him, no way to ID him at all.''

''Oh, well, but...didn't you say the body is frozen? Are the extremities turning black?''

''Yeah, his fingers and nose are black, yeah.''

''So you can't autopsy till he thaws out anyway. At least twelve hours. Could be twenty-four. Let me make a deal with you, okay? We'll get him finger-printed sometime tomorrow, and then we'll schedule the autopsy as soon as we can. Maybe in the mean-time we'll get lucky and get a match on the prints. Trudy and Brian are getting very good with our AFIS program—''

''She's been bragging about it.''

''Well, it's good on repeat offenders. If your vic-tim's been arrested lately in the U.S., we'll get his name for you.''

''And if you don't get a match, you'll do a DNA test, right?''

''We'll do that in any case. Automatic, now, for homicide.''

''Damn thing takes forever, though, doesn't it?''

''Maybe not. Our new STR method only takes a couple of days, and it's the most accurate of all. And I can justify using STR if you've got a John Doe homicide.''

''Awesome.'' I had no idea what STR was; Jimmy always seems to be one or two clusters of initials ahead of me. ''What else should we do here, then? Besides the pictures? We've got some bloody snow under the body, can you test that?''

"Yes. Have Pokey collect some in a test tube or any clean glass container. Have you got blood in several locations, or—"

"No. Just under the head."

"Well. Almost certainly the victim's, right? Still, you better send me some if you can. The weapon, do you have the weapon?"

"No. And no tracks. I just realized this, Jimmy, there are no tracks in the snow around the victim."

"Well, of course with this wind—"

"Maybe. But I didn't see any when I got here. I'm gonna go take another look. If we find any we'll try to make casts, if the plaster doesn't freeze before it sets up. I'll call you when the body's on its way."

I hung up and began digging through three layers of clothes for my camera. I couldn't remember where I'd finally put it. Hanenburger watched my contortions with interest. "You got the itch?" he asked me sympathetically.

"No. I keep my camera in my shorts," I said. It was a dumb joke, but I was trying to keep my spirits up while my hands froze.

I finally identified the bulge in the zippered pocket and fished out my Minolta. "We're gonna be ready to transport this body before too long," I told him. "Will you call dispatch? Tell them to find an undertaker who'll send a hearse out here ASAP, with a driver who's prepared to drive to St. Paul. And listen, both you guys?" I turned to look for Cooper and found him behind me. "Take another close look around, will you? I don't see any tracks around this body, but they have to be here. He was on top of the snow when you found him, right?"

"Just like you see him, sure," Hanenburger said.

"So he got here after it quit snowing this afternoon, right? So where are the tracks?"

Cooper started shining his light around while Hanenburger crunched off toward his car phone. Beyond him, I saw Milo Nilssen's felt-lined boots emerging from the driver's side of his taupe sedan. He struggled out from under the steering wheel, his usually svelte silhouette bundled inside many layers of clothing and a down-filled overcoat the size of a love seat. He could barely lower his arms. When he reached the front of the two squads, he stopped, blinded by the glare of the headlights, and inquired of the group around the body, "Howsgoin'?"

"Doin' pretty good till you got in my light," Pokey said. "Move over." Crouched above the blue-white body, trim and wiry in his ancient pea coat, Pokey seemed impervious to cold, his appearance a reproach to the thickly padded shapes around him. It's something I've noticed about him before: he ignores routine hardships like weather and traffic. I guess Soviet work camps taught him to save his energy for the big stuff.

Milo said, "Sorry," stepped sideways, and edged toward me across the disorienting circle of light. "Hey, Jake. You know who this is yet?"

"Don't have a clue. Help me look around here, will you? You see any tracks or footprints around this body?"

"Um, no." He looked some more. "Do you?"

"No." I kept shooting pictures while we talked. "It's starting to bug me. How did this man get on top of this snowbank if he didn't walk and he wasn't carried?"

"Dang, Jake. If I'd known there was gonna be a

quiz, I'd have come prepared." Dead bodies spook Milo; he tries to cover up with smartass attitude. "Do you need the answer tonight?"

"No. But you're gonna need it before very long, if we find a suspect to charge with this crime."

"Aw, come on, you're gettin' ahead of yourself a little here, aren't you? What makes you so sure you're lookin' at a homicide?"

"You ever see a suicide that took off his shirt and one shoe, made a perfect vault into a snowbank and spiked the landing, shot himself fatally in the head, and then threw the gun so far away nobody could find it?"

"No," Milo said quietly after a pause, "but there's a lot I haven't seen yet, I guess." He sounded suddenly much older.

"Me too," I said, sorry to have needled him. "I wasn't even calling this a gunshot, till Pokey found the entry wound. Here, let's get him to show you." I leaned into Pokey's patch of light, said, "Show Milo the gunshot wound, will you?" then stepped back so Milo could use my space while Pokey showed him the almost bloodless wound under the hair on the victim's temple. When Pokey beckoned, I stepped up to the frozen knees, and together we rolled the body just enough so Milo could see the bloody crater on the lower side.

Milo said, "Jeez, he's really torn up, huh? Why's he so red on the underside of his body?"

"Lividity looks like that in cold weather."

"Really? I never saw that before. You really think the same bullet made both these holes?"

"Pokey thinks so," I said.

"Autopsy gonna prove it," Pokey said, "no use

freezin' our butts talkin' about it here. You seen enough?'' he asked Milo.

Milo nodded, and I said quickly, ''But how about holding the body right there while I get a couple of close-ups?''

''Shee,'' Milo said, ''you want me to run get your tripod first?''

''Nah,'' I said, ''just a cup of coffee and a raised doughnut with sprinkles.'' I hurried through half a dozen shots. They put the body back in its shallow groove in the snowbank, and I began shooting close-ups of the top side of the face.

Before he got shot and frozen, I thought, this stranger had been quite presentable. If he'd been living on the street, it couldn't have been for long. He looked adequately fed, and his dark, wavy hair had a decent trim. His few clothes—dark twill pants and navy blue cotton knit socks—were ordinary but not ragged. The jockey shorts that showed above the waistband of his pants were clean except where they were blood-soaked on the lower side.

Something glinted in the viewfinder. I lowered the camera and saw that he wore a fragile gold chain around his neck. When I lifted it off his chest, a bright fragment slid away. I lowered the chain again, and a thin gold ring, like a wedding band, slid back into view. I looked at his left hand. No wedding ring there.

I took several pictures of the jewelry gleaming faintly against the ghastly blue skin of his chest, and went on and finished with close-ups of the hands and feet. Then I put the lens cap on, zipped the camera back into my pants pocket, and stood staring down at the body.

''What?'' Milo asked.

"I'd like to get that ring and chain off him."

"Can I help?"

"I don't think so. Hardly room here for me and Pokey."

"Okay. Guess I've seen enough, then," Milo said abruptly. "Be in touch tomorrow, huh?" He crunched away across the snowpack toward his car.

Pokey glanced at his big car coat slouching away and said, "Milo seems kinda grouchy, huh?"

"It's lonely at the top, I guess," I said. Pokey muttered something Ukrainian that I knew I didn't want translated.

Leaning far out across the frozen body on the snowbank, I slid the fragile chain around the victim's unyielding neck, looking for the clasp. My fingers were stiff with cold and awkward in the plastic gloves. My eyes wept and my nose ran, and I couldn't spare a hand for a wipe. The clasp was almost too small to see, and by the time I got it in my hands, my fingers were so cold they were barely moving. I pushed the snow-clogged keeper back at last, and pulled the tiny metal loop out through the barely visible space. Holding my breath, I shook open a paper evidence bag, held it under the chain, and carefully slid the ring off, knowing I'd never find it if it dropped in the snowbank. When it plopped into my paper sack, I stood up and blew air through my mouth. Pokey was looking at me with amused disbelief.

I realized I'd been counting backward by threes and fours from four hundred, murmuring the totals to myself while I struggled with the frozen clasp. Counting backward by varying numbers helps me endure frustration and pain. I opened my mouth to explain, decided it was folly to explain anything about endurance to a man who was a teenage slave in the Soviet outback, and smiled.

"I'm trying to stop swearing," I told him. Pokey vented one quick humorous snort, shook his head, and went back to peering through his little light.

The tiny gold chain slid out from under the frozen neck without sticking. When it was safe in the bag with the ring, I stood up and tucked my frostbitten hands into my armpits.

"Jake?" Buzz Cooper stepped suddenly out of the darkness into the circle of light beside me, making me jump. "Got time to look at something?" He was breathing hard, and his eyes were bright.

"Sure. Where?"

"Up there." He pointed to the bridge above our heads.

"What, up on the highway?"

"Yeah, the overpass."

"You been up there? What—how'd you go up?"

"Over the rip-rap."

"Jesus. Hard going."

"Not as bad as it looks." He started up, and I followed him. It seemed to me it was even worse than it looked. The broken rocks were loose, just big enough to break an ankle if they rolled over, and very slippery under the snow. Car lights illuminated the lowest part of the slope, but the midsection was dark as the inside of a boot. "I guess we coulda driven around to the on-ramp," Cooper said.

"Yeah," I said, "mighta been better." After that I didn't talk. Climbing was making me breathe harder, and I was afraid of getting frost in my lungs. If we break our stupid legs up here, I thought, we might look quite a bit like that corpse down there before anybody figures out how to get us off this rock pile. Then Cooper's silhouette appeared against the bridge lights at the top of the slope. He panted back at me, "There's a gap in the railing right here at the end of the bridge, see?"

The wind slammed into me as soon as I stepped up on the bridge. "Jeez, blowing pretty good up here," I said, grabbing my scarf just before it left for Canada. An eighteen-wheeler roared past us, creating its own whiteout. We stood silent till we could see each other again. "More traffic up here, too, huh?"

"Yeah. Come over here." Cooper hunched inside his jacket and sidled to the middle of the bridge. I edged over to stand beside him, looking down over the railing at the toylike group around the body below.

"Look at the railing," Cooper said. He turned his light on. "Isn't that blood?" There was a rusty smear along the cement guardrail, with pale streaks of snow slithering across it. "Lookit down here." He aimed the beam to the bottom of the railing, where a double line of orangey spatters marched across the curb, from the roadway to the railing. "Doesn't that look like blood to you?"

"Sure does." I stared at it, admiring. "Goddamn. Nice job. How'd you think to look up here?"

"You kept saying the body didn't get onto that snowbank by itself. I just started pokin' around." He adopted an aw-shucks tone to hide his pride, but he knew he'd earned an attaboy. While Hanenburger mooned over his lunch break, Cooper, the backup officer, had almost certainly found the place where the body got dropped off.

From what? A hundred tire tracks crisscrossed the roadway. I snapped some pictures, asking, "You see any tire tracks, rub marks, anything like that on the curb?"

"No." He beamed his light along the curb. "Down here, sure—" He swung his light a few inches farther into the roadway, and we squinted together at the hopeless tangle of tracks in the road.

I stared into the snowflakes blowing past the bridge lights. "Guess I better go down and get Pokey," I said, "to help me with blood samples. I'll bring him back up here by the entrance ramp." Cooper led the way, going back down the rip-rap like a mountain goat; he had all the good rocks spotted by now. Across the circle of light, I saw Pokey closing his bag.

I ran and caught him getting into his Jeep. "Hang on a minute," I said, "I've got something else for you to look at." I told him about Cooper's find.

"Yah? How much blood? Enough to scrape?"

"Um, probably not. There's a pretty good smear on the railing. Little drops on the curb that have soaked into the cement. Snow's blowing over everything."

"Don't hafta worry about snow, too damn cold tonight for snow to mix with blood. Lessee. We need wads of cotton—here. Damn, almost gone. Well, I got Q-tips, they're okay. You got a good light?" I borrowed Cooper's Streamlight. "Plenty of evidence bags? Paper ones?"

"Of course I've got paper bags," I said, "I'm a cop, I've even got a gun, see?"

"Some guys use that stupid plastic junk belongs at picnics," he said. "Hope I got some distilled water."

He pawed through bottles in an old Styrofoam cooler that serves him as a warmer in cold weather. "Ah, yah." He was enjoying himself, I realized. At a ghastly crime scene in bone-chilling cold, in the dark of night in a rising wind, getting ready to undertake a tough, intricate job in poor light with makeshift equipment, Pokey was having fun.

"Get in," he said.

"What, in your—? No, let's take my truck."

"No use movin' everything. Oh, here, door's kinda funny on that side." He twisted the handle the wrong way, and the passenger door creaked halfway open. I wedged myself through the narrow space and perched on the high small seat with his bag between my feet. The inside of the ragtop was as windy and frigid as a tent in Antarctica, but with more sharp corners. I bounced off the seatback and the door frame while he manhandled gears through three quick turns to the approach ramp, roared up to the overpass at top speed, and stopped abruptly six inches from the bridge abutment. With my nose grazing his windshield, I had an excellent view of the thirty-foot drop-off onto Burton Hills Drive. I handed him his bag and crawled out over the gearshift console, vowing never to ride with Adrian Pokornoskovic again.

We sidled along the curb to the middle and stood with our backs to the traffic, grimacing and pinching our butts up tight every time a big rig roared by.

"It's here, see?" I turned the Streamlight on. Loose snow blew across the smear of blood on the railing. I lowered the light beam to where a little drift was building against the curb. Pulling on a fresh pair of surgical gloves, I brushed it gently away. "And right here."

"Ah. Yah." Pokey crouched, hugging his knees to get close. "Uh-huh. Gotcha."

"You think you can get some samples?"

"Yup. Think so. Let's try top one first." He dampened a Q-tip in distilled water, waved it in the air a minute, rubbed it gently over the blood smear on the railing, and held it under the light. It showed a rusty stain, and he grunted approval, waved it in the air some more, and dropped it into the paper evidence bag I held open for him. I labeled it simply "railing," leaving the rest of the writing for later at the station.

He took four samples from the railing and four more from the drops on the curb, making sure I marked the last four "curb." My part of the job, holding the light and writing one wobbly word on a paper bag, allowed me plenty of time to notice that my wet left foot was freezing to my boot. I ducked my chin into my scarf as deep as I could and hugged myself in the wind, trying to stop shivering.

Finally Pokey said, "That oughta be enough to blow his skirts up, huh? That Jimmy Chin." He pretends not to be able to remember Jimmy Chang's surname, a shameless put-down from a man who speaks five languages.

On the street below, I saw a long refitted limo pulling into the circle of light beside the body.

"Hearse is here," I said. "I better get down there. Here, I'll take the bags and the light. You be okay with the rest of this?" I scrambled down the rip-rap. After the ride in Pokey's Jeep, it seemed safe and easy.

In the front seat of the hearse, taking my time because his heater was working well, I wrote a label for the body bag. "Bag's not gonna go on him, I bet," the attendant said. "Betcha his arms won't bend at all."

"Put him on the gurney," I said, "and lay the bag on top. They can do what they like with it in St. Paul." My beeper chirped. I went back to my truck, found my phone, and called the station. "Chief wants to talk to you, hold a sec," Woody said. Frank came on and said, "I just called the Highway Department. This storm is worse farther north; they're closing Fifty-two between Cannon Falls and the Cities, and they might have to close the Interstate too. You gettin' ready to transport that body?"

"Just packing up, yeah."

"Tell you what, Jake, I think it's better if we keep it overnight. Your victim's not gonna get any deader, no use getting a driver stranded on the road someplace, huh?"

"Right. So, what, send it to Hampstead County then?"

"Yes. I called, they say they got room. Lemme talk to your driver there." I handed the phone to the attendant. He said, "Yeah?" and then, "Yes, sir," and, "Right," and "Fine," and handed the phone back to me. "He says take it to the pathology lab. Boy, he won't get no argument outta me. Lookit that stuff come down." It was snowing much harder, suddenly; the lights at the end of the block had become dim yellow moons, and even the nearby headlights were indistinct in the swirling storm.

"Okay," I said, "let's move it before we're all stuck here." He got the gurney out of the hearse, and I walked with him to the body, where Hanenburger and Cooper waited, stamping their feet.

"You still worried about tracks here, Jake?" Cooper asked.

"Nah. Snow's blown over everything anyway." The officers took the shoulders, the driver and I took the feet; I counted to three, and we heaved the body onto the gurney. The frozen string of tissue and bone fragments came along all right, but the arms stuck out awkwardly over the side. The driver pulled the body bag up to the victim's hips and laid the top section across his belly with the tag uppermost. "Best I can do, I guess," he said, looking guilty.

Pokey parked his Jeep as we closed the back door of the hearse.

"You wanna send snow samples along?" he asked me. "I got 'em here in my car."

"I'll take 'em," I said. "The body's staying here tonight, the roads are all closing." I stood dialing BCA while the hearse disappeared in the swirling storm. When Jimmy answered, I said, "Turns out we can't get our body up there to you tonight."

"I know, I was just about to call you. It's getting just ridiculous up here. My other van is stuck on Lyndale Avenue now."

"Stuck in traffic, you mean? Or the snow?"

"Both, actually. It's stuck in the middle of a great many vehicles, most of which are hopelessly mired in the snow. You think it's some kind of cosmic retribution? Kanaloa's mad that I moved to Minnesota?" Jimmy's from Hilo.

"Up here it's more likely to be one of those Norse guys, Odin or one of them. Somebody shit on a runestone or something. You know, seriously, I'm starting to wonder if we shouldn't go ahead and schedule this autopsy down here."

Jimmy sighed. "Well, you know—" he sighed again "—maybe it would be better. By the time I get a full crew in here, we're going to be so damn far behind—"

"I hear you. Let's do it. We'll still ask you to do the blood work, though, okay? And listen, I'll have my guys take the fingerprints, and then we'll send them to you for comparison. Sound okay?"

"Agreed. I'm sorry about this, Jake."

"Can't be helped. It's starting to really come down here, too. We better get home while we can still see the street."

Pokey came back carrying a brown paper sack, and I asked him, "Any chance I can get you to schedule an autopsy at the pathology lab here for late tomorrow, or first thing Tuesday morning?"

The wind picked up a whole snowbank and swirled it around us; Pokey disappeared for a couple of seconds and emerged a step closer to me, beaming. "Gonna let old Ukrainian asshole have a crack at it, huh? What, big-city Hawaiian kid got spooked by a little snowstorm?"

"Will you talk to the clinic in the morning?" I asked him. "And then call me and let me know what time?"

"Sure sure sure." He watched me put the paper bag, with its two glass jars full of bloody snow, in the back seat of my truck. Then he stood there squinting, looking dissatisfied, while the wind blew snow down our necks.

"What?" I said.

"You won't mix up blood samples from overpass, huh? You can keep straight, top ones from bottom ones?"

"I marked each one as you gave it to me. I'm not gonna change it. Although I never did see why you were making such a big deal out of where each sample came from. I mean, it's all gonna be the same blood, right?"

In the shifting headlights, he shrugged, ducked his chin, looked around. "Maybe not."

"Whaddya mean? We only got one body. What makes you think we might have blood from anybody else?"

"You notice how blood drops on curb was lined up? In two rows, kinda?"

"Uh, yeah...I guess it was. So?"

"Wasn't any wound on that body we just loaded up," Pokey said, "that woulda made spatter pattern like that."

THREE

MY FIRST YEAR AS A COP, I figured out a way to lower the crime rate.

"Make the lawbreakers file the reports," I told Frank McCafferty.

"You got a sick mind, Hines," McCafferty said. He wasn't chief of police then, just the acknowledged best shot in the department and my assigned tyrant, aka field training officer.

"Trust me," I told him, "only a handful would ever commit a second crime."

"Are you still fightin' the problem with report forms?" Frank shook his head sadly. "Get over it, for God's sake. Record keeping is just a fact of life, like bunions."

"More like bleeding piles," I said. "Or a strangulated hernia."

"Jesus, what a bitcher," Frank said. Everybody in the department had told me I was lucky to have him for a trainer, and most of the time I believed it. I only really wanted to kill him when he yelled at me about my driving.

He was also prone to fits of temper about my handwriting and spelling. An indifferent student to begin with, I had moved through half a dozen school systems during my childhood in Minnesota foster care, and there were holes in my basic education you could throw a cat through. Math aptitude got me into college, and I finessed civil service exams with multiple choice. Now, trying to become a cop, I was handing in typed reports that were mazes of whiteout and upper-case *X*s.

Computers came along just in time to save me. I loved electronic correction so much, at first I didn't notice that Spellcheck did nothing for the grammatically challenged. Then I got Grammarcheck and clung to it fervently till I realized it wouldn't keep me from using "eight" when I meant "ate." Finally Frank found me a bonehead English course in night school and helped me arrange my schedule around it for a couple of semesters. With my job on the line, I finally learned enough about my native tongue to write short declarative sentences. I keep a cheat sheet in the top drawer for toughies like "their" and "there."

Mastering basic English didn't make me love record keeping, which is boring and gobbles up too much time. But now that I'm a police detective, I consider information my lifeline, and think that cops who can't keep good records ought to find another line of work.

So on the Sunday night when we found the frozen body in the snowbank, I was at the station till past midnight, filling out many forms. In fairness, I shouldn't count the first ten minutes, which I spent in the break room hugging a cup of coffee.

The space around the microwave was crowded with night shift cops on break, waiting to nuke the leftovers they brought from home. They peeled off layers of padded clothing, blew their noses, and monotonously cursed the weather.

"I spent a whole friggin' hour directing traffic around that pileup on Eighth Avenue," Huckstadt said. "Shit, I thought my feet were gonna freeze right to the asphalt."

"You think you got troubles, I'm out at Perry Homes tonight," Manahan said. Perry Homes is a grim place even in good weather; big blocks of low-cost housing painted vomit green. "Wouldn't you think we coulda planted a windbreak on the north side of that place? Jesus. Right out on the flats, and the wind blowin' about fifty miles an hour... I think we must be tryin' to freeze those poor buggers offa welfare."

"Fine with me. Serve 'em right." Putratz had transferred his anger from the cold to the clients. "You know that Stan Bischoff at Stan's Auto Parts? Talk about a dumb shit," he ranted, "Sets his automatic alarm and then forgets to lock his back door. Wind comes up and blows the door open, alarm goes off, wee-ah, wee-ah, wee-ah—" He bugged out his eyes, twirled a finger above his head, and became an alarm system. "Kranz and me get the call an' blaze out to the Beltway, run around wavin' our Remingtons at that big friggin' warehouse about the size of a goddam *Metrodome* for chrissake, miracle we didn't shoot each other. Chill factor must be thirty below at least out there, freeze the balls off a brass monkey." He pulled off another sweater as rage warmed him up.

When I couldn't take any more weather reports, I carried a second cup of coffee to my office, grabbed the week's duty roster sheets off my clipboard, posted one outside my door, and handed the second one to Woody at the dispatch desk, saying, shamelessly, "Here's a replacement for that lost duty sheet." Back at my desk, I wrote all the evidence inventory forms for the blood samples that were still in my truck, took a last big swig of hot coffee, and put my coat back

on. Outside in the parking lot, working by the overhead light in the cab of my truck, I sealed the blood
samples up in sample kits. I wrote dates and initials
all over the seals, brought the kits inside, and put
them in the freezer in the small evidence room.

I washed my hands then, pulled on fresh surgical
gloves, and dug the gold chain and ring out of my
briefcase. They slid noiselessly out of the paper bag
onto a clean paper towel on my desk and lay gleaming
under the light, the only real clue I had to what kind
of life had ended out there on Burton Hills Drive
tonight. I sat quietly in front of them, waiting for them
to tell me whatever they could.

The chain was nearly weightless. It looked clean
and quite new. The ring appeared older and somewhat
scuffed. It was an unadorned gold band, too small to
go on my little finger, with nothing printed inside. I
guessed it to be a woman's wedding band, and esti-
mated it had been worn for some time. Neither piece
looked expensive. Their inappropriateness as male
neckwear suggested some sentimental value or a
good-luck charm.

Nothing about the fragile trinkets seemed to belong
in the same picture with an almost naked man shot
through the brain and tossed in a snowbank like trash.
Staring at them, I remembered thinking, while I pho-
tographed the corpse, that his luck had not been all
bad; he had had a decent haircut and a clean pair of
shorts. Now I added to his list of better-than-even
breaks a woman who cared enough about him to hang
her keepsake jewelry around his neck. I put the ring
and chain in a fresh bag, tagged it, and wrote up an
evidence inventory form for it. I unloaded my camera,
fished two used rolls of film out of my coat pockets,

bagged and tagged the three together, and wrote up a photographer's file sheet for them. I took the whole stack to the table outside the evidence room, entered everything in the log book there, unlocked the deposit door in the wall, slid all my bundles through, and locked the door. I dropped the report forms in the box by the door.

Now the ring and chain, my film, and the victim's blood had become part of the chain of evidence. These previously unremarkable items picked up dignity and status as they slid through the wall into the evidence room. They had numbers, now, identities of their own, and they had their rights. Till this case was closed, nobody could touch them again without signing a form that said they had done so. I couldn't even get them back myself unless I signed for them, and if I checked them out of the evidence room, I had to account for where I took them, and why.

Back in my office, I turned on my word processor, pulled up the Initial Crime Report form, entered the number Woody had given me earlier, and began to fill out the first homicide report of the new year. The cover sheet is a lined form with many questions, most of which I couldn't answer. I didn't know the victim's name, address, or phone number. I had no place of business for him and no vehicle, no suspect and no witnesses. I checked the boxes that indicated he was an adult white male. I noted his meager clothing, named the responding officers, recorded the order in which the rest of us appeared, and went on to the blank lines facing me on the supplementary report page.

I had very sparse notes, but the scene under the overpass was fresh in my mind, and I described it in

detail, typing fast. I've learned to put down everything I can think of about the victim and the surround-
ings. I tell everything I know about the weather—
temperature, wind speed, precipitation, if any—and
describe the traffic in the area, and the way everything
looked and felt to me—colors, sounds, smells, tex-
tures. I don't worry about the fact that much of what
I put down will prove irrelevant. You never know.
Tomorrow, next week, I might get a fresh piece of
evidence, come back to these pages, and see that it
fits with something I thought was useless but wrote
down anyway.

Also, when the time comes to take this to the
county attorney, no matter how many details I've put
down, he's going to want more. It's a knee-jerk thing
with attorneys; they're always hoping to bury the op-
position by knowing one extra fact.

Besides, like everybody else, I'm trying to cover
my own ass. Months, even years from now, I might
have to answer questions about this case on a witness
stand. When I do that, people will expect me to answer, confidently, "Yes, I remember—" and pour out
a stream of details. But that's impossible, really, because by then I'll have looked at many other distress-
ing scenes. I can't keep all that misery on the front
burner; I'd self-destruct. Most of the memory I claim
to have about this incident on my day in court will
have to be recalled by reading this report.

The bizarre appearance of the body in the snowbank took the most time. I noted the position of every
limb, the marble-hard blueness of the naked upper
torso, the cherry-red color of the lividity on his lower
side, the missing shoe, the chain around the victim's
neck and the ring hanging on it. I put down every-

thing I could remember about the undamaged-looking upper side of the face: the glazed eyes, the neat haircut, the ample flesh, the blackened nose and chin and darkening cheeks, and then described the discovery of the neat little bloodless hole hidden in the hair of the sideburn. The ruined lower side of the face was easier to describe; there were no subtleties about the gaping wound and the string of bloody tissue that hung out of it. I mentioned again the extreme low temperature, windchill, and drifting snow, to explain the rigid, blackened extremities and the fact that BCA could not send an investigative team at once. I gave Cooper full credit for finding the blood stains on the overpass and detailed the sampling we did on the railing.

When I finished, I printed up the forms, put one copy in the new case file for the county attorney, left my copies on my desk for the file I'd start in the morning, and took the third copy to the slot in the records room door. On my way back I detoured past Ed Gray's desk. He quit barking at his night shift staff long enough to collaborate on a homicide report for Monday's BOLOs, the Be on the Lookout notices that are read at all the shift changes.

Back in my office, I made six copies of the report forms and stapled and stacked them ready to hand out to my crew in the morning. I wrote a note to the chief that summarized the most important information and pinned it to the corkboard on his door.

Chores done, fingers flexing again, and left foot warm and dry, I was ready to go home, if I could make it. I dialed the Highway Department and got a tape that said the road was closed north of Cannon

Falls. My house was in Mirium, twenty miles south of the roadblock.

I decided to chain up and go for it, even though my bedmate would not be waiting for me there. BCA staff does one week a month in the outreach van; Trudy still had five days of her week to go. She was counting on me, in her absence, to keep an eye on the frailest features of our ninety-year-old house in the country.

"Wait till you see it," Trudy told her sister Bonnie, the weekend after we signed the lease. "It's got a huge yard with beautiful big old trees. And a half-brick barn."

"What's a half-brick?"

"Brick on the ground floor, I mean. Red painted siding above."

"What do you need a barn for?" Bonnie asked her. "You gonna raise pigs? I suppose they do that in Mirium."

"Of course not. It's not downtown in Mirium anyway. Sort of on the outskirts."

"Oh, *that's* good. Out of the high traffic area."

"Why are you making fun of it?" Trudy asked her. "Mirium is a nice little town."

"I know, Trudy, we go there all the time. Doesn't everybody? I usually pick up a few items at the feed store, and then Mel likes to have a beer at the bar with the nude dancers."

"I might have known you'd know about Peepers. Listen, that won't be there long. Some fly-by-night outfit rented an old bar. The city council's not gonna let them transfer the liquor license."

"Way to go, Trudy, abrogate their civil rights, that'll show 'em."

Bonnie lived in Owatonna, a pretty town filled with great restorations of century-old buildings. It was too far west for us, even if we'd wanted to be that close to Bonnie, who had turned mean when she heard of our plans. She said she thought people who wanted to live together ''ought to get married and be done with it.''

''I don't want to be done with it,'' Trudy said, ''I want it to go on and on.''

''Fat chance of that. Men don't buy the cow if they can get the milk for—''

''Okay, Bonnie.'' Trudy got up, spilling her coffee. ''If you're going to talk like that, this conversation is over.''

''You know it's what Mama's going to say—''

''I have to take it from Mama,'' Trudy said, ''but I don't need to hear it from you.'' She threw things in her purse and headed for the door. ''I thought you might like to help me shop for a hutch for my new dining room, but I see I came to the wrong place.''

The sisters were close, but contentious. I tried to stay out of the way when they fought. Bonnie saw me as the evil seducer, and I wasn't going to defend myself against a charge like that. Trudy and I were not ready to consider marriage, but our desire to spend time together was passionate and serious. We worked in towns eighty miles apart; one of the small towns on the highway between St. Paul and Rutherford would allow us to split the commute.

Trudy flounced out of Bonnie's kitchen, Bonnie ran after her, and they yelled at each other in the yard for several minutes till they realized how much fun they were affording the neighbors. Then they jumped in Bonnie's car, slammed the doors and blew the horn by mistake, and skidded out of the driveway. They were back in a few hours, chatting happily about the corner cupboard they'd found in a secondhand store in Kasson. I hauled it home the next day in the back of my pickup. It wasn't too ugly if we kept it full of dishes.

The rest of the house was more of a challenge. The first time I saw it, I felt certain we'd come to the wrong place.

"No, this has to be it," Trudy said, peering at a classified ad she'd clipped. "The first house on CR 82 at the end of Burr Oak Avenue."

"It's just an abandoned farm. We must have missed a turn."

"What turn? CR means County Road, doesn't it? That's a county road." Directly ahead, the paved street morphed into a crushed rock road that wandered toward several farmyards. Trudy was pointing at the house in the nearest yard.

"Hey, I like the green shutters. Side porch, wow. And great trees, huh? Wonderful big yard." She glowed. "You suppose that barn out back goes with it?"

"The attic window is boarded up. Sweetheart, this can't be the right house."

"That barn—the whole bottom story is brick. How long since you've seen one of those?"

"I don't look at barns much." I put the truck in gear. "I'm more of an outhouse man, myself."

"Why am I not surprised? We'd probably find out more," she said, "if we got out of the truck. Pull in the driveway right up there."

"You're not going in, are you? It's a farm, for God's sake."

She opened the door on the passenger's side. "Okay, I'll walk from here."

"Oh, sit still, I'll drive you to the door. Jeez." I pulled onto the roadway to make the turn, earning an indignant horn blast from a Beetle that swerved to miss me. "What did you put in your cocoa this morning? You're really fired up."

She had the door open before I stopped the truck, and as soon as her feet touched the ground, she started up the gravel path toward the house. The storm door was sheathed in chicken wire and plastic sheeting, which bellied a little in the wind. As Trudy lifted her hand to knock, a thin girl in jeans opened it.

"I was watching you through the front window," she said. "Thought I was gonna hafta run out and wave you in."

"We weren't sure we had the right place," Trudy said.

"I've often wondered the same thing." She motioned us in. "My name's Cammy."

Trudy got right into the details: how much to run the propane stoves, whether the garden patch was included in the rent, where to do laundry in Mirium. Whenever I could get a word in edgewise, I said something like, "Of course, it's too big—" or, "We need something modern." The happy stream of their conversation parted around my clinkers and flowed on.

We were outside, opening half-doors on the front of the barn, when the phone started to ring, and Cammy sprinted for the house. Trudy secured the doors and walked ahead of me into the dusty gloom. Peering up into the hayloft, she mused softly, "Room enough up there to put a loom and a potter's wheel, I bet.''

"No lights up there, though. And no way to heat it.''

She turned and stared at me thoughtfully. "Are you getting cold feet about living together, Jake? Because it's not too late to back out—''

"Trudy, come on. This was my idea, remember? But *this* place is too old and too big for us. We'd have to be constantly fiddling with it instead of—'' I moved closer and touched her "—you know...''

"Aw, baby—'' She put her hands at the back of my waist, pulled me close, and chuckled warmly into my chest. "We're going to do plenty of *you-know*. We'll be doing you-know morning, noon, and night, wherever we live, how can you doubt it?'' She held me like that, rocking a little.

I asked into her hair, "In the barn, maybe?'' I don't know where the idea came from, but as soon as I said it, I felt our bodies start to respond.

"Hey, *yeah*,'' she whispered. "Up in the loft, huh? Forget weaving. We'll buy this big load of hay—'' I felt her hot breath through my shirt.

"Take up some old blankets—'' I said.

"And a big jar of pear butter —'' Her rocking was taking on a regular rhythm.

I raised my head, laughing, and saw, in the light that filtered down from the cupola, how the floor sloped away toward sliding doors across the back of the barn.

"Hey,'' I said, "look at that.''

"What?'' She straightened, blinking.

"This barn's got a ramp. And double doors along the back.''

"Well—sure. Easy access. So we can bring in plenty of hay for the orgies." She grinned up at me, realized that my body wasn't in the game anymore, and stepped back. "What are you thinking?"

"I bet you could pull a boat and trailer straight in through those double doors. Park it along the wall here without ever backing up once."

Trudy began to look at me the way a cat looks at a bird. I'd been grumbling because Noonin, my partner in a fishing boat, had been hired by a big accounting firm in Oregon and wanted to sell his half of the boat. I might find a new partner, but I had no place to keep the boat. I was afraid truck payments and boat storage fees might make me short for my half of the expenses when I moved in with Trudy.

"Your boat would fit in here just fine," she said, smiling gently.

"How much extra to rent the barn?"

"Haven't you been listening? The barn comes with the house. Which we can get even cheaper than she said, if we dicker a little."

Cammy came back from her phone call and showed us asparagus beds and raspberry bushes. I began to think about yardwork, a lost pleasure since my divorce.

That afternoon in a realtor's office, we signed a rental agreement that said we'd pay for anything we broke, and could move out on thirty days' notice. We added a clause that said Cammy had to give us first refusal before she sold.

"But we're not committed to anything till we see how we like it," Trudy said.

"Oh, you're gonna like it all right," Cammy said, looking sad. "I love this place."

The leaves were red and gold in the yard as we moved in, the second weekend in October. I unpacked boxes in the bay window of the dining room while Trudy tried out the kitchen stove, baking something with cinnamon that made me crazy.

"Hey, Tarzan heap hungry in here," I yelled.

"You ready for a break? I made some coffee." Munching warm cookies at the kitchen table, she said, "The good news is, the kitchen stove works. The bad news is, hardly anything else does."

"What, for starts?"

"No power to any of the outlets. Refrigerator won't start."

"Oh, well, that's just a circuit breaker somewhere, I'll fix it in a minute." I chased a lot of spiders away from a pocked metal door by the cellar stairs. There weren't any circuit breakers; it was one of the real old-timers with a big spade fuse at the top and a bank of round screw-in fuses below. I replaced a couple of dead ones. Trudy yelled down, "Okay, refrigerator's on," and then, "Now the lights work, too." I made a note of fuse sizes and added them to my hardware store list. We had lists all over the refrigerator: order firewood, bring out more blankets, buy paint.

We still had our apartments in town, that first month. When the Saturday shadows grew long across the yard, we would throw tools and trash in the back of the truck, drive to the dump, and then go on to her place in St. Paul to take showers and make love. When we got up, later, ravenous, we would cook a huge dinner and sit over it, drinking another glass of wine and making more lists. It was like playing house.

Golden October light poured over everything in the

afternoons, and the morning air had just enough snap to lend an edge. Raking leaves one Saturday, I stopped to watch a couple of jays grazing in the cornfield across the road, and felt something stir in my memory.

"Days like this make me think about Maxine," I told Trudy.

"Who? Oh, you mean the foster mother you told me about?"

"Yeah. The good one."

"Why do days like this make you think of her?"

"She liked fall. I remember jumping in a pile of leaves and having her cover me up."

"Hey, if that's what you like," Trudy said, "I can do that."

"Better still," I said, grabbing her, "why don't you lie down on these leaves and I'll jump on you?" I didn't finish the raking till much later.

On the thirty-first, on my lunch hour, I did a final walk-through of my tacky old apartment in Rutherford. The place had never been anything but a temporary squat, and the only memories it held for me were of the rage and regret that followed my divorce, and the mostly indigestible meals I had eaten there alone. Turning in the keys was a pleasure. I drove to the farm that night feeling like the big winner in some cosmic lottery.

Trudy opened the door as I drove up, holding a bouquet of balloons and a hand-lettered sign that said, "Country People Do It Better."

"Come out here," I said. When she stepped across the doorsill, I picked her up and carried her back inside. She is an athletic woman who could probably carry me if she made up her mind to, so I put her down quickly and kissed her till our knees started to buckle.

Dinner was late that night, but hilarious when we got to it. As soon as the washing up was done, Trudy said, "I'm going to take a shower tonight, so we're not competing for that in the morning."

"Fine with me," I said. "I'm gonna put up the towel bar where you said on the end of the kitchen cabinet." I got my tool chest out of the truck, rigged an extra light on an extension cord, found a rock station on the radio. I heard Trudy get out of the shower, humming, and start the hair dryer. I set the point of the drill bit against the mark I'd made earlier, hit the trigger, and watched the room go dark. And silent. Till Trudy stuck her head out of the bathroom, yelling, "Hey, my hair dryer just—" and saw me kneeling on the kitchen floor with the dead drill in my hand. We looked at each other in the silence. "Fuse," I said.

Water flew off her long hair when she nodded. "I guess we have to learn how many things we can run at once."

It became second nature, keeping track of the limits: we could not use the fry pan while the vacuum was running, or make coffee while we ironed, or run the hair dryer with anything else. But by the time we'd figured all that out, the weather was turning cold, and keeping the house warm took priority over everything.

The windows bled heat; I covered the worst-fitting ones in plastic sheeting. I sealed up the side door onto the porch, and we hung a quilt over it. When the wind blew from the north, we locked the kitchen door and folded a throw rug over the sill.

The heaters and the main kitchen stove all ran on propane, which was expensive and ran out fast. I checked the gauges often, since running out might mean freezing the plumbing, a prospect too horrid to contemplate. We closed up the parlor soon after Halloween, and retreated from the dining room as soon as we'd cleaned up from Thanksgiving. After that we concentrated our efforts on staying comfortable in the big kitchen and the bathroom. At bedtime, in long johns and wool socks, we sprinted through the icy rooms to our bedroom, where we shivered under many blankets, waiting for our body heat to warm up the sheets.

"Once I get this spot comfortable," Trudy said, "I'm not turning over for anything." She did, though, toward morning, and I helped her out of the underwear and later, giggling, back into it, kissing her and thanking her for being the sexiest woman on earth. "So soft," I said, "and you smell good and look good and have these lovely—" and soon I had to help her out of that damned underwear a second time.

We hit the snooze alarm twice that morning. Then she turned into a remorseless Norse maiden, yelling, "Get your ass out of the sheets, Jake Hines!" and scrambling nimbly into her freezing jeans and sweaters. She braided her yellow hair while I started both vehicles, and we snarfed handfuls of cereal on the way out the door. I followed her through downtown Mirium with a cup of coffee steaming in the cupholder, and waved as we pulled into opposing streams of traffic on the highway. I was already planning my next heat-saving maneuvers: a baffle for the trapdoor into the attic, a shag rug for the bathroom floor. We bought more long underwear, and got used to a life lived almost entirely in the kitchen.

DRIVING CAUTIOUSLY INTO the swirling snowstorm now, I thought how fast we had accepted our difficult lifestyle and found pragmatic solutions. In the driveway, my headlights lit the monster icicles that hung all around the roof, mute proof of the heat leaking through the shingles. I shifted into four-wheel drive, kept the speed up, and drove right past the house to the shed in back, where I'd rigged a tent of plastic sheeting over the end of the lean-to. I snapped it open, drove in, lit the tiny propane space heater I kept there, and snapped the plastic snugly shut around my improvised garage. In town I'd have been ashamed of this tacky lash-up, but out here it seemed ingenious and I was proud of it.

The phone was ringing in the kitchen as I came in. I grabbed it up and answered, and Trudy said, "Aha, there you are."

"Man, am I glad to hear from you. How're you doing? Somebody finally dig you out of that snow-bank?"

"Oh, they're still working on the van. See, the first tractor, the one we hired from the farmer there? He just dug himself another hole next to the van, only deeper. He said, 'Shit, I think I might be here till spring.' It's a mess up here, Jake, snowing hard and a terrible wind blowing. But I found a builder in Thief River Falls, he's got a thing, I think they call it a Wisconsin loader?"

"Michigan loader." I snaked the phone cord over to the propane heater and turned the heater button to high.

"Okay. My tractor guy suggested him. It took some persuading, but he came out after I promised to tell him all about the crime scene. I know I can't, but I'll make up something. Bless him, he's digging out our van as I speak. How did we ever manage before we had cell phones, can you remember?"

"My group used smoke signals." I slid a beer out of the refrigerator, snapped it open, and rummaged through the shelves for snacks. "What about the crime scene you went up there to see? You still gonna try for it?"

"We're working on it now."

"How'd you get to town?" I found some cheese, pulled a box of crackers out of the cupboard, and carried all my goodies to the shelf by the sink so I could snuggle with the heater while I ate.

"The sheriff's office has a Jeep with chains on all four wheels. I found a kindhearted deputy—" I'll bet you did, I thought. I well remember how kindhearted I started to feel the day I met Trudy Hanson. "We off-loaded the main things we knew we'd need out of the van, and came over here and got started. Good thing we did—" she lowered her voice "—some crazy guy went berserk here, Jake. Looks like in the middle of robbing a 7-Eleven he just totally lost it and killed the clerk with a shotgun at close range. Then he turned it on himself. He blew out the front window with the second shot. Bad move, wow. Temps up here are way below zero."

"Here too."

"I heard. Anyway, we're scraping freezing blood and brains off a wide selection of high-calorie snacks."

"Babe, I gotta tell you, you're spoiling my cheese and crackers."

"Too flamin' tough. How come your poker game ran so late? I've been calling you for hours."

"We had a DOA. On Burton Hills Drive. That was nice and cool too."

"And you took the call? On Sunday night? Your whole crew took sick over poker?"

"Long story. I'll tell you later. Any predictions when you might get home?"

"No. We'll be done here in a couple of hours. After that it depends on when they get the van out of the ditch, how damaged it is, when they get the road open. I probably won't get back to the farm till my week's up, though. Jimmy's got calls stacked up the yazoo, we'll all have to grab naps on the road and keep going."

"Poor poor Trudy. Keep in touch, will you?"

"Sure. Wear all your fuzzies tonight, sugar muffin," she murmured, close to the phone. "It's gonna be cold in that bed."

"I know," I said, "I'm gonna miss you all the way down to my toes." I hung up and finished my beer while my long johns warmed on the radiator. Adding ski socks and two sweatshirts to my nighttime attire, I turned slowly in front of the heater until all my sides were equally toasty. Then I believe I achieved a personal best on the stairs to the bedroom.

FOUR

KROC REPORTED fourteen degrees below zero on my truck radio at seven-thirty Monday morning. Expect a high of five below, the man said, with gradual clearing. Sunrise tinted the undersides of pewter-colored clouds. Snow had stopped falling, and the plows had been out, so morning traffic flowed toward Rutherford at its normal rate, which is ten miles above the speed limit with an occasional crazed lane-jumper bombing through at eighty-five.

Inside Government Center by seven forty-five, I kept my head down, skirted morning chat groups, and bore toward my office with a single thought: Time to make work lists before the crew gets here. My phone rang, though, while I was unlocking my office door, and when I picked it up Lulu Breske said, "Chief wants to see you," and hung up.

Lulu's probably not rude on purpose. She's been the chief's secretary since the day he was sworn in, and she focuses on his needs exclusively. It works out well for Frank, for whom she greases the wheels. The rest of us have to live with how infuriating she is. Damn! I hurried into his office.

"Morning, Jake," McCafferty said, without looking up. He'd evidently been at work for some time; he had fancy-looking brochures, spec sheets, and high-gloss folders spread all over his desk.

I didn't sit down. "You get my note?"

"Yes. Thanks. So Pokey's doing the autopsy after all?"

"Right. With one of the docs at the clinic. Probably this afternoon or tomorrow morning."

"Okay. And you'll be there, huh?"

"Yes. I'd like to take Kevin with me, get him started on that."

"*Uh-huh.* Good idea. Now—" His prominent blue eyes dragged themselves away from the bright-colored folder in his hand and focused on me. "I know you're already plenty busy, but I have to ask you to help me with one more thing this morning."

"What's that?"

"Remember this project?" He waved the brochures. "Paper-free records?"

"Brave New World?" Frank had been holding meetings about all-electronic reporting for so long, the idea had earned its own derisive nickname, based on one of the contending systems, which was called New World. I had attended several meetings and sat on one committee, but I never took it seriously. Cops trusting their arrest records to a machine that has fainting fits in a thunderstorm? Please. We copied important stuff in quadruplicate.

Admittedly, all those copies were creating problems of their own. The department had grown by a third in the last five years, and thanks to computers we were churning out reports faster and faster. It was easy to envision a day in the future in which the records room, swollen to grotesque proportions, collapsed and buried us all under a paper mountain.

Lately we'd all noticed Frank holding serious talks with the cool guy in the Italian suit who brought brochures to one of our paperless-records meetings last year. Sometimes the suit brought along a studious youngster in round glasses who did a lot of silent nodding.

"The engineer's here," Frank said. "He wants to start today."

"What? You mean…I thought you said…we're actually gonna do this?"

"Sure. I told you the council approved the first payment."

"But isn't that just for the study? I thought you said we were starting the study in March."

"I did. But then they ran a study in Iowa City, and everything worked fine. So for us they want to go ahead and build a parallel system. Run it for a while in tandem with what we've got. They can always take it out, they keep assuring me, if we're not satisfied with it when it's finished."

"But we're not gonna wait till March?"

He flailed his big arms around. "Another big job got delayed, so they've got a programming genius sitting here in Rutherford going to waste. They wanna start our job now."

"Chief, I've got a brand new homicide, I really can't—"

"I know that! Don't get in a lather, now, this doesn't need to take much of your time right away. He's gonna be mostly working with the people in the records room anyway. Just detail one person from your crew to visit with him a couple of times a day for a while, help him get a sense of your priorities—"

"Which are what?"

"I don't know!" His voice rose. "We'll all find out as we go along, damn it, I told you that."

I saw too late that I had touched a sore spot. Frank

was the smart guy who sold the city council on computer-aided dispatch, tweaked hell out of the budget to put laptops in the squads, and had been pushing paperless records ever since the idea was born. But though he loved computers in theory, personally he found them confusing. Lulu produced all his letters, and though he had a PC on his desk and knew how to use it, he still sometimes typed his private notes on the old Selectric in the corner of his office. The move to paperless records, I realized, was going to be harder on the chief than anybody.

"I need one person from each division to act as liaison." He pronounced it *lays-on.* "Gotta make sure we don't lose any…uh…functions." He punished the springs of his desk chair and kicked his desk. His feet are too big for most of the spaces he occupies. "Who's the best gearhead you got in there? Next to yourself, of course." His upper lip curled, just slightly, and I glimpsed the looming hazard: I'd always understand this new system better than he would, and he would always resent it.

"Lemme think about it." I wanted to get out the door. "We meet this guy in the records room? What time?"

"Nine-thirty. Okay, we set on that? Now. You dealt with the media yet on this homicide?"

"No." I looked at my watch. It was three minutes after eight. "Will you? It's all in the note I left you—" We went over it again: white male, early thirties, name and address unknown. "I'll have more for them in a couple of hours, but—" I could hear my crew in the hall. "I gotta get everybody going on this, Frank."

Bo and Lou were waiting silently in the small

meeting room, and Ray walked in with me. I could hear Darrell Betts talking excitedly in the break room, his voice rising as he reached the punch line of a joke that made Rosie Doyle explode in laughter.

"Go get Rosie and Darrell in here, will you?" I asked Ray. "Where's Kevin?"

"Records room, I think."

"Get him, too. We've got a ton of work to do right away." The phone was ringing again in my office. I ran and answered.

"Got lab space for four o'clock," Pokey said.

"At Hampstead County?"

"Yah. Got Dr. Stuart, too."

"You're sure the body's going to be thawed out enough—?"

"Yup. Stuart says is almost ready now. You gonna be there?"

"You bet." It was good luck, getting Stuart. He'd given us substantial help on a spooky pair of mutilations last year; he's smart, and he seems to be unruffled by Pokey's idiosyncrasies. "How soon do you figure my guy can take fingerprints?"

"Oh—anytime after ten, probably. Just make sure he's done before time for us to start, hah? Lab's only got one hour free, no time to fool around."

"We'll do it." I punched Off, grabbed the stack of papers from my desk, and hustled to the small meeting room. Ray and Kevin stood in the hall, talking intently. Rosie and Darrell gabbed merrily at the table while they arranged their coffee and notebooks. "Come on in, guys," I said. "Darrell, put a sock in it, willya? We gotta hump it this morning." I don't waste time on formalities with my crew. They know I don't harass them for the fun of it.

"That DOA I got called to last night is definitely a homicide." I passed around the copies of the ICR I'd prepared the night before. "Read these as soon as we're done here, but right now—" I looked at my watch; it said twelve minutes after eight "—I'm going to assign your new jobs for this case. Don't drop your existing cases, work them around the new jobs. Bring any promising leads to me right away. First thing we need is identification on this John Doe.

"Darrell, when we finish here and you've read the ICR, check out the rolls of film I put into evidence last night, take them to Jay Billingsley, tell him we need two sets of prints ASAP. Then come back here and check out everything else I put in evidence last night. All the blood work is in the freezer, be sure you take the paper bags as well as the kits." He was scribbling notes at top speed; misspelled or not, he always seemed to be able to read his own notes. Darrell's track record for doing everything I send him to do is beyond reproach. "Third, go to Hampstead County Pathology Lab and pick up the fingerprints one of our guys will be taking from the victim. Don't forget to sign his evidence form. Take the blood work, the prints, and the jewelry to BCA—the road's open all the way by now, isn't it?" Nobody knew. "Call the State Patrol, find out. And listen, the stuff that's in the freezer? Get the cooler out of the cupboard in the evidence room, take it in that.

"Oh, and at the Hampstead County Lab, pick up the clothing from the body and take that to St. Paul too. Make up our evidence forms for it—copies to everybody, and don't forget to file them when you get back here. In St. Paul, follow BCA guidelines for how and where they want the stuff checked in up there. Don't get into any pissing matches. Any questions, call me. Come back as soon as you can; I really need a clone for every one of you today.

"Ray, I want you to go back out to the crime scene and search for the gun and the missing clothes off the body, the shirt and the shoe."

"Is it marked? Where you found the body?"

"We left the tape up. It was blowing like hell out there, though, so some of it may have blown away. And you can expect a lot of drifting."

"Otherwise you think my chances are excellent, correct?"

"Ray, we have to say we tried." He nodded glumly.

"Lou, we've got a DOA here with no identification whatever. Fingerprints may take a couple of days and DNA much longer, meantime we need to get lucky. Check Missing Persons and Attempt to Locate reports for the five-state area. Do some networking around the state, see if anybody you know is looking for anybody.

"Rosie, same thing—check all the homeless shelters, town and county as well as Twin Cities."

"How about battered women's clinics?"

"Absolutely, good thinking, he could be a spouse of one of them. Spread the victim's description around, ask them to talk to all their clients.

"Bo, I want you to get in touch with every snitch you can reach this morning, find out if there's any action going on out there that might have generated a nearly naked body here last night."

"He was under a highway, right? I better call Chicago and Milwaukee too."

"Right. Start nearby and keep expanding the circle.

Kevin, I'm gonna want you to go along with me to
the autopsy at four o'clock. Meantime contact all your
POP officers, tell 'em what we've got, get 'em all
networking, see if anybody's got a clue who this guy
is." I looked at my watch. It was eight-thirty-three.

"Okay, everybody but Rosie, go to it. Beep me the
minute you learn anything. Rosie, one more thing—"
She sat with her pen poised over her notepad.

"Complete change of pace here," I said. "Remember all-electronic reporting?"

"Brave New World? Sure."

"You won't believe this. The chief says it's actually happening. Today."

"Oh, fantastic!"

"Well, glad you're pleased. Because right now the
problem is this: the technical genius is on his way
here, and the chief says we need one watchdog from
each section, to show this guy where the forms are
and make sure we get all the access and reporting
space we need. I want you to do it for our crew."

"Oh, Jake." She slammed her case file on the table. "*Jeee-sus!*"

"What?"

"When I tested for this job, didn't I beat all the
guys I went up against?"

"By a country mile," I said.

"Okay," she said, "and didn't you promise me if
I came in off the street, you'd still treat me like a real
cop?"

"Haven't I always?" I asked her, stuffing reports
and my cell phone into my briefcase. I slid my cuff
back. It was eight-forty-three.

It was a mistake for me to look at my watch. Rosie
Doyle picked up the stack of papers in front of her

and threw them into the air. "Then why do you keep trying to turn me into a secretary?" she yelled out of the paper blizzard surrounding her. Little combs flew out of her curly red hair, and the freckles on her nose looked suddenly vivid against her white skin. "You always give me the phone calls and the records searches! Pretty soon you'll be asking me to make coffee every morning!"

Frank warned me when I recruited her that Rosie Doyle was a top high school athlete and very competitive. "Her father and two of her uncles were Rutherford cops," he said, "every one of 'em stubborn as a post. Always sure they're right. Second generation's just the same, look like 'em, talk like 'em, argue till hell freezes over if they have to, everything's their way or the highway. Her brother Brendan's in the State Patrol, and her cousin Jerry's a sheriff's deputy."

"Since when is that a reason not to hire her?"

"It isn't. Just be prepared for the fact that she's used to competing with men, and she's anything but a pushover."

"Fine with me," I said. "What would I do with a pushover if I got one? I've got work enough for ten investigators and a budget for six. If she can hack it, she can have it."

Now I saw what Frank meant: Rosie's sharp edges were not so much feminism as force of habit. The only girl in a house full of tough male competitors, she had been guarding her turf since preschool and had a sharp eye for chauvinism in all its aspects.

"Rosie," I said. "Sit down. Sit down, damn it! Now listen," I tried a trick that sometimes works with angry prisoners; I hitched my chair closer to her, leaned in close, and lowered my voice. "This job I just handed you is positively not gender-specific. I gave it to you because you're a whiz on computers, far and away the best in the section." She shot me a little quick look, loving the praise but not wanting to get suckered. "But okay, if you still hate it after a couple of days, I'll change it. Only please, right now I don't have time. Go to the records room at nine-thirty, meet the guy who's starting to plan the new workstations, his name is…uh—" I looked at my notes "—Stacey Morse. Help him all you can. Will you?"

She dabbed at her sweaty freckles with a piece of Kleenex and said, reluctantly, "Okay."

"Rosie, lemme tell you something. The chief is nervous about this job—there's a lot of money riding on it, and he's not as confident as he'd like to be that it's the right answer. I promised him we'd make it work if we can. Help me deliver on that promise, and I'll owe you a big one. Okay?"

She rose to that bait, cautiously, a team player before everything. "I don't mean to be hard to get along with, Jake."

"You're not." The other thing prisoners have taught me is to get out of the room while you're ahead. I gave her one quick buddy tap on the shoulder and left her in the small meeting room, sheepishly picking up papers and putting combs back in her hair.

Lou French was standing in the doorway of my office, waving a piece of paper.

"You got something?" I said. "Already?"

"Hey, we aim to please." He handed me the print-out, an Attempt to Locate request from the manager of Clearwater Truck Lines in Minneapolis. A long-haul truck was past due at its destination in Duluth, and the driver wasn't answering his cab phone.

"Probably not our guy," Lou said. "Not much information on the driver, mostly ID on the truck. But there's a number to call."

"Come on in," I said, "let's try it." The number rang twice before a secretary answered, and then a man's voice said, "Dietz."

I told him about my DOA. John Dietz thanked me, but said my location was all wrong. "The rig I'm looking for would have been over on Interstate Thirty-five, somewhere between Albert Lea and Minneapolis."

"Still," I said, "if it's lost—why don't I just give you this man's description?" I told him everything I remembered about the body—his size and the complexion I figured he had when he wasn't frozen, his hair, his pants, and his one shoe. A note of uncertainty crept into John Dietz's voice.

"That does kinda sound like Wayne," he said, "but it can't be."

"Is it possible you could come down here and take a look?"

"Um, well…I'm supposed to be…well, never mind, I'll work it out. Yes, I think I'd better do that. Tell you what, I'll make one more try to locate this rig of mine. If I don't get any answer, I'll come right away." I gave him the address of the lab and told him I'd meet him there, and he agreed to let me know if he found his truck and wasn't coming.

Lou said, "We got a hit?"

"Possibly. Don't quit looking. A lot of things don't fit. This Dietz might call back any minute and say he found his truck and driver broken down in Iowa."

"Right. I'll stay on that search and do some more work on the break-in at the bowling alley." He went back to his cubicle looking jaunty, elated by his possible quick find.

I dialed Russ Swenson, who was ramrodding the morning shift. "Who've you got on duty that's qualified for fingerprints?"

"Lessee...Green's on duty today. And Kranz... Green's already out in a squad, though, but Kranz is just standing here picking his nose. If he can find his hankie, he should be just the ticket for one of your keen-eyed scientific in-VEST-uh-gations." Russ is talented; not everybody can manage to insult two guys at once like that.

"May I speak to him, please?" I have a long-standing promise to myself not to acknowledge Russ Swenson's taunts. He's an insufferable bullying bigot who can't stand to see dark-skinned people get ahead, but hey, who notices? Certainly not Jake Hines.

"Yo," Kranz said.

"Nick, I need you to go to Hampstead County Pathology Lab at ten o'clock to take fingerprints from the John Doe DOA we found last night. Can you?"

"Guess so," Nick said. "Beats taking guff offa Russ Hitler here."

"Good. And then wait there, will you, till Darrell Betts gets there, and give the prints to him. He's making a run to BCA this morning."

"Oh. So take along the folders and stuff, huh, the mailing stuff?"

"Yeah—go ahead, seal 'em up like you were sending them. Let's not give anybody a chance to bitch at us later." Since O. J.'s trial everybody's antsy as hell about carrying anything around, but the Supreme

Court has ruled that sending evidence by U.S. mail preserves the chain of evidence. So now when we hand-carry evidence to St. Paul, we seal it up as if we were going to mail it. It's getting a little ridiculous; lately we've been signing the seals on the packages and dating our signatures. What's left? Initial the date, maybe.

I stuck my head in the door of Frank's outer office, found his door closed and Lulu stapling pages as if her life depended on it. Standing in front of her desk, I wrote a note that said, "Meeting witness at lab for possible ident. of DOA—Jake." I folded it twice and started to put it in Frank's In basket; Lulu, glaring, grabbed it out of my hand, stuck a Post-it note on it, ran it through the date-and-time stamper, and then put it in Frank's In basket.

"Have a really great day, Lulu," I said. I found a Polaroid camera loaded with film in the records room, put it in my briefcase, got a fresh cup of coffee and a glazed doughnut from the break room, and juggled the whole load outside to my pickup against a stiff breeze that cut like a knife. I could have taken a division car out of the nice warm basement garage, but as long as this storm system kept dumping snow on us every few hours, I liked my own four-wheel drive. Heavy-looking clouds moved in fast out of the north while I scraped my windshield, and by the time I turned the corner on Fourth Avenue and headed into the Hampstead County parking lot, the sky had darkened completely, and a few flakes had piled up against the wipers.

Before I went inside I called BCA, asked for Trudy, and was told she and her crew had returned from

Thief River Falls, caught a quick nap on the cots in the supply room, and now were headed for St. Cloud.

"Huh. I thought she told me Red Wing was next in line."

"It was," Lucy said, "but the road's plowed to St. Cloud."

FIVE

THROUGH THE GLASS DOOR of the lab, I watched John Dietz get out of his company car and come up the walk, a tall, strong man wearing a fleece-lined windbreaker with a Clearwater Truck Lines logo on the chest. Once inside, he took off his glasses and stood staring at them nearsightedly, waiting for them to defrost. When he could see, he took his coat off and stood with it over his arm, wearing a blue oxford-cloth shirt with a company logo on the pocket.

I walked up to him, said, "Jake Hines," and showed him my badge. I took my time shaking hands, to give him a chance to get used to my face. It startles people I've talked to first on the phone. Because I grew up in Minnesota and have a midwestern accent, they're expecting pale skin and blue eyes. Instead they see almond-colored skin, Asian eyes, a nose like Crazy Horse, and dimples. I can't help them sort it out, either; I have no idea who my parents were.

I gave him the department card with my e-mail address and phone number, and he fastened it carefully under the clip on his clipboard, then pulled a company ballpoint out of his pocket protector and wrote my name next to the card. The busywork steadied him.

He got a little spooked again, though, as we went through the door of the morgue. Waiting to view the body under the sheet, he stood rigid, with a nerve jumping in his hard-clamped jaw.

Thawed overnight, the victim lay flat on his back, with arms at his sides. The skin of his face had faded to waxy marble. The big wound on the right side of his face drew the eyes away from the undamaged left side, so that the whole face now looked abused. John Dietz drew a ragged breath and said, "Aw, shit."

"You know him?" He nodded. "Is he your missing driver?" He nodded again and mumbled something. "What?"

"Wayne Asleson," he said. "That's his name."

We went out to the little waiting room. I sat in a corner with Dietz while he collected himself. In a couple of minutes he cleared his throat and began to tell me what he knew. Wayne had worked for Clearwater Truck Lines for five years. He did short hauls in the Twin Cities area for the first eighteen months, Dietz said, and when he built up points enough—the company had some rating system that measured trustworthiness and good judgment—he began to make long hauls, to North Carolina first, and then to southern California.

"Then for the past eighteen months or so," Dietz said, "he's been on the Nogales run regular. Drivers like to get fixed routes with regular schedules, and Nogales is one of those. A load down and back in ten days, then five days off. Stays the same year round, they get a schedule they can count on, even get certain places where they meet buddies to eat and shoot the shit with. Makes it less lonely on the road. Once Wayne got on the Nogales run, he never changed."

"So," I said, staring at my notes, wishing I knew anything about long-haul trucking, "What does Minnesota get so much of from Arizona?"

"Not from Arizona," he said. "Mexico. That's

where the *maquiladoras* are, all those factories that take American parts and assemble them cheap. Then they ship 'em back across the border to warehouses in Nogales, Arizona, and we pick 'em up there and bring 'em to places like, well, for instance, the load of CD players and amplifiers that Wayne had this time, that's headed for a music store in Duluth. Where is it?'' he asked me.

"What?"

"Where's the rig?"

"We don't have your truck, Mr. Dietz," I said. "We had no idea our DOA was a truck driver till we talked to you."

"Well, but—" He stared at me. "What about his partner, then?"

"He had a partner?"

"Sure. That's how long hauls work, usually. One guy drives while the other one sleeps. So the truck keeps moving without drivers getting overtime."

"Overtime's too expensive, huh?"

"Oh, it's not our rule. The government—OSHA and them—they got laws that drivers can't drive more than ten hours a day, or seventy a week."

"I know the trucks have beds in them now, but don't they have to stop to eat?"

"Not always. Lotta drivers carry provisions for two meals a day and only stop for one. That space behind the seat has a toilet, refrigerator, most of the comforts of home." He shrugged. "Except a shower. But a lot of the truck stops have those."

"I see." It was obviously a big subject. I was already wondering how much it was essential to know, which facts I didn't have to take the time to learn. "Okay, well—what's the partner's name?"

"Roger Carr. On this trip. Before that Wayne was partnered with Tom Deever, ever since he got the Nogales run. But Tom transferred to North Carolina because his wife wanted to be near her mother, she's getting on in years—"

"And Roger Carr, he's new with your company?"

"No, oh no, Roger's been with us—uh—about a year longer than Wayne, actually. But he lost his partner, see, just before Wayne did, because Buddy Hall, who was Roger's partner, wanted to get off long hauls, because he said being away from home so much was starting to affect his marriage—"

My eyes were glazing over. "So these two drivers, Roger and, uh, Wayne, they were new to each other."

"But I figured it would work out," John Dietz said, "because they both wanted long hauls, they were experienced drivers, and Wayne knew the Nogales run well. It's tricky matching up long-haul drivers—" he rotated his head uncomfortably, as if his shirt collar hurt "—because if they don't get along, that truck cab can get too small in a hurry. But this first run seemed to go smooth as silk, they made every checkpoint on time, and nobody had any complaints."

"But then this morning they didn't show up when you expected?"

"Right. Well, not show up, they weren't due in Duluth for a few hours yet, but they didn't check in when they were supposed to. They're supposed to send an e-mail every eight hours or five hundred miles, whichever comes first."

"The cabs have computers now?"

"Yes. Laptops mounted on the dash. I got to work this morning and found my night dispatcher very concerned, because he'd just checked his list and found one rig, Wayne's rig, that hadn't checked in since three o'clock yesterday. So right away I sent an e-mail to Wayne and Roger. I waited ten minutes, and when they didn't reply, I called their cell phone. Although, their last morning out, and they were due at the Mall in Duluth anytime in the next two or three hours, you'd expect them to be in that cab, humpin' for the finish line. But anyway, our standing orders are, if you're out of the truck, take the phone along. So I called. But they didn't answer.''

"You didn't think they were just stuck somewhere in the snowstorm?''

"Not likely in one of our rigs. Besides tremendous power, we've got communication systems up the ying-yang—our drivers don't just drop off the screen, anything goes wrong, they get in touch right away. Our whole system's based on knowing where everybody is all the time. But just to make sure, I called the music store in Duluth. They said, 'No, they're not here yet, but we expect 'em in a couple hours.' Which I knew, of course. That's when I called the police.''

"And Roger Carr has still not called in?''

"No.'' He squinted at me unhappily. "Do you know what happened to Wayne's face?''

"That's a gunshot wound, Mr. Dietz.''

"A gunsh—ohmigod.'' He swung sideways on his chair and clutched himself. He rocked a while, grunted a couple of times. When he could talk, he asked, "How could a gunshot make that great big hole?'' I explained the effects of a bullet fired at close range. Hearing it made him sick and miserable; his skin got a greenish look. His mouth hung open and a little trail of spit ran out the left side and down to his chin. When it looked about ready to drop off, I handed him a Kleenex. He jerked erect and mopped his face sheepishly, staring into the corner and muttering "Godalmighty" several times.

"I know it's hard to accept," I said. "You haven't had any other trouble with your drivers recently?" That snapped him out of his daze; he faced me, and his eyes got sharp and angry.

"I certainly have not. Eleven years, I've been managing this office. Eleven years! And I was assistant manager at the Chicago branch for five years before that. And no serious trouble, ever! This is the first driver I ever lost. Ask anybody! I stay right on top of everything, my crews don't fool around."

"I believe you." To quiet him down, I got busy with details. "Let's see, let's get some information here—" He gave me all the numbers off the truck, both the tractor and trailer. I asked for all the information he had on his two drivers, and he gave me meticulous employment records that included height and weight, date of birth, education. I got Wayne's address and phone number, and Roger's. Roger had a wife named Connie. He gave me the name of the restaurant where she worked. "And the name of Wayne's wife?"

"Wayne's not married."

"Girlfriend?"

"Never saw one."

"Hmm. Was he gay, do you know?"

"You kidding? A long-haul driver? He'da had the shit beat outa him years ago."

People always think they know, but they don't. I put down "Mgr thinks not gay," and said, "Will you excuse me a minute? I want to get some people working on this."

I called the station, got Kevin on the line, gave him the short version of everything Dietz had just told me, and asked him to go see Connie Carr at the restaurant where she worked. "Tell her we haven't found her husband, he may be fine, but just ask her what she thinks. Stay with her if she needs help, get Victim's Services to get in touch with her. Now gimme Lou."

I went through the information again with Lou, adding, "The victim's address is in Mantorville, you know anybody there?"

"Everybody," Lou said. "My mom grew up there."

"Everybody in Mantorville is what, three or four hundred people?"

"Closer to a thousand now. And okay, there might be some kids and a few newbies I don't know, but I'm tight with all the old-timers that count."

"Well, good, then, call some people you know over there, and get all the skinny you can on Wayne Asleson. Including, did he have a girlfriend. Or a boyfriend," I added as an afterthought.

"A boyfriend? I can't ask a question like that in *Mantorville,* for cat's sake."

"What, Mantorville can't stand a reality check? The bell doesn't toll for Mantorville?"

"Aw, Jake, gimme a break."

"Find out all you can," I said. "He wasn't wearing that ring and chain for no reason. Gotta be somebody in his life he cares about."

I went back to John Dietz, who was getting back into management mode, smoothing his hair and looking at his watch. "One thing I wanted to ask you," I said. "Was there anything particularly valuable in this load Wayne was hauling?"

"I brought you copies of the bills of lading," he said, handing over a big rustling stack of paper. "This load was music equipment mostly, CD players, sound systems, entertainment centers. Pretty high-end stuff. I guess the whole load would go, retail, probably half a million dollars."

"Whoa, that much? Well—but I suppose there are all sorts of alarm systems and so on, huh? A load like this would be tough to steal?"

"Well—" John Dietz shifted in his chair and examined the ceiling light for a while. "It would be tough to steal *part* of a load. We have a great records system for keeping the drivers and shipping clerks honest. But—it's never happened to me, but whole loads have been known to disappear, on rare occasions. Usually in seaport towns, of course."

"You saying the whole thing, truck and contents? Stolen and sold?"

"Presumably. The only missing loads I know about have never been found."

"So they went to some other country."

"You have to think so." The conversation was making him very uncomfortable.

"The truck part of the deal would be worth something too, huh?"

"Oh, hell yes. This one's new, so—a sleeper cab, latest electronics, full refrigeration hookup, and compressed air suspension? Well upwards of a hundred thousand."

"Wow. You folks aren't playing beanbag, are you?"

"Nope. Big game, keeps us on our toes. Loads have to keep rolling, trucks clean, deliveries on time, customer confidence high. An incident like this—I hate it. My insurance company hates it worse—you'll be hearing from them, I expect." He gave me another card. "Anything you can do—"

"It's important to us, too. I'll put my best people on this." My entire staff was already working on it, but why worry the man? My beeper gave three blips. John Dietz stood up and said, "Okay, well—" shook hands, and left. I called the department.

Lou said, "I found her!"

"Who?"

"The dead guy's girlfriend. Everybody in Mantorville knows she's been living in Asleson's house since last June. Her name is Cathy Niemeyer. After enough people said that, finally I just called his house. She was sleeping; I woke her up."

"What did you tell her?"

"That his rig is missing. And I asked if we could come to see her. She said yes, any time before three or so, she goes to work at five." He gave me the address and directions.

"Is Ray back?"

"Haven't seen him."

"Okay. I'm going to Mantorville right now to talk to her. Page me if there's anything new. Oh, and will you make sure everybody knows we ID'd the body? No use wasting any more time on that." I pulled the Polaroid camera out of my briefcase, went back in the morgue, and took a couple of full-face shots of the victim.

Driving out of town, I detoured to Burton Hills Drive, where I spotted Ray, crouched high on the rip-rap, peering under the overpass. I pulled onto the shoulder ahead of his car and blew my horn. He waved and climbed down, stiff and awkward on the loose rock.

"I haven't found a thing," he said, standing by my window knocking snow off his pants.

"Hell with it then," I said. "Let's go to Mantorville." The sudden silliness of it pleased him so much he almost smiled; his eyes lit up and his long flat mouth turned down at the corners.

"My car—" he said.

"Follow me," I said. "We'll leave it at the car wash."

In the parking lot, he climbed into my car without question and sat silent with his long hands folded over each other in his lap. I was tempted to see how long he could last without asking me what the hell we were doing, but we only had twelve miles to go, so I started talking right away and downloaded details as fast as I could. By the time Highway 57 turned into Mantorville's Main Street, he'd heard everything I got from John Dietz, and knew we were on our way to see Wayne Asleson's girlfriend.

Mantorville's on the National Register of Historic Places, one of those proud little hamlets that cling on through bad times and good till they become too unique to ignore. Once a Pony Express station, later a stagecoach stop, it was a busy market center about a century ago. But the railroad closed the branch line, new highways went to bigger places, and the town unwillingly turned itself into a living historical museum by hanging on to what it had: well-built structures from a dozen eras back to the Civil War. There's a clutch of antique shops, an elegant Victorian bed and breakfast called the Grand Old Mansion, and an outstanding 150-year-old restaurant called the Hubbell House on a boardwalk in the center of town.

Wayne Asleson's house was nondescript but solid, with white-painted wood siding and small windows, set close to the sidewalk three blocks south of Main Street. There wasn't any bell. I raised my hand to knock, but just then the door opened a crack. I held up my badge and said, "Jake Hines. Rutherford Police Department."

She looked back and forth from my face to my ID several times, and said, "Are you the man who just called me?"

"That was another man in our department. I'm Lieutenant Jake Hines, chief of investigations, and this is Sergeant Ray Bailey." Ray held up his badge too. Finally she opened the door all the way, saying, "Come in. I'm very confused. And I'm not exactly dressed for company, I'm afraid. I just got up."

"I apologize for coming on short notice," I said, "Ms. Niemeyer, is it?"

She nodded. "Cathy." She shook hands with each of us, looking serious. She was a lanky woman who appeared to be in her late twenties, with sallow skin and mouse-brown hair hanging limp to her shoulders. She wore a haphazard assortment of knit clothing and no makeup. A percolator was making glupping noises on a gas stove behind her. She looked straight into my eyes and asked, "Have you found Wayne yet?"

I moved toward the gateleg table under the window, set my briefcase down, and asked, "Okay if we sit down?" She might be the fainting kind.

"Sure. I guess this coffee's about ready, would you like a cup?"

"No thanks," I said quickly. I didn't want her

starting all that business with cream and sugar. I pulled out a chair and stood beside it, remembered she was just waking up, and added, "But you go ahead, though. Please."

Ray said, "Could I get it for you?"

She sensed we were being too kind, suddenly, and stopped with her head cocked sideways, like a person listening to distant thunder. She looked from one to the other of us, licking her lips. The coffee boiled over. She backed to the stove, turned off the heat under the pot without looking at it, and said, "What's going on?"

"Cathy," I said, "we found a body in Rutherford last night that we believe is Wayne Asleson."

She frowned and shook her head. "Couldn't be. Wayne wasn't in Rutherford last night; he was over on I-Thirty-five, going through the Cities on his way to Duluth."

"The manager of the truck line has identified the body we have as Wayne Asleson."

"He's made a mistake." She was adamant. "Wayne called me yesterday afternoon, north of Des Moines, said they'd be in Duluth by this morning. He's up in Duluth right now, unloading his truck."

I pulled the two Polaroid shots out of my pocket and laid them on the table. "Cathy, is this Wayne Asleson?"

Still in denial, she stood over the pictures, not looking at them, shaking her head. Then she let one sidelong glance wander to the left-hand picture, and it got stuck there. She picked up the picture, stared at it with shocked eyes for a couple of heartbeats, and began to cry. She cradled the picture in her left hand and stroked it with her right, wailing to it on a rising note,

"Oh no no no no no honey no baby no baby no no no—" The sound of her horrified grieving grew louder and louder till it seemed to fill the little house and press hard against the windows and doors.

I leaned toward her, ready to catch her if she fell. Ray stood close to her other side. When tears and snot ran off her face onto the table, he reached to a box of Kleenex and quietly mopped up. Cathy didn't notice. She was in some painful private space with her lover, begging him nonono, don't do this baby, come back come back. Ray set a straight chair behind her and she sank onto it gradually, planted her elbows on the table, and leaned closer to the terrible picture, wailing, imploring it to come back come back, don't leave me baby. It was very hard to watch, and it went on for a long time, trailing off into an eerie silence in which she sat curled above the picture with her shoulders shaking. Ray and I stood over her listening to the refrigerator turn on and off.

Finally she sat up, mopped at her face with capable-looking hands, and whispered, "Can I see him?"

"As soon as you're ready." She got up shakily, turning her bloated face away, and disappeared into the bathroom. Water ran for a while, then she came out and went into a bedroom down the hall. She came back soon in jeans and a sweater, wearing dark glasses. She picked boots and a coat out of the jumble by the door.

"It's still below zero," Ray said, and she added a wool cap and mittens.

"Anybody have a grudge against him that you know of?" I asked her on the way to town.

"Wayne? He was the sweetest man I ever knew. Why would anyone want to hurt him?"

"We don't know. All we know is, somebody did. It would help if we knew why."

"Well, my best guess is, it was some kinda crazy nut. Anybody whose head was working right would have no reason to fight with Wayne."

She got through the ID at the morgue with just a brief storm of weeping, but looked exhausted when it was over. We took her back to the station with us. She came along without comment, like somebody who didn't know where she was going and didn't care. We went in my office and closed the door.

"You weren't worried about Wayne, huh? He wasn't late as far as you're concerned?"

"No. He told me they had a complicated load this time, off-loading might take all day. And I worked till one o'clock, so I was still sleeping when your office called me."

"You didn't expect him to come to Mantorville last night?"

"No, today. He was due today."

"You were expecting him sometime this afternoon?"

"And maybe not then. I have to be to work by five, so we agreed, if I didn't see him before four I'd leave supper in the fridge and see him after work."

"How long have you been living together?"

"Six months—almost seven. We were saving up to get married," she said, "but see, there's a problem. I'm already married." I looked up in surprise. She was a plain, straightforward woman; involvement with two men at once did not seem to suit her style. "Yeah," she shrugged, apologetically. "What a mess, huh?"

"So first you had to save for a divorce?"

"Yes. I have to pay an attorney and go through all this legal maneuvering because he won't sign for a no-fault divorce."

"Your husband?"

"Yes. Eugene Niemeyer. I thought he was all right when I married him, but he turned out to be...not all right. Kind of crazy, in fact. He used to get drunk and come home and want to do things—'' She blushed behind the dark glasses and looked uneasily at the tape recorder. Ray got busy turning over a page of his notebook; he fastened the edges with two perfectly placed binder clips. "And he got mean when he didn't get what he wanted. When I tried to leave him, he said he'd kill me first, and before I got out of there he almost did. He beat me up good; I spent a week in the hospital. So then I hired a lawyer, who got a restraining order to make Gene stay away from me. Also, she helped me keep my car after Gene emptied out the bank account. I'm sorry, I know you don't want to hear any of this—''

"Talk," I said. "We get paid to listen."

"You want some coffee?" Ray asked, "or some water?"

"Water would be good." She drank a whole glass, thirstily, and he brought her another.

"How'd you meet Wayne?" I asked her.

"At the truck stop in Rutherford where I used to work. I work in Mantorville now, at the Hubbell House, but back then I was working at the restaurant at Buck's Texaco. Wayne wasn't very noticeable at first, but gradually I realized how decent and nice he was. A lot of guys, with a waitress, are—you know. But Wayne treats everybody like a human being." Her mouth formed a shocked O suddenly, and she put her fingers to her lips. When she took them down, she said huskily, "Treated, I mean." Her eyes filled, and two tears ran over. Ray handed her a Kleenex and she wiped her cheeks absentmindedly.

"We didn't really date or anything," she said finally. "I wasn't looking for anybody, you know? I just wanted to be quiet and heal up. Wayne talked to me friendly when I waited on him, is all. Then one night when my girlfriend and I were getting off shift, we said something about a movie we'd decided to go see, and he asked if he could go along. After that the three of us used to do things—once we tried roller-blading. We were all so pitiful, we fell down just from laughing at ourselves."

She was quiet a few seconds, remembering. "Another day, a bunch of us took a bike ride. I didn't think about it at the time, but I guess Wayne had figured out my shifts and was coming by the truck stop when he knew I was due to get off. Then one night he asked me did I like to dance." The shadow of a smile moved across her face. "We went to that country-western place, Mac's Bar. Just the two of us…that night changed everything. About a week after that, I moved out to Mantorville to live with him." She turned her hands up, lifted her shoulders, and said, "He changed my life completely."

"What was he like, Cathy? What did he like to do?"

"Well, he liked to make me happy, for one thing." She brimmed over again. We waited. "He was a fixer. Always tinkering with a hinge or something. His house may not be fancy but, boy, I mean to tell you, the doors and windows all work.

"He enjoyed his garden. I guess you couldn't see

it under the snow, but we planted almost the whole backyard last summer. I've got a freezer full of vegetables downstairs. Pickles. Jam we made together—'' The jam undid her for a while. Ray got more water.

''He was systematic and patient. I used to worry that he'd get fed up with my problems. Like my car breaking down—he had to help me with the repair bills that month. Which made one whole month when we couldn't save a dime. I said, Wayne, you don't need this mess in your life. I mean, to have to help your girlfriend save up to get a divorce before you can plan your wedding? Who needs that?

''But he always said no, you're the best thing that ever happened to me and I'm gonna make you believe it.'' She shook her head with a wondering smile. ''He wrote down what he said were the three most important dates in our lives, and the next time he came back from a trip he had this bracelet.'' She held out her wrist and showed us a chain bracelet with dangling charms. ''Each one's a number, see? Here's twelve and twenty-five, that's my birthday—yeah, I was born on Christmas—and then four and fifteen, April fifteenth, which he said was the date we went to that first movie, can you imagine a man remembering that? And here's a five and a twenty, the twentieth of May, that night we went dancing.'' She held the numbers cupped in her hardworking hand, and said fiercely, ''*This* is the kind of a man Wayne Asleson was.''

''Did you give him the chain he was wearing around his neck?''

''With my mother's wedding ring on it, did you find the ring?''

"Yes. We have to keep it for now, but we'll be sure you get it back."

"Thanks. She gave it to me when she died. It was my most precious possession, so I gave it to him when he gave me this bracelet. I said 'I'll have it made bigger,' but he liked it small, so I bought him the chain."

"Okay. One more thing, did Wayne own a gun?"

"A gun? No. Not that I ever saw." She stared at me a minute with her color rising and asked, "You're not thinking he shot *himself,* are you?"

"No, we're not."

"Because he wouldn't, ever. He was a happy man. We were gonna have a *life.*"

I knew she'd like my next question even less. "Do you own a gun?"

"Do I own a...why in the world would I..." She looked at Ray, puzzled and indignant, and I saw him lean toward her in an involuntary gesture of support. I made myself sit still and wait; I needed her denial on tape.

"No," she said finally, stiffly, "I don't own any stupid guns, for heaven's sake."

My phone rang. I picked it up, and Mary said, "Julie Haydon is here. And Kevin said remind you it's after two-thirty, and you're due at an autopsy at four."

"Thanks." I put down the phone and said, "Cathy, will you excuse us for just a minute?" In the hall, I told Ray, "The caseworker's here from Victim's Services. It's Julie Haydon; will you introduce her to Cathy? And then stick with them till they seem comfortable? I've got to get ready to go to the autopsy.

First thing they better do, by the way, is arrange for her to get some time off from her job.''

"For sure."

"And then as soon as you pass off Cathy to the aid worker, write up your notes on the morning's work, will you? Everything you've got on tape and whatever else you remember. Put down *everything*. Be thorough. Because I might not get to my notes for some time."

I found Kevin and said, "Had lunch?"

"Lou brought a pan of leftover lasagna. There's some left, you want it?"

"Fantastic." I got a carton of milk from the vending machine and sat in the break room eating twice-warmed-over lasagna, somewhat crusty around the edges but still tasty. Kevin sat across from me, thoughtfully eating one peanut butter cookie after another from a bag.

"Tell me about your interview with Connie Carr," I said.

"Never happened. She's not at work, she called in last night sometime and said she just got word her sister was in the hospital and she had to go."

"They know where she is? Which hospital?"

"The person who took the message didn't get that information. I explained it was important we reach her, and they said she's supposed to call in sometime this afternoon and let 'em know about tomorrow. They promised they'd tell her to call us."

"Wow. So she doesn't know yet that her husband's missing."

"No. But some lucky person here gets to give her that news when she calls in from her sick sister's bedside."

"That better be Lou. I'll tell him. Does he want his pan back?"

"Nah, he said pitch it when I was done." I went down the hall to Lou's cubicle, found him on the phone, and made a time-out signal. He said, "Hold on a sec," and punched hold. I explained the Connie Carr situation and asked him to call dispatch and the front desk to be certain the call was routed to him.

"And you're going to be hiding where during all this?"

"Hampstead County Lab," I said, "watching doctors cut up a body."

"What a wimpy excuse," he said. "Go away."

I went back to my office, where Kevin was looking at his watch.

"My car's at the front door," he said. "What else do we need?"

"Tape recorder," I said, and passed it to him. "Thirty-five-millimeter camera. Plenty of film?" There were four rolls in the case. "Okay. Something for notes?" I grabbed a spiral notebook, looked at my watch again. "We've got fourteen minutes. Can you do it?"

"No sweat." He bullied his way through a couple of lights just as they turned red, and we pulled into the lab's parking lot just behind Pokey's Jeep. The snow had stopped falling, but the clouds hung dark and heavy-looking.

Pokey squinted at us curiously. "Two of you gonna watch?"

"Good chance for Kevin to observe an autopsy," I said. "And I want you to show him that little entry wound under the hair."

"Ah, yah. Little entry wound smart detective

couldn't see till I showed 'im.'' Pokey was tickled literally pink; his foxy little face glowed in the brooding light. He strutted in ahead of us and found Dr. Stuart, gowned and gloved, directing two men who were wheeling a gurney into the first examining room on the right. They shifted the body onto the high steel table in the room, and I took a couple of whole-body shots.

Stuart pressed a button to start the tape machine, spoke the date and time into it, and called out more numbers as they weighed and measured the body. Kevin started our recorder and began copy-catting the information into it.

"See this smear?" Pokey pointed to the victim's chest, and Stuart nodded. "Noticed it last night. Looks like dirt, but could be some blood in it, too. Let's get couple samples, hah?"

"Sounds good," Stuart said. They took a couple of scrapings and a smear of the marks on the victim's chest, then looked the body over front and back and peered into all his orifices.

"Ain't been in any fights lately," Pokey said.

"Subject has smooth healthy skin, shows no obvious marks or scars, has full set of teeth in good condition—" Stuart told the tape.

"Ain't been sodomized lately," Pokey said.

"—and shows no evidence of rape or abuse." Stuart took a blood sample and said, "Okay, let's look at the entry and exit wounds, now. Then we can open him up."

"Gotta razor?" Pokey asked.

Stuart looked alarmed.

"Wanna get hair off here—" He pointed to the victim's temple. "Whatcha think, I'm gonna cut his throat?'' He chuckled merrily while Stuart rummaged through drawers.

It's a kick, watching these two doctors work together. Pokey is animated and cheerful, as informal in the lab as on the street, chattering pretty much non-stop, cussing if he feels like it and laughing at his own jokes. Stuart's appearance is beyond clean and neat; he's the high priest of antisepsis, and he speaks, if at all, with clipped precision. I'm always surprised that they seem to stay on the same page and understand each other.

''Before I shave him, though,'' Pokey said when Stuart came back with an electric clipper, ''let's see can we get better look.'' Stuart adjusted a light. ''You see any gunpowder soot around wound? Hard to see in hair, but—''

''No,'' Stuart said. ''I don't think I do. But let me try a swab.''

''Couldn't see any last night, but light was so damn bad—and snow in everything—'' They looked anxiously at the scrap of cotton.

''Nothing,'' Stuart said.

Pokey went to work with the clipper, straightened, and said, ''*Now*, Kevin, you wanna see good example of close range entry wound? Look here—'' His bony finger pointed.

The hole had shrunk a little more, and glazed over.

''Looks like a rash around there,'' Kevin said.

''That's called stippling,'' Stuart said, leaning in so our four heads formed a kaleidoscope pattern above the body. ''Burn marks. From the unused gunpowder that blows out after the bullet. You might want to try several different f-stops,'' he suggested as I raised my camera, ''to see if you can show those.'' I switched my lens to the macro setting and crouched by the table. "Can't you get any closer?" The man was an expert in all things.

"Nine to ten inches is the best I can do with this lens," I said. He sighed.

"So, are you saying the gun was right up against the head?" Kevin was taking his first autopsy like a champ, crouched over the body with his clear blue eyes shining, looking carefully where the doctors pointed.

"No," Stuart said. "There's no gunpowder residue around the wound. And the wound shows no sign of that star-shaped bruise you'd see if the gun was right up against bone like that. And then this stippling, that suggests a distance of maybe six inches. Possibly eight, hmmm?" Pokey nodded.

"Wow. Hard to get that close," Kevin said.

"Not if he was tied up," I said.

"No marks of that," Stuart said.

"No." Pokey did one of his thoughtful multistage shrugs. "But no signs of struggle, either. No bruises, anyway. We send what's under his fingernails to BCA, hah? But don't look like much to me."

They had a lively chat, mostly in Latin, over the clotted mass of tissue and bone fragments hanging out the right side of the victim's head. They drew a big vial of blood, and took scrapings from the victim's mouth and anus. Then suddenly, with no warning, Stuart reached into his tray of shining instruments, picked up a scalpel, and made a deep V-shaped cut across the dead man's chest. He brought his knife back from the top of the V to its lowest point and, with one graceful motion, sliced straight down from sternum to pudenda. I took a quick peek at Kevin. He looked pale and a little sweaty, but he was standing firm, staring through the Y-shaped opening at Wayne Asleson's internal organs.

Which didn't tell us much, according to the doctors.

"Blood and tissue tests gonna take a couple days," Pokey said, as they were finishing, "but from what I can see I'd give couple years' pay to be in shape like this fella, hah?"

"God yes," Stuart said. "Killer cholesterol numbers, I'll bet—blood you can see right through. Heart looks good for another eighty years at least. We'll see what was in the urine, but the kidneys look perfect."

"So," I said, "you think he died from the gunshot?"

"Right through the brain stem," Stuart said. "Never made a sound, I would bet." He was packing body parts back into the cavity they'd come out of; he glanced at the clock above the door and said, "The next crew's waiting for this room, gentlemen, so—"

"Right." Kevin and I loaded up our gear and moved together toward the front door.

"Ah, jeez, it's snowing again, lookit that," Kevin said. The wind had come up again, too; we watched it blowing gusts of snow against the glass front door of the lab while we stomped into boots and pulled on padded coats, hats with earflaps, wool scarves. "Just think, we only got about three more months of this stuff to get through." He had survived his first autopsy without throwing up and had not grown faint even during the hardest part, the moment when the whining rotary saw began carving a wedge out of the skull. Now he was enjoying a burst of euphoria because it was over; he was feeling giggly and was trying to cover it up in the time-honored Minnesota way, by bitching about the weather.

Once in the car, driving back to the station, he grew thoughtful. "Boy, he sure got lucky, huh? That shooter."

"Maybe." I stared a while at snowflakes pelting the windshield. "You ever make any lucky shots?"

"Never. Every good shot I ever made, I worked for. You know, when I was first in uniform I was a firing-practice fanatic. I attended every bull's-eye match I could get off for, and at home, watching TV, during commercials I'd dry-fire at a doorknob till my mom threatened to throw me out of the house. A couple of times in those years I got up to a Grand Agg score in the mid-eight hundreds, and I made the Master Class. But guarantee you I could kill a man with one shot, with a handgun? Forget it. Hell, Jake, the winner at one of the state shoots usually scores, what, in the eight-eighties?

"Somewhere in there."

"So shooting at a fixed target, with no distractions, the best handgun shooters we've got in the state still miss the ten ring maybe twenty percent of the time."

"Well, but that's from twenty-five yards. You could be sure of a kill from six inches."

"Sure, if I could figure out a way to get the victim to hold still till I got that close." We watched the snow come down for a while, and then he said, "How would *you* do it?"

"Very quickly, I suppose. After careful planning. With a cartridge in the chamber and the hammer, if any, already cocked. And nobody else around. But that makes it harder, doesn't it? Well, in a crowd then?"

"Sure," Kevin said, "and then they'll all help you take off most of his clothes and throw him off the overpass."

"There you go," I said. "The more you think about it, the harder it gets."

SIX

"WHERE'S KEVIN? Never mind, the rest of you bring all your notes," I told my crew Tuesday morning, "and be in the meeting room in ten minutes."

"I have to be in the records room by nine," Rosie said.

"Bo's not here yet," Lou said.

"Ray, your phone's ringing," Darrell said.

I'm proud that my crew contains no ass-kissers. But sometimes I think longingly about a dog whistle tuned to whatever frequency would make investigators run to the round table in the small meeting room and sit down. I went in my office and scribbled a few hasty notes, called Mary at the support desk and asked her to hold our calls for an hour, stuck my head in the break room, and found Kevin making fresh coffee.

"Never mind that," I said. "Come to the meeting room right away." I swept Rosie, Darrell, and Lou in ahead of me. Bo hadn't come in yet, and Ray, down the hall, was still muttering into his phone.

"Let's start anyway," I said. "Rosie, tell us first, how'd you get along in the records room?"

"Oh, fantastic." She rolled her eyes up. "Mary and Stacey and I inventoried every form we've ever used since 1985. That's when we got the first computer system."

"I remember it. OARS, it was called. Information used to enter that thing and disappear forever. It was so user-hateful, for the first few months they'd only let senior officers use it; they were afraid all the beginners would quit.''

"Uh-huh. Only traces of it remain. We got the present system in 1992.''

"I've always thought it was pretty good. But you say the new one's gonna be better?''

"By orders of magnitude, Stacey says.''

"Stacey is the systems guy, right? What kind of a guy is he?''

"Dorky but cute. Corduroy pants, analog watch. Talks about subsets a lot.''

"And he wants you to count the sheets of paper in each form, or—''

"No. We counted the lines on the forms. And we figured out how many bytes in the answer spaces.''

"Shee. It's not exactly rocket science, is it?'' Darrell said. Rosie gave him a look that would have melted his shorts if he'd been paying attention.

"Okay,'' I said hastily, ''let's move along. Our DOA worked for Clearwater Truck Lines, do you all know that?'' I passed around copies of all the information John Dietz had given me. ''Then Lou found the victim's girlfriend—'' I told them about the interview in Mantorville, adding, ''Ray's got the notes on that, did he give everybody a copy? Good.''

"Wait a minute,'' Rosie said, ''I thought Ray went out to the crime scene yesterday to look for the gun.''

"I did,'' Ray said, walking in, ''Never could find squat. So I rode along with Jake to the big city of Mantorville.'' Rosie's bright eyes turned back to me, and I watched them darken as the thought formed: Ray goes to Mantorville for an interview, Darrell takes evidence to St. Paul, I work in records.

"Listen, I've got something now, though,'' Ray

said. "Sheriff's office is on the line. They got a call from a snowmobiler out near Oronoco, found a jacket and shirt in a field. The jacket's got writing on it that says, 'Clearwater Truck Lines.'" He looked around. "They say both garments have stains all over that look like blood."

"Are they bringing them here?"

"If you want them to."

"I'd like to see them, sure."

"Gotcha," he said, and walked out as Bo walked in. Bo took one of the two empty chairs and began looking through the pile of papers in front of him. I looked at him till he looked up and nodded shortly. His face looked set and hard.

"Okay, new jobs for today," I said. "Darrell, check for guns registered to either or both of these drivers, will you? And Lou, I want you to see if you can find Cathy Niemeyer's estranged husband. His name is…uh…" I shuffled through papers.

"Eugene Niemeyer," Ray said, coming back in. He sat in the last empty chair and shuffled through his notes. "Eugene, but they call him Gene, or sometimes Gee." He had done a good, thorough job of writing up the notes; he almost knew them cold.

"Yeah. You got a last known address? Give it to Lou. Lou, find that asshole, make him prove his whereabouts for the last four days. He's a wife-beater, maybe he found out about Wayne and got jealous.

"Ray, I want you to go over those weigh bills for the load Wayne's truck was carrying, look for anything odd or offbeat or extra valuable. Then get me a figure for the value of the whole load. And Bo—" My pager sounded; three loud beeps. We all jumped. I trotted down the hall and called Mary.

"I know you asked me to hold calls," she said, "but I've got the manager of Clearwater Truck Lines here, sounds like he's ready to bust."

"Put him on."

"The State Patrol just called me," John Dietz said

"Yeah?"

"They've found our missing truck. The tractor anyway—they say the trailer's missing."

"You're sure it's yours?"

"They read me the numbers; it's Wayne's rig all right."

"Where is it?"

"Up near Pine Island, in a patch of woods behind a farmer's barn—" he read me the directions. "They say it's got a lot of blood inside."

"You got a name for this farmer?"

"Uh...yes. Norman Schellhammer."

"Okay. You know we'll have to impound the truck?"

"I figured. I'd like to see it, though."

"Of course. We'll be sending it to the Bureau of Criminal Apprehension in St. Paul, for them to do the fingerprint and blood work and so on. You can see it up there. I'll call you with the address of the storage facility as soon as I know it."

"It's a break, isn't it?"

"Absolutely. Great news."

"All this blood—" his throat sounded dry "—I guess you have ways to prove, don't you, if it's all Wayne's blood?"

"Yes." I didn't want to talk anymore, but the man was plainly distressed, so I said, "We'll know a lot more as soon as we run some tests on this vehicle, Mr. Dietz, and we'll make certain you get all the facts as fast as we learn them.'' People find the promise of more information reassuring even when it's rotten news they're waiting for.

But I realized, after I hung up, that I'd forgotten to tell him about the jacket and shirt that the State Patrol was bringing in.

Which gave me an idea. I went back into the meeting room and said, ''Rosie, when those bloody clothes get here, see if you can find a size tag in any of it, or any marks or stuff in the pockets, to tell us if it's the victim's or his partner's.''

''Okay. You want me to check it in, too?''

''Yes. Write it up and check it into the evidence room. I'm gonna check it right out again to take to St. Paul, but let's not skip any steps. And then call John Dietz, will you, and tell him what we've got? Be gentle with him, he hates talking about blood.''

''You got it.''

''Fine. Everybody else but Bo, let's go ahead with what we've got so far. I just got a call that a farmer thinks he's got the victim's truck, so Bo and I are gonna go out and have a look. Kevin, mind the store, will you? We'll be back ASAP.''

They all watched out of the sides of their eyes as Bo and I walked out. Their faces were carefully noncommittal, but I could feel them wondering, Why is he getting a ride to Pine Island instead of a couple of days of processing gun permits? They know how I feel about promptness. Since he mostly does narcotics and vice cases, Bo has a lot of autonomy to start with. All the more reason for them to resent any sign he's working the system to his advantage.

I took a department car, because I wanted Bo to drive and I can't stand anybody driving my pickup but me. While he negotiated North Broadway and turned left on Thirty-seventh Street, I made phone calls. By some fluke, everybody answered that morning.

I gave the chief a quick rundown on the case and told him where we were headed now, and he promised to get Lulu working on the impound papers and the tow truck.

"Touch base with me later today if you can, huh?" he said. "I need a few new details every so often to feed the media."

"What say we give them the truck this morning," I said, "and keep the shirt and jacket till after lunch?"

"Good. I'll do it. But keep in touch."

I called BCA, got Jimmy Chang, and told him about the jacket and the truck.

"I'll add them to my growing list, Jake," he said. "We're not promising curbside service this week."

"I know that. Don't be so hostile. Which storage yard do you want this vehicle sent to?" He gave me the information, and I asked him, "Any chance you've got my significant other chained to a desk there someplace?"

"Hell no," he said. "My rule for van crews this week is that at no time are their butts to touch a chair in this building."

"You building a lot of team loyalty that way?"

"They've all begun to talk about fleeing across the ice to Canada."

"Rats. I was hoping to keep that woman. Any idea where she is right now?"

"About halfway to Montevideo. Some fool went postal in the feed store over there."

"Is that gonna be another all-nighter?"

"No. He mostly blew holes in grain sacks and feral cats, but there's one death. It doesn't sound complicated. I expect them back this afternoon."

"You mean I might get a glimpse of her if I brought the jacket up there myself?"

"Save your tires," he said. "Trudy convinced me they really do have to have some rest before they go out again, so I'm laying on an extra crew for twelve hours. Your lady can spend tonight in her own bed."

"Why, Jimmy," I said, "you're turning into an old softie."

"No, actually I was facing a possible OSHA fine for too many consecutive hours of hazardous employment."

Jay Billingsley answered the phone in his store, sounding harassed out of his mind, and said my pictures would be ready by midmorning. I called the station and asked Darrell to go get them by eleven.

Then I put the phone back in my briefcase and asked Bo Dooley's stone-hard profile, "Okay, tell me about it."

"About what?"

"Don't shit me, Bo. You were late twice last week and again this morning, and last Thursday you snuck out at four o'clock. What the hell is going on?"

He shifted in his seat, pulled in a deep breath, and let it out. Mumbled something.

"What?"

"Diane's back on the stuff."

"Oh." A truck passed us, and I watched our wipers scrape holes in the mess it threw on the windshield. "When she got out of detox last year, you said—"

"Yeah. She seemed so sure of herself, like she'd really...seen the light or something. But then...it was hard for her that Nelly hardly remembered who she was. I said, Look, it's just gonna take a little time. But it made her ashamed, Nelly turning away, asking me for everything. They told me, at that hospital in St. Louis, the first time she was in treatment, that women have a harder time than men coming back. That time she said, If I could just get away from here, I wouldn't have to see people I know. So I transferred up here. Now she says the trouble is she doesn't have any friends here. Didn't. Looks like she's made a couple now." He choked a little, and I saw desperation in his face.

"What happened?"

"Well...I kind of knew a while ago, from little things...she got slipshod around the house. Had trouble sleeping. I smoothed things over, I guess, I didn't want to know. Then Friday before last I got home and found Nelly in the house alone."

"Jesus."

"Yeah. I asked her, 'Where's Mommy?' and she said, 'Mommy went to the store.' She had jam all over her face, and the bread was out of the drawer. I said, 'You had a snack, huh?' and she said, 'Mommy had to go with the man, so I made lunch.' I think she'd been there almost all day by herself."

"You think? Haven't you asked Diane?" He shook his head. "You mean she hasn't been back?"

"Oh, she came back, toward morning, but she wasn't in any shape to talk. Stayed in bed all day, got up for supper, and disappeared again sometime that night. Since then she comes and goes on her own schedule and we don't speak."

"What are you doing about Nelly?"

"I found three different baby-sitters. None of them

can take her full-time. One she really doesn't like and another one I don't like, the one that made me leave work and come get her last Thursday. Something came up. Goddamn. I'm sorry I just ran out."

"Say no more."

"I shoulda told you sooner, but—I hated to narc on my own wife, you know?"

"Sure. You gotta do something pretty soon, though, Bo."

"I know. I'm scared shitless she'll burn the house down. Or I'll come home and find one of her new friends there and kill him with my bare hands."

That was a possibility, I thought, watching the nerve jump in his jaw. Bo has manners a girl would not hesitate to take home to her mother, but there's something in his face that would look right at home in a knife fight.

The sign for the Goodhue County line flashed by, and then the Pine Island exit.

"Slow down a little, can you? Lemme look at these directions again. Okay, within a mile or two here, we're looking for a graveled road on the right, with four mailboxes together—" I read aloud the names to look for. When we found a wagon wheel fixed on a post carrying four boxes with the right names, Bo turned east.

I'd been wishing I'd brought my truck since I noticed how much snow there was out here; the trees and even the fences were heaped with it. When the sun broke through the clouds, the glare on that vast expanse of white was blinding. But the road we turned onto was freshly plowed, and Bo got along all right.

We poked along, reading mailboxes again, till we

found one with "Norm Schellhammer" printed on the side. The driveway wasn't plowed, but half a dozen vehicles had carved a track; Bo poured on speed and fishtailed into the yard, stopping midway between the house and barn. A beefy guy walked out of the barn. We got out and showed him our badges.

"Norm Schellhammer," he said, shaking hands. "You wanna see the truck?"

"Yes," I grabbed my camera out of the backseat. "Is it far?"

"It's right out back of the calf pasture," he said. "Easiest way is through the barn." We followed him into the yeasty gloom, past the black-and-white rumps of a dozen Holsteins, and stepped out into a reeking brown space where a tractor with a scraper blade was parked by a colossal pile of manure. Schellhammer led us to a gate on the far side and into a pasture, where a dozen small copies of the cows inside peered at us out of a small corral.

"Couple of my calves got out, is why I found it," Schellhammer said. "Knuckleheads knocked the gate down. That's why they're all penned up, they can't come out till I get the gate fixed."

"So you had a big calf roundup this morning, huh?"

"Well, fortunately I heard the commotion, and so did Charlie." The dog looked up at the sound of his name and nudged his owner's knee. "We got ahead of all but three of 'em, chased 'em into the corral there, and then went looking for the rest. Right out here, I'll show you—" He and Charlie led us out through the damaged gate and along the rough track that Schellhammer and his animals had just stomped into two feet of loose snow. "I was following their tracks around this little grove of trees here, looking down. We came around the corner and Charlie barked—'' he pointed ''—and there she was.''

Taller than a room, looking top-heavy and truncated with its trailer missing, the cab was nosed into the small trees on the south edge of the woodlot. Its door logos advertised Clearwater Truck Lines. The sunlight glinted off its chrome. I set my camera for minimum exposure to the glare and took a few pictures.

''Right there's where they came in,'' Schellhammer said. He pointed across his plowed field toward the highway. ''See that track, under the snow? They pulled off down there on the dirt road that runs between my two wheat fields, and then just headed across the field to here.''

''Shee-ee,'' Bo breathed, in descending tones of awestruck tribute, staring up at the gleaming expanses of bright red paint and flawless chrome.

''Tell me about it,'' Schellhammer said, ''this here's one very sexy rig, ain't she? Or was, anyway, till somebody made that mess inside.''

''You looked inside?''

''Yup. It's not locked.'' He looked from one to another of our dismayed faces. ''What?'' he said, and then defensively, ''I didn't take anything!''

''I understand,'' I said quickly. ''I guess we'll have to ask you to let us take your fingerprints, though. So we can eliminate them from the others we find in there.''

''Oh. Damn, I never thought of that. Well, sure,'' he said, looking chagrined, ''you can do that. Sorry to put you to all that trouble.''

''That's okay,'' I said. ''If I found this baby in my yard, I'd look in it too.'' I fished two pairs of surgical gloves out of my coat pocket; Bo and I put them on. I climbed up on the high step and opened the door on the driver's side. Bo broke trail around the front, opened the passenger door, and said, "Oh."

"Careful," I said, "it's mostly on that side." He closed the door and came back around to my side. I stepped into the space behind the seat. "Well, there's a mess in the bunk, too." I took one careful step sideways, and Bo slid in beside me. Sunlight flooded across the awesome array of gauges and gadgets on the dashboard, the nifty little laptop cantilevered above it, and the complex gearshift box on its high console between the seats. In the brightness we could see, with merciless clarity, the gory mess of blood and tissue and bone fragments that had turned John Dietz's fancy new tractor into a slaughterhouse.

The biggest splash of blood and tissue seemed to be concentrated around the front doorpost on the passenger's side. The glass on both sides of it had been cleaned off, but blood had soaked the door padding and the seat, the floor in back, and the covers on the bunk. Blood had run down the door in streaks and pooled on the doormat, and the passenger's seat was black with blood.

"BCA will take pictures of all this," I said. "But as long as I brought the camera—" I reset the exposure, turned the flash on, and started.

"Some above your head too," Bo said. I looked up. A double track of tiny blood spatters marched across the ceiling.

"Now look at that," I twisted my neck half off to get the picture. "It looks like the blood spatters we found on the overpass. Two rows of little drops. Wait'll I tell Pokey. He said there wasn't any wound on the body that would make a spatter pattern like that. But this blood had to come from over there. Didn't it?''

''Hard to see how, though.''

''Let Jimmy Chang figure it out,'' I said, flashing away, ''blood spatters are his specialty. I wonder how that tow truck's doing?''

''When you're done taking pictures,'' Bo said, ''can we look under the bunk?''

''Uh…I don't think we'd better mess around, Bo, till the lab guys have finished with it. Bad enough Norm got in here and looked around.'' Good lawyers win appeals by showing crime scenes have been compromised.

''Okay. Then if you don't need me, I'm gonna take a look outside.'' By the time I climbed down he was under the truck, on his back with only his feet showing.

I knelt and peered under; he was feeling up the back of the jockey box under the step. ''Need any help?''

''Nah. Be out in a minute.''

I walked back to the car, dug out my phone, and called the station. Lulu said the tow should be along shortly and was bringing the impound papers. I got her to transfer me to Rosie's phone and said, ''Have you processed the clothes yet?''

''I just got 'em, Jake, I'll go to work on it right away.''

''Good. And remind Darrell to go get my pictures, will you? We should be back there in less than an hour, and I want to pick up the jacket and pictures and head right out for St. Paul.''

While we waited, I called John Dietz and gave him

the address of the storage yard where his truck was going, but cautioned him not to touch it if he got there when the BCA crew wasn't around. I gave him a number to call at BCA, to coordinate his visit with theirs. Then I hung up and stood in the yard, watching steam rise off a bare spot on the barn roof.

Norm Schellhammer stuck his head out the barn door and asked, "When do you want me to come in, then?"

"What?"

"For fingerprints."

"Oh...you don't have to do that, Mr. Schellhammer—"

"Norm," he said.

"Okay. Norm, well, you certainly don't have to come all the way in town. We can send a team out here at your convenience."

"No, listen, I feel bad, putting my stupid hands where they didn't belong, I shoulda thought. Besides," he said, brightening suddenly, "I've always wanted to see how that fingerprinting stuff works. Where do I go? That government center there in the middle of town?"

Norm Schellhammer wanted to get a look at our bells and whistles, I realized. Probably he needed a midwinter break from chasing calves and watching snow melt off his barn. I gave him directions to the station and the number to call.

When the tow truck arrived, I walked the driver out behind Schellhammer's manure pile to show him the problem. He said, "Okay, yes, well...," wheeled his outfit back out to the highway, and came in across the field on the original track. Bo crawled out from under the high cab while the tow truck turned and backed up to it. He stood beating snow off himself while the driver hooked on, hoisted the rear wheels in the air, and followed his own track out to the road. We were all out of there in fifteen minutes.

"Besides getting your pants wet," I said when we were headed back to town, "what were you doing under there?"

"I didn't think about it till I saw the truck," Bo said, "but these guys were on a regular run to Nogales, weren't they?"

"Yes." I waited through one of his impenetrable silences and finally said, "So?"

"I haven't seen it lately," Bo said, "but once in New Orleans and a couple of times in St. Louis I worked on big trucks like this that had been customized to haul drugs. Long-haul tractors assembled in a plant in Sonora, Mexico. They'd built special compartments under the bunk and behind the jockey box, and in those round fuel tanks that are lashed under the cab. They make 'em like a false bottom in a trunk, invisible from the outside, hard for an inspector to spot unless he takes the whole thing apart."

"You're suggesting this shooting might be drug-related?"

"Think about it," Bo said. "A shot like that, at point-blank range. Two guys on a long haul to the Mexican border, and they're new to each other. Maybe one of them got his arrangements disrupted. Or they started to make a deal, and it didn't hold up."

"All good ideas. But we've talked to their boss and one significant other, and they both describe steady guys with regular habits over many years."

"Bosses and bedmates don't always know everything they think they know." He watched the road for a while, and a long silence grew between us. Finally he said, "I guess I need to ask you for a favor."

"What?"

"Lemme take a day or two off. I gotta get Nelly lined up with full-time day care, this is too scary for her."

"Absolutely. What about Diane?"

"I'll deal with her when I can deal with her. If she doesn't go back into treatment, she's gonna end up in jail. But getting her to see that…I have to catch her when she's not too high and not too low."

"Or find her dealer and put him away."

"That would be nice too. But there's always another one of those." He sounded a hundred years old.

"What if you call the hospital where she was last in treatment and ask them to intervene?"

"If they drag her in there kicking and screaming, she'll just run away. Treatment doesn't work at all unless the client's willing."

"I know." I'm not an expert on substance abuse, but I'm a cop, so I do know how seductive crack is, how close to impossible it is to break its iron grip once it's got a good hold. Yet some people do it. "You've got vacation time coming, haven't you? Or sick leave?"

"Sure."

"Why don't you take off as soon as we get back? At least get Nelly settled, do what you can about Diane."

"I know how overloaded you are," he said. "I won't take any more time than I have to."

"Of course." A brilliant idea was blossoming in my brain. "Listen, you need somebody to monitor your cases while you're out, though, huh?"

"Oh...there's a few things oughta be followed up on, yeah. But hey, I won't be gone that long—"

"I know. But I'd like you to pass 'em to Rosie before you go."

"Rosie?" Bo's polite, and quiet; it's not his way to enter loud objections. But his expression said volumes.

"I've been giving her a lot of shit work, and she says I'm treating her like a girl."

"She is a girl. You don't want her bumpin' chests with bikers."

"She's a cop. She wants to get her turn at bat like everybody else. She can get in touch with you if she needs advice, can't she?"

"Sure. Whatever you think, Jake," he said, quickly tired of arguing. "I won't be gone long."

"Take all the time you need. I mean it. We'll manage." I called the station then and got Kevin. "Now that I've seen the truck," I told him, "I want to initiate a full-scale search for the other driver. Put out an Attempt to Locate on him, will you? Good. Now put Rosie on the phone, please." I told her we'd be there in ten minutes and asked her to meet us in my office with the clothing and the pictures.

Bo waited, impassive as a monument, while Rosie showed me the jacket and shirt and then sealed up the evidence bag. Her eyes got brighter and brighter as I explained that Bo's wife was sick, that he needed time off to find a good baby-sitter and was going to pass on to her some contacts that needed tending while he was gone. Then she followed Bo down the hall, writing rapid notes and looking happy as a fox in a hen house.

I stuck my head in Kevin's office and said, "Help

me.'' He trotted after me, loading evidence and gear into my pickup while I told him everything I knew about the truck we'd found in the field.

"Now we need to find the trailer," I said. "Get it into BOLOs, will you? Put out a Need to Locate. And then pass all this along to the chief, will you? He needs to feed the media beast. Oh, and here's my camera. Have Darrell unload it and reload it and take the used film to the developer.''

I told him Bo's wife was sick and mentioned Rosie's new assignment. He raised his eyebrows all the way to his hairline, but made no comment. I asked him to keep an eye on her for signs of stress, and he said, "Me take care of Rosie? That'll be the day." Kevin loves being in charge, though, so he didn't argue. In fact he did everything possible to speed my departure, and I was back on the road by eleven forty-five.

The sun had disappeared behind dishwater clouds. At the oil refinery at Pine Bend, massive columns of toxic-looking white smoke rose straight into the murk. Beyond it, a few farms still clung to a marginal existence on the fringes of exurbia, then State 55 split off to go into Minneapolis and I continued on U.S. 52. I crossed the hectic traffic around the 494 bypass and negotiated the noisy insanity of the Lafayette Bridge. By the time I parked my pickup in front of the red-brick rectangle on University Avenue that houses the Bureau of Criminal Apprehension, South St. Paul had worked its usual magic, and I was giving thanks for life in a small town.

Jimmy Chang was hunched over a book and a sandwich at his desk.

"Rats," I said, "I was gonna take you to lunch."

"No time," he said. "Wanna join me here?"

"I didn't bring anything—"

"Use that machine in the hall. Hardly anyone dies from it. This one is—" he scowled at it "—I don't know. Guess."

I went and got a ham on whole wheat that tasted like cardboard boxes, and a can of otherworldly purple soda. I moved a tall stack of unopened mail off a chair, pulled it up to his desk, and asked him, "What are you reading?" He held up his book and I read off the spine, *Parasitic Infestations of the Lower Bowel.*

"Catchy title. Are you dying to find out how it ends, or can we talk?"

He sighed and put the book down. "Let me guess. You brought me some items that you hope are evidence in a capital crime, and you want me to analyze various aspects of those items."

"How nicely you put it. I've got a blood-soaked jacket and shirt that were found in a field about a mile from my crime scene. The blood might belong to my victim, or his partner whose body we can't seem to find, or I suppose some of it might have come from the unknown assailant who blew my victim's brains out. It would help us a lot to find out which."

"We can do that," he said, "when we get to it."

"Good. I also have a stack of pictures, a couple of which I'd like to show you when you have a moment."

"Crime scene pictures," Jimmy said, "now there's a treat."

"They have a spatter pattern that I think matches the one in the line-haul tractor we sent to your Maryland Avenue yard this morning."

He looked up. "Spatter pattern? Show me."

I showed him the pictures on the bridge. "See these little marks on the curb? It's tough with all the snow, but—"

"Mmmm. Pretty faint."

"But you can see it's two rows of spots. See? And again in this one." He took the two pictures to the window for a better look. "You can see the pattern much more distinctly in the cab of the truck," I said, "and I think it matches."

"Tell you what," Jimmy said, "I'm still on my lunch break. It wouldn't really be putting you ahead of the others in line if we went there right now. You done with your sandwich?"

"I hope so," I said. "How soon will I know if ptomaine is starting?"

"Bitch bitch bitch. Will you drive? I'm resting." He slumped against my passenger seat, dozing, till we got to the yard, but once inside the cab of the tractor he came alive. Standing behind the driver's seat, eyeing the mess on the doorpost, he said, "Tell me about the victim. Describe the wound." I told him about the tiny entry wound and the way the gunk on the doorpost matched the string of matter hanging out of the right side of Wayne Asleson's head.

"Pokey and Jason Stuart did the autopsy, and they agreed on about a nine-millimeter gunshot at very close range," I said. "Six to eight inches. There was no blood visible around the entry wound when we found him, we didn't even know we were dealing with a gunshot victim at first. Yet you can see how massively the exit wound bled. So where does this double spatter of tiny drops on the ceiling come from?"

"No other wounds on the victim?"

"No."

"You said the other driver's missing? A spatter pattern like this could come from self-defense wounds on a second victim. Somebody who fought, got a wound, and then threw his hands up like this, see?" He illustrated how blood might fly from the arm or hand, in a fight, and get thrown across the ceiling.

"Of course the shooter had to be in pretty much this same area. Victim shot at point-blank range on the left side? The shot had to come from about here then," he said, leaning into the space in front of the driver's seat, "to put that bloodstain on the doorpost. Did you find the casing?"

"No. I didn't want to mess around in here till your crew was done with it."

"Excellent, go to the head of the class. Pokey didn't find the bullet either?"

"No. He thinks it went right through the victim."

"It must be in that doorpost then," he said. "I don't see any holes, do you?" We peered into the gore.

"Can't see any light coming through," I said.

"Must be buried in that mess of blood and tissue then. We'll find it if it's there. The other possibility, of course," he said, turning to look again at the drops on the ceiling, "is that this spatter pattern was thrown by the shooter." He pulled a tiny metal tape measure out of his pocket, measured the space between the rows of drops, and said, "Looks about right."

"For what?"

"For the kind of railroad-track wound that a retracting slide will put on the dorsal aspect of a shooter's hand if he holds it too high on the stock. If the shooter has a very large hand and a small gun, it can happen—or sometimes an inexperienced shooter who holds onto the gun with both hands—'' He mimed clutching a handgun with his left hand over the top of his right. "Never seen a wound like that?"

"Once, come to think of it," I said, "while I was an FTO, I took my recruit up for his qualifying rounds, and one of those fluky things happened; he just couldn't miss. By the time we were halfway through the format they had set up for us, he was totally pumped up because he was smoking every other rookie out there. Next time the targets turned, he screamed like a wounded bobcat and started spurting blood. He had his left hand too high over his right, and that slide made two slices as neat as a fillet knife."

"Exactly. That's just how it happens, from carelessness or excitement. We might be looking at something like that. We can compare this pattern with some samples I've got in the lab. And of course if we find the casing—'' He swung around the front seat to climb out and suddenly began to laugh.

"What?" I said.

"You're leaning on it," he said.

I straightened up and looked down, and the casing fell at my feet. "Now where did that come from?"

"It must have been caught in the covers. You pulled it loose when you leaned on the bunk," Jimmy said. "Wait, I've got gloves with me." He put one on his right hand and picked the casing off the floor. "Beautiful," he said, beaming at it. "Now—'' he glared suddenly at his watch "—you must take me back at once."

He grabbed another little nap on the way back. Curled sideways on the passenger's seat with the shell casing cradled in his hand, he looked like a clever child exhausted by playing doctor.

He snapped awake and aged twenty years as soon as I parked. "You have other evidence to check in, right? Take it to the second floor, Judy will help you. I'll take this casing to ballistics and ask them to expedite. Even so, I can't promise when they'll get to it. I've got a crew already scheduled to test the truck, though. This afternoon."

"You're gonna get a call from a man named John Dietz—"

"Already did." The elevator arrived, and we got in together. "He's coordinating with the head of the truck crew. You get off here," he said as the door opened. "I'm busy for the rest of the day and evening. Don't bother me anymore."

"Okay if I go back to the storage yard and nose around the outside of that tractor some more?" I asked him, holding the door.

"If you don't touch anything. Let go of the door now, or I'll kill you with my foot." I smiled and blew him a kiss as the door slid shut between us. Jimmy doesn't know any more about Asian martial arts than I do; all the men of his family are teachers, and he's spent his whole life with his nose in a book. His attempt at mordant humor was a very good sign, though, I thought. My fresh spatter pattern must have pleased him more than I realized.

I waited a long time at the evidence desk, behind a mobile crew checking in a great many bottles and bags that, judging from the smell, I didn't want to know anything about. When I got to the clerk, she picked a printed form off the stack on the desk and said, "Fill this out." Damn, I forgot about the evidence entry form. I could have been doing that while I waited.

I was bent over the long white page, concentrating on making legible block letters, when somebody goosed me firmly from behind. "Hey, snookums," Trudy said.

"You're back!" I hugged her hard. She smelled like roadkill, with an overlay of grain products.

"I just called you in Rutherford," she said, "and they told me to look for you up here. You know I have tonight off?"

"I heard. Do you have to do another run first, or—"

"Not if you beat me with ropes," she said. "We've got a couple hours' work to do, checking stuff in here, and then we have to get the van ready for the next crew. After that I'm outta here. Is there anything at home to cook, or shall I shop on the way?"

"I had a better idea." I nudged her elbow, and we stepped out in the hall. "Why don't we stay in town?"

"What, you mean—"

I bent close to her ear. "I'll go rent a room and buy a bottle of wine—"

She began looking at me as if I'd just invented air. "A room? You mean a clean, warm motel room where there's so much hot water it never runs out?"

"And when you get hungry you send out for pizza or something."

"And people take stupendous showers and get half plotzed and then just…lie around…"

"Lie around together, there you go. Sometimes they even practice mating rituals."

"*Genius.*" She gave me a smile that lit up the entire hall and parts of the stairway. "I love it!" She hugged me again, quickly, and ran off, calling back over her shoulder, "I'll hurry, but it's gonna be two hours, minimum. You gonna call me, tell me where to go?"

"Count on it." I went back to the evidence desk and forced myself to concentrate on a clearly printed description of a bloody jacket and shirt. After that, though my heart wasn't in it, I drove to the lot where Dietz's truck was stored.

The manager loaned me his creeper. I slid faceup under the tractor, where I spent a long time peering into the spaces above and behind the hundred-gallon cylindrical fuel tanks slung beneath the chassis on steel straps. I was hoping to spot an extra seam or rivet that might be the sign of a pocket built into a tank, but both tanks looked perfect to me.

I measured the toolbox under the passenger-side step, slid back underneath, and measured again from there. The dimensions matched precisely. I spent a lot of time staring at all sides of the massive dual mufflers. Something about the arrogant gleam of their chrome standpipes invited suspicion, but I couldn't see a spot on them anyplace that wouldn't be too hot for contraband.

I was back on the creeper, checking out mudguards, when a familiar voice near the front of the truck said, "I certainly hope there's a live body attached to those feet."

I slid out and said, "Hey, Ted."

"Jake Hines, I presume," Ted Zumwalt said, pulling the straps of several Dacron bags off his shoulders.

"You taking the pictures today?"

"Of course not. I go everywhere festooned with cameras." To compensate for his small stature and baby face, Ted Zumwalt has developed an ironic, imperious manner and a folksy twang, an unlikely combination somewhere between a country judge and Caligula. "I will also be dusting for prints," he intoned, "and quite possibly, before I'm done, lending a hand with the blood work and interviewing the innocent bystanders. The bureau is encouraging versatility this week."

Megan Duffy appeared beside him, burdened with more gear. "C'mon, Zumwalt," she said, "hustle your buns back outside and bring in the rest of the bags I left by the rear door, huh?"

Zumwalt gave a windy sigh. "This woman," he said, "has got no respect." He went grumbling, but he went, clearly no match for the redoubtable Megan. She had matured since I saw her last summer; the reversed baseball cap that had always covered her ponytail was replaced by a fetching knit cap over a neat single braid. When she took off her padded car coat, I saw she wore a pretty sweater instead of a shapeless T-shirt boosting some pro athletic team. Wasn't there something else?

"Hey," I said, "you got your braces off."

"Yup. Even orthodontia doesn't last forever. Whatcha got down there, Jake? Something good under the truck?"

"Not that I can find," I said. "Bo Dooley thought we might be looking at a drug heist. Did they tell you the body we found was the driver of this rig?"

"Nobody tells us much of anything this week," she said. "We just go scrape whatever Jimmy says to scrape."

"Oh. Well, we found a frozen body Sunday night, no ID. Matched it up with an Attempt to Locate report and established that the body we've got is the missing driver of this truck. We found the truck this morning up near Pine Island."

"Huh. Awesomely mysterious. And Bo thinks it's some kind of dope-smuggling deal? Why isn't he here?"

"His wife's sick. He'll be back in a couple of days."

"Well, you want us to test for traces of crack?"

"Yes. Please. And heroin. Also—" I told her about the missing bullet and showed her the mess on the bulkhead where I hoped it was. Ted was back by then, and I showed them both the spatter pattern on the roof of the cab.

"Fear not, my good man," Zumwalt said. "We know how our glorious leader feels about spatter patterns. I expect we'll probably cut this whole thing right out of there and transport it to the lab intact, don't you think, Megan?"

Somebody cleared his throat nearby. We all turned and saw John Dietz in the open doorway, looking in at the ruin of his beautiful new Peterbilt. He seemed to age as we watched.

"Do what you gotta do," he said hoarsely. The mess in the bunk held his mesmerized attention for a few seconds longer; then he began to look ill and turned away. I climbed down from the cab and walked with him toward the front bumper.

"I'm afraid it's going to be quite a while before you get this unit back in service," I said. "I hope you have good insurance."

"The company does, yes. I'll start the paperwork. Any word about Roger?"

"Who? Oh, the other driver. No."

"How's Connie taking it?"

"We haven't been able to talk to her yet. She's out of town somewhere visiting her sick sister. We'll reach her soon."

"Okay. My other drivers—nobody wants to talk about it much, but they're anxious."

"Understandable." He wanted reassurance, and I had nothing for him. I dredged up the chief's old favorite, "Rest assured, Mr. Dietz, we'll keep you informed." Dietz looked as if he knew snake oil when he smelled it.

He went gravely back to work, a deeply troubled controller forced to acknowledge circumstances beyond his control. I said good-bye to Duffy and Zumwalt, who were in the bunk area, wrangling over who'd get first use of which space. I returned the creeper to the owner of the yard, found my pickup in the parking lot, and went in search of a motel in my price range with smoke-free rooms, good ice machines, and decent locks. When I had the key in my hand, I scoured the neighborhood for fast food, party favors, and chilled wine.

After I called Trudy with the address, I uncorked the sauvignon blanc and nested it in a bucket of ice, unwrapped a plate of nachos, and tied a bouquet of silver balloons to the foot of the bed. By the time my beloved knocked on the door, I was vamping behind a hand-lettered sign that read, "Viewer Discretion Is Advised," wearing nothing but a party hat and a welcoming smile.

SEVEN

PADDING SILENTLY into the bathroom Wednesday morning, I turned on a light and looked at my watch. Damn, only four-ten. I was wide awake and seriously hungry.

We had gone to bed in late afternoon, after one giggly glass of wine and a deliriously sensuous shower. Slippery with soap and horny as a two-peckered billygoat, I had done a lot of boasting, under the hot spray, about my intention to ravish my lusty bathmate all night. But one glorious climax left us relaxed and murmuring endearments, in the course of which we fell asleep. Exhaustion overcoming sexual ambitions, we slept all night.

Now, hours before dawn, I was hungry enough to eat lug nuts. I turned out the light and got back into bed, where I lay twitching, listening to my stomach growl.

"Jake?" Trudy said softly in the darkness.

"Hey, babe," I whispered. "I'm sorry I woke you."

"You didn't."

"It's way early," I said. "Go back to sleep."

"I can't," she said, sitting up. "I'm starving."

"You are?" I turned on the light and beamed at her. "Fantastic! Let's go eat!"

She'd brought the duffel of clean clothes that she keeps in town when she works on the van. "I'll stop at home on the way to work," I said, getting back into yesterday's duds.

"It's a shame to leave the balloons," she said. "But I guess...here, you take the wine." She followed me to the twenty-four-hour diner I had spotted the day before. We ordered three-egg omelets, plenty of sausage, and mounds of hash browns. The first cup of coffee tasted so good it made my eyes water. I fetched the *Pioneer-Press* from a rack in front, and we passed the sections back and forth, commenting on headlines, sneering at politicians, and arguing with the editorial page, till our food came. After that we were silent for some time.

"I was thinking," Trudy said, leaning back and stretching over her third cup of coffee. "Since it's so early, would you like to come over to the lab with me before you head home? I could scan the prints from your victim into my database."

"We already identified my victim."

"I know. But I could show you how our new software works. It's so cool. And who knows? We might get lucky, get a hit, find out your victim has a notorious past."

"A spy in deep cover as a teamster. I like it. You're sure you've got time?"

"Yeah, the rest of my crew won't be in till seven. Lots of time."

We strode through the almost empty, echoing halls, took the elevator to the third floor, and pulled up stools to a cluttered workstation in a corner. "Let's see," Trudy said, pushing stacks of slides around, "Ted said he...oh, here." She peered at the labeling on a couple of plastic boxes, said, "Yeah, okay," and inserted a slide in the digital scanner by her elbow.

She touched the keypad on the bench, and the screen in front of her flashed PRINTRAK and then displayed a fourteen-inch image of a latent print.

"Is PRINTRAK the database?"

"No, just the software. Well, the hardware too, it's all built together. Wait, now," she said, clattering away, "the good part is coming." Trudy can talk fast and type flawlessly at the same time, a skill that makes my teeth ache with envy.

"Are we going into this AFIS thing now?" She's been crowing about this national fingerprint database that's coming on-line, so comprehensive, so fast, fast, fast. No need to hand sort, ever again, no sending away for copies.

"I'm gonna try MAFIN first, the Midwest section. It's smaller, so it's quicker and you're most likely to get a hit close to home anyway." Her hands danced on the keys. "I'm asking for the nearest twenty matches. Watch this." The CPU groaned like a tired housewife with lower back pain until a second thumb-print appeared on the screen. Or was it the same print? "It looks the same to me," I said, "but what do I know?"

"Well, it should look pretty similar. The computer always delivers the nearest matches first."

"But you look at all of them?"

"If I don't get a match on the first one, sure."

"I should think there'd be less and less chance as you go along."

"Not always. Fingerprint matching's mostly science and partly art. It takes a human brain to make the judgments. See, you start with the core—" She moved a tiny cursor to the central portion of each image, a place like a cowlick in the middle of each thumb. "The one in the print from the victim leans a little to the right, see? And, actually, the one in the sample leans the same way—I'd call that a pretty good match."

"Everybody's got a core?"

"Unless it's an arch pattern. And a delta. We'll look at that next—" Cursors appeared above a three-way intersection of lines on both prints.

"Close, huh?" I squinted. "Though maybe the angle's a little sharper on the left."

"Exactly. See, you're getting it already. Now, if both of those two basics are close matches, you go on and compare minutiae." She placed cursors at half a dozen locations on each screen and then pointed out broken lines and places where a line split into two ridges. In a few seconds she had enough differences to eliminate the first print.

"Wow. You're fast."

"After you stare at a few hundred thousand of these, you know how to look."

"But the software couldn't do that for you?"

"It did what I asked, brought me the nearest matches. It measures the points of similarity and shows me the ones with the highest count. Then it's up to me to judge what it shows me. It might award a lower score because of a difference that I think is probably an injury. Or what looks like a difference to the computer might look to me like a print taken from a slightly different angle. The human brain isn't just muddling along on zeroes and ones, y'know. We've got common sense, experience, intuition—"

"Superstition, bias, myopia—"

"Yeah, yeah. But babies can sense their parents' moods from facial expressions and tone of voice before they're six months old. What would you give for a computer that subtle?''

''Actually I probably wouldn't let it in the house. I don't need a filing cabinet that understands my shortcomings.''

''Shee. Talk about guilt.''

''All us rogues have that. Can we look at another one?''

We eliminated three more near matches. ''Of course you realize,'' Trudy said, ''these are just from our five-state area. We'll go on and compare with the national database if we don't get a match here. And I guess—'' she looked at her watch as we heard voices coming up the stairs ''—it's almost seven o'clock. I better get my tushy off this chair and go see what goodies Jimmy's got lined up for me today.''

She gave me a quick, fierce hug and said, ''I owe you big-time for one fabulous break in the workweek, Jake Hines.''

''My pleasure. When will you get out of this jail?''

''Depends what happens. If our crew catches a new case around lunchtime Friday, I'll be late. Otherwise, I'll be headed home by midafternoon.''

''I'll focus on a crime-free Friday.'' She gave me careful directions to the firearms lab, where she said the early shift would be starting. I found it after only one wrong turn.

I eased in quietly and stood by the nearest workbench. After a couple of minutes, an otherworldly creature in a lab coat, wearing a plastic mask, earmuffs, and surgical gloves, emerged from somewhere and began to fire rounds from an ancient-looking Smith and Wesson into a space behind a wall. The noise was punishing; I covered my ears. When the hooded entity had emptied the chamber, it brought the revolver to the table where I was standing, removed its headgear, and morphed into Stan Spencer.

"Hey, Jake," he said, "whaddya doin' ? Anybody helpin' you?"

"I promised Jimmy I wouldn't get in anybody's way," I said. "He said you're all busy."

"That's Jimmy for you, all heart and soul. Whaddya need?"

"He brought in a shell casing. Jimmy did. Yesterday afternoon. I wondered if anybody's had a chance to look at it yet."

"Let's find out. C'mon." He led me into the next big room, where a wall full of mounted handguns backed a long worktable littered with tagged weapons and evidence bags. A small gray-haired man in a sweater was peering into a microscope.

"Willy? Did Jimmy bring a casing in here yesterday afternoon?"

"Uh-huh."

"You looked at it yet?"

"Uh-huh."

"Whadja do with it?"

"It's in that pile at the end of the table." Stan moved toward the pile. Willy raised his head suddenly and cried out in alarm, "Don't get them mixed up!" He peered at us myopically, eyes still focused for the microscope. "I haven't done the paperwork yet!"

"I was just hoping you could tell me the make of gun—" I said.

"The make of gun that fired that casing Jimmy brought in? Hell, I knew that before I looked at it under the scope," Willy said. "Walther PPK nine-millimeter."

"Okay, I'm impressed," I said. "What makes this casing so easy?"

"That's an old bullet. See how dull the brass is? And it was fired from a collector's gun. Brought home from Germany in World War II, probably. Has very distinct markings from the ejector mechanism. We don't see many of the old originals anymore. There's an American-made copy on the market now, piece of junk. It was a hot item on the world market when it first came out." Like most experts, Willy knows a great deal more about his subject than I have any use for. He's a good talker, too. "The first of the double-action pistols. Here, I've got one, I'll show you." He pulled a short-barreled pistol off the wall and let me hold it. "The PP stands for Polizei…uh…something German that means police pistol. The K is for *kurz*, which means short. Just over six inches long, see? Ideal for concealed carry. Most of the able-bodied men in Germany were armed with these things during the war, my dad told me, even the railroad workers had 'em to guard the trains if they were attacked. Except when the time came they were so sick of the war they handed them over to any GIs who would take them. Hundreds of these guns came home as souvenirs."

"Did your father get one?"

"No. He was sick of the war too, he said."

"This a manual safety?" I turned a lever on the slide, and a red dot came into view.

"Exactly," he said. "Allows you to carry it with a live round in the chamber. Jimmy got very excited when I told him his casing was fired by a Walther."

"He did? Why?"

"Oh, he's got the hots for some pattern of blood spatters in the cab of that truck. He's decided to write his Ph.D. thesis on blood spatter patterns, and he gets all warm and fuzzy when he finds a set he can nail for sure."

"A Walther helps with that?"

"Oooh, yes." He showed me how the Walther helped. I began to feel that peculiar satisfaction that occurs when information meets need to know

HELLISH RUSH-HOUR TRAFFIC was headed into St. Paul, but I was headed out, so I reached U.S. 52 still driving a one-piece red pickup. The temperature was up to fifteen degrees at the Minneapolis airport, the radio said, and no snow was forecast. For today. The announcer wanted me to worry about the low pressure system hanging over eastern Montana, but I decided to take one day at a time. I switched to a country station where Carlene Carter was singing about falling in love as if she'd just done it that minute. Country rompin' and stompin' carried me past the turnout to Mirium before I remembered my intention to change clothes. I wasn't about to go back; my crew would be coming to work shortly, needing assignments and advice. I called the duty sergeant's desk and got Russ Swenson.

"Kevin's already here," he said. "Somebody put a firecracker up his ass today."

"Everybody's here but Bo," Kevin said, when he got on the line, "and we've all got a shitload of work, so take your time, Jake, we don't need you."

"That's cute," I said. "What's everybody so busy with?"

"A couple of break-ins last night. Downtown. I'll send Darrell and Ray to cover them, okay? Rosie said last night she's gonna be making about a hundred phone calls that Bo gave her, plus she's working in the records room. Lou's still working on the bowling alley break-in, plus he's got his usual collection of beat-up women calling him. You got something that won't wait? I'll do it."

"Any word from Connie Carr?"

"Yes. She called in yesterday afternoon. Lou told her about her husband being missing, and he said we'd like to visit with her a few minutes as soon as she could manage that."

"Visit with her? That's how he said it?"

"Yeah. He said she was understandably upset, so he didn't want to get her any more steamed up than she already was. She told him she'd be back in town sometime this morning, and she'll call as soon as she's back."

"Excellent. Perfect. I'll see you in a few minutes."

I heard Lou coughing as I came up the stairs. The smell of wintergreen leaked from his office, where he was pounding on his keyboard and sucking a lozenge. "Got some news for you," he said, but the effort of talking set off a fresh paroxysm. I waited. After a minute he was able to wheeze, "Found that guy. Cathy Niemeyer's ex." He dug through a pile of notes. "Eugene Niemeyer. Gene to his friends, which I don't know why he would have any. He's in jail in Austin, awaiting sentencing on assault charges brought by his new girlfriend, uh—" He continued grubbing fruitlessly through the litter of paper hiding his desk.

"Never mind her name," I said. "How long's he been in jail?"

"Eight days. And he'll go direct from there to Oak Park Heights. The charge was attempted murder, and he couldn't make bail. Dumb prick attacked this woman in the checkout line at the supermarket at the height of the afternoon rush, so there's about a zillion witnesses, mostly women, and they all want to hang him. When he finally sobered up enough to talk to his pro bono mouthpiece, he pleaded no contest to aggravated assault."

"All right. Guess we can't hang him for shooting Wayne Asleson then."

"No. Damn shame."

"Heard you talked to Connie Carr, too."

"Oh. Yeah. I actually got that one typed up. Here." He fished it out of a pile and handed it over.

"How'd she sound to you?"

"Uh…pretty much what you'd expect for a woman who hears her husband's missing while her sister's dying of cancer."

"But she said she'd be back in town this morning?"

"She's driving back, yes, and she's going to call as soon as she gets here." His coughing started again.

I asked him, "You want to go home?"

"I'm better off here," he gasped. "Mamie cleaned out a closet. Dust—" He waved his hands helplessly and reached for a cartridge respirator he keeps on his desk.

"You want somebody else to take your calls?"

"Nah. Most of my clients just want me to listen anyway." Lou's specialty is clucking sympathetically to battered wives till he persuades them to blow the whistle on their abusers. Nobody in the section wants to take Lou's calls, and we all dread his retirement.

Kevin followed me into my office, where we traded a lot of information fast.

"You want me to come with you to see Connie Carr?"

"If Darrell and Ray are back by then, I'd like it, yes. Otherwise I'll have to leave you here. Bo's out, and Lou's pretty shaky. How's Rosie doing?"

"I don't think I ever saw her so happy. She's got all Bo's deviants to talk to, and she says that little programmer geek that's working in the records room is just stone brilliant. She says wait'll we see the cross-checking we can do with this system when it's finished, we're gonna wonder how we ever got along without it."

"Well, good, then, if all of our arrest records evaporate in a thunderstorm next summer, we'll just blame Rosie, won't we?"

Lulu wasn't at her guard post in the chief's outer office, so I walked in without having to prove I was pure of heart and had pressing business. As soon as my foot crossed his doorsill, though, I heard her voice.

"You want kissy-kissy here?"

"Little farther down," he said. "Do a little stroking first."

I started to back out, but he looked up and saw me.

"C'mon in, Jake," he said. "We're almost done."

They were answering his mail. Over the years, they have had to work out a few shortcuts, because Frank is the softest touch in the western hemisphere. Besides all the usual civic and church affiliations expected by any chief of police, he belongs to every do-good or-

ganization, fishing fraternity, and Hibernian Branch
of Christknowswhat that's ever come after him. Besides, he was born in this town, into a big family, so
a vast swarm of relatives and friends, friends of
friends, second cousins of uncles by marriage, and so
on are proud of their connection to the police department and panting to take advantage of it. No day
passes without somebody soliciting his support for a
new crossing light, after-school program, extra traffic
control for their horseshoe tournament or flower show
or square-dancing contest.

Fending off this army of supplicants could easily
become a full-time job. And Lulu's legendary impa-
tience was sorely taxed by taking dictation from a
man who couldn't explain conflicting dates between
an Eagles picnic and a Scout jamboree without making it into an act of contrition. One day while he was
agonizing through one of his tormented apologies, she
snatched the letter off the top of his pile and said,
"Okay, I gotcha, give them a firm no with some
kissy-kissy before and after."

A star was born. Within a couple of weeks they
could power through a stack of mail in a few minutes,
using the crude argot they quickly developed. "Kiss-
ass thanks" go to the mayor and council members;
"Warm strokes with cool maybe" are for overbearing
pests whose demands are totally unreasonable; and
"Ha-ha no" takes care of ridiculous schemes from
boyhood pals. Lulu transforms these gutturals into elegant letters under the department crest, incorporating
appropriate nicknames, sports metaphors, and subtle
permutations for rank and status.

My personal favorite piece of their code is
"Wimpy ha-ha," their response to all the cop jokes

people constantly send Frank. He hates them but doesn't want to seem ungracious, so Lulu acknowledges every one with a smarmy note insisting he was delighted to hear from this dear old buddy, and intimating he laughed so hard at the stupid cop joke he wet his shorts. Frank tries not to read these responses; he just sits there kicking his desk and signing fast.

As soon as Lulu was on the way out with her armload of paper, Frank said, "Sit. You need coffee? You look a little mussed up."

"Sorry," I said, smoothing my hair with spit. I didn't want to get into the details of my social life. "Have you got a minute? I'd like to review this homicide we're working on."

"Yes. About ten minutes, actually," he said, and then, looking at his desk clock while he picked up the phone, said, "Well, fifteen." He asked Lulu, "Hold my calls, will you?" and sat back, looking contented. Frank once told me the trouble with being chief is that it leaves no time for police work.

I reviewed the autopsy, told him about finding the truck in the field, and reported on the other evidence we took to BCA. Then I went into detail about the information I brought back from the crime lab.

"Jimmy had two guesses about the spatter patterns on the ceiling of the truck. It could have been from defense wounds from a second victim, presumably the second driver. Or it could have been made by the shooter. The second guess seems to fit with Willy's statement that the gun that did the shooting was a Walther."

"A Walther? That little German pistol from the war? The James Bond gun, we used to call it. I've seen one or two. Long time ago," Frank said. "Remind me. What does it do that would make a spatter pattern like that?''

"This gun has a short grip as well as a short barrel; it was designed for concealed carry. So if a guy has big hands, or more likely if he shoots two-handed and gets the supporting hand cupped too high over the shooting hand—'' I showed him ''—when the bullet ejects, this baby has sharp little metal slides that will slice a beautiful railroad-track wound across the top of that supporting hand. And the natural thing when you're hurt like that, I guess, is to flinch back like this—'' I threw my hand in the air ''—and throw a double spatter of blood drops across whatever's in the way.''

"Okay, I can see how that could have worked on the ceiling of the truck. But out on the overpass, why—''

"Harder to envision, I grant you. But it stands to reason the shooter is the one who threw the body over the railing. And his hand could have still been bleeding, and dripped on the curb. If the drops on the overpass match the drops on the ceiling—which DNA will tell us—then we eliminate the idea that the spatter in the truck could be defense wounds from a second victim.''

"Uh-huh. The second victim that you've been thinking might be the second driver.''

"Exactly. And if the second driver's not the second victim, he starts to look better as the shooter.''

"Well—what does their boss say about these two men? What do their wives say?''

"The boss is firm—both are long-term employees with good records. Drivers have to work up to these long hauls, only reliable types get them in the first place, and both these men have been long-haul drivers for years.''

''But this was their first trip together, you say?''

''Yes. And they were off their route; they should have been over on I-Thirty-five heading for Duluth. Nobody has a clue why they detoured to Rutherford. And the other wild card in this is the freight they were hauling. We found the truck, but the trailer's missing.'' I told him about the surprisingly high values Dietz had quoted for his gear and its load.

''That isn't all,'' I said. ''In fact, I feel like I'm playing Rope-a-Dope here, bouncing from one theory of this crime to another.'' I told him about Bo's experiences of finding drugs in long-haul trucks, and the fact that items in the load were assembled across the border from Nogales, somewhere in Mexico.

''Well. That's another whole road to go down, isn't it? Bo's working on that?''

Time was short, so I skipped Bo's problems and said, ''He's looked at the truck, and he's talking to his connections about news of a shipment.''

''Well—'' he was looking at his clock and squirming ''—did you say you've talked to both wives?''

''We interviewed the live-in girlfriend of the victim. She insists that the guy was steady as a rock, Mr. Goodperson.''

''Of course he's dead, she would say that.''

''Sure. All the other testimony and the visible evidence fits, though—he was nice to her, took care of his house, raised a big garden. About as straight-arrow as they come.''

''All right, and the missing driver's wife?''

''She had a family emergency out of town, she was gone when they turned up missing, and we didn't find her till yesterday. Lou talked to her on the phone; he said her reaction was just what you'd expect, distraught. She's due back in town this morning and I'm going to see her myself.''

"Okay. Sounds like you're covering all the bases. The thing that keeps kind of biting on me is the fact that this was the first trip together for these two drivers. Have you talked with the two fellas they drove with before?''

"Uh, no. Good idea.''

"They might have some insights you haven't heard from anybody else. And you might try contacting the warehouse at the other end where they picked up their load. Otherwise, the most obvious thing is, you gotta find that load. You got all your lines out on that?''

"Yes. Time to check them again, though.''

"Okay. I gotta go. Keep me in the loop, Jake.''

"You'll take care of the media?''

"Oh, sure.'' He knows I'm not ready for prime time. When loud, cheeky questions get hurled at me from behind a video camera, I get a sneaky expression and start to act like I did the crime myself.

I went back to my office and called Kevin.

"Connie Carr called,'' he said. "We can see her at one o'clock.''

"Good. Are Darrell and Ray back?''

"Darrell is. He's turning in his evidence right now. Ray called in and said his case was getting complicated. It's a burglary in a sporting goods store with partners, and the more they go over the damage and what's missing, he says, the more he thinks maybe one of the partners might be involved.''

"Did he want help?''

"Not so far—he says it's a mess, but he can handle

it. He's got a couple uniforms there to help if he needs anything, Greeley and Priebe."

"Okay. Can you come in a minute?" He came right away, with his hands full of phone messages. "Anything there that won't wait?"

"Just the Connie Carr message, I guess. I wrote her address and phone number on it."

"Okay. I'll take that. Now let's talk about the load."

"The what?"

"The load, the trailer, the freight for Clearwater Truck Lines. It's missing, and we've got to find it."

"I'm sure the company's anxious," he said, "but does it really come ahead of finding out who offed the driver?"

"The money part doesn't. But as long as the load is missing, we don't know whether it's the reason the driver was killed. If we find it and the load's intact, and there's nothing there but CD players and woofers, we know we've gotta look elsewhere for a motive."

"I put it in the BOLOs like you said," he said, "and I sent an Attempt to Locate to all the departments in the Twin Cities metro area."

"Good. But now, think about it. The man who was killed in the truck was dropped off the Fifty-two overpass here sometime late Sunday. The tractor, without the trailer, was found in a field near Pine Island yesterday morning. Isn't it reasonable to suppose that the trailer might be somewhere between those two places?"

"Unless it's what the killer was after," Kevin said, "in which case it might be just about anyplace else by now."

"Exactly. So let's go to work on it this afternoon.

I'm having trouble getting a focus on this homicide because there are too many possibilities. We need to eliminate something. Let's go find Darrell.''

He was in his workstation, underneath the vanity wall covered with pictures of himself in muscle shirts and tight nylon shorts doing bone-cracking lifts. He looked up from his word processor when we stopped at the door and said, ''How do you spell refuge?''

''Refuge? Like a hideout?''

''No. Refuge, like trash.''

''Look it up,'' I said.

''You sure that guy's gonna be an asset?'' the chief asked me once, about a month after I recruited Darrell.

''He's strong as an ox,'' I said. ''He does everything I ask him, and he never complains.''

''Never complains, are you serious?'' Frank said. ''What the hell's he doing in the police force?''

''Can you leave that a minute?'' I asked him now, ''I've got a job for you.'' He turned obediently toward me at once, clipboard in left hand, pencil in right hand, shoulders bulging like boulders in his neat cotton shirt.

I told him to call the sheriff's office in all the counties bordering I-35 from the Iowa line to Minneapolis, and U.S. 52 from Rutherford to St. Paul. ''Tell them it's evidence in a homicide and give them all the numbers and stats that you'll find in the report I filed Monday night. When you finish talking to sheriff's offices, talk to all the POP officers here in town, we've got what, now, six? Seven? Find all of them, on duty or off, tell them on their next shift we want them to scour their sections, look in every gas station, parking lot, anyplace that trailer could be. You understand me, Darrell? I want that big hummer.''

"I hear you," Darrell said.

"Stay on it," I said. "Drive everybody nuts till they find it for you."

"Next thing," I told Kevin as we headed back to my office, "I want you to call John Dietz and get the names of the two drivers who were partnered with Wayne Asleson and Roger Carr before this last trip. Get him to tell you how we can find them now."

"For what?"

"Evidently Asleson and Carr had these other partners for some time. When they're out on the road they go a week, ten days, in a row, cooped up together in that little space about the size of a bathroom, at the front of an eighteen-wheeler. They must get to know each other pretty well. They almost certainly know each other better than their boss knew either one of them, and they might even know things about each other that the wife and girlfriend don't know. See if you can find them this afternoon and ask them how they felt about their former partners."

Wanting a little time to myself before the next interview, I went out, got in my stiff, frosty pickup, and drove to a grocery deli, where I helped myself to a salad bar and ate at a tiny plastic table, in a cement-floored area echoing with the scrape of chair legs. Afterward I carried a Styrofoam cup of coffee out to my pickup to get away from the noise, and used the steering wheel for a writing desk to make a list of questions about Roger Carr.

When my list was complete, I went looking for Connie Carr, after calling Kevin back and making him swear the address he gave me was not a joke.

And sure enough, there really was a Granny Goose's Mobile Home Garden, on a dead end off Twenty-ninth Street Northwest. It was beyond the used furniture store and just before the cornfield, next to a creek on the extreme west edge of town. The first street inside the gate was named Wee Willy Winky Drive.

Speed bumps enforced the signs demanding I slow to ten miles an hour. I eased past painted signs for Jack Spratt Road and Peter Rabbit Way. The whole place had been cutesied up with Disney cutouts, and the cheap kitsch was already yielding to hard wear and neglect. A couple of spaces had out-of-order signs on them, and the yard behind the office held two old car bodies on blocks.

A faded jigsaw cutout of a blond female child in pantaloons, holding a shepherd's crook, marked the hard right turn onto Bo-Peep Lane. On the shabby single-wide in space forty-five, a carved wooden sign read "The Carr's." An ancient Lincoln Continental sat on bald tires in the far end of the aluminum carport. In front of it, barely under the shelter, was an eight-year-old Escort. Out of old cop's habit, I noted the make, model, color, and license number on both vehicles.

Connie Carr pulled the door open to the end of the chain, glanced once quickly from my badge and ID card to my face, slid the chain off, and opened the door. She was a small, pretty woman in her early thirties, with very fine brown hair that curled in child-like ringlets all over her head. Her brown eyes, darker than her hair, looked shadowed with fatigue and red-rimmed, as if she might have been weeping. She was neatly dressed in basic casual, faded jeans and a navy blue T-shirt.

"I'm sorry to take up your time when you have so many troubles," I said. "I just need to ask you a few questions." She nodded the smallest of nods. All her movements seemed cautious and minimal, as if she were guarding her strength.

"Come in." She backed into the small space, and I followed her. We stood for a couple of seconds facing each other on the old shag carpet, till she turned away and sat down in the overstuffed plastic-covered chair. I picked a spot on the matching sofa, on the end nearest her, as close as I could get without letting our knees touch. I asked her some chitchat questions about the road conditions and weather between Winona and Rutherford while I got out my notebook and set up the tape recorder. She answered in monosyllables and then sat watching the tape rotate.

"I need to record our conversation, is that okay?"

"Okay."

"When was the last time you saw your husband?"

"The morning before he left for Arizona."

"That'd be—"

"A week ago last Friday."

"So he was gone for New Year's?"

The question evidently struck her as inane. "Well," she said, "yes."

"Have you talked to him since then?"

"Uh-huh. He called me from a truck stop east of Tucson the afternoon of the day they started back, I guess that was Wednesday last week, and again Sunday from someplace in Iowa."

"Does he usually call you like that? From out on the road?"

"Yeah, he usually calls a couple of times during a trip. Always on the day before he's due in, to check on my schedule and see if there's anything I need."

"So when he called you Sunday, what did you tell him?"

"That I'd had a call from my family in Winona, and they said my sister's cancer—she's had cancer for some time, but she had chemo last year, and it was supposed to be in remission. That's what they said. But last week she had another test, and it's spreading again. Spreading like wildfire, is how my mother said it, and she said if I wanted to talk to her, I better come. So I told Roger I wouldn't be here when he got home, I said I have to go *right now,* and I'll just have to let you know when I can get back."

"And how did he seem to you then?"

"How did *he* seem?" She shrugged. "Same as always, I guess. He wasn't the one with a problem, I was."

"He didn't say anything about worries on the job, trouble on the road?"

"No. He said he missed ol' Buddy, that's what he always called the partner that he had before. But everything was going fine with this new guy, he said, they were right on time and they'd be off-loading Monday morning in Duluth. But now you say his partner's missing?"

"His partner's dead. We found his body. We didn't know there was a truck and trailer involved till later. Now we've found the truck without the trailer, and we don't know where your husband is."

"I just can't imagine anything like this happening to Roger."

"Why? You think he's particularly good at looking out for himself?"

"Himself and the company both. And proud of it. Don't worry about Mr. Reliable, that's what he always tells me. He loves to brag that he's been on the road twenty years, and never lost a load. Never had a wreck, not even a fender-bender, with his rig."

"And on the earlier calls this week, he never gave you any indication of trouble?"

"No. It was a new route for him, and he talked about the sights mostly. He said it sure was dry country down there by the Mexican border, but he was enjoying the heat. Said we oughta think about taking our next vacation down there, and maybe we'd cook up a baby." A trace of color came back in her face. "Lately we been thinking it's about time to start a family."

"How long have you been married?"

"Five years this June."

"Okay, so that last time you talked to him—Sunday? What time was that?"

"Uh...maybe three o'clock, three-thirty."

"Were you at work then?"

"No, home. I work six to two."

"Where do you work?"

"At Ben's House of Pancakes. Downtown."

"And where did he say they were at that time?"

"North of Des Moines. Said everything was on schedule, he'd be back here at the house by Monday afternoon, and he'd wait to hear from me."

"And did you call him then? Monday afternoon?"

"Late afternoon, maybe seven o'clock. I thought he'd be home by then for sure, but he wasn't."

"Were you alarmed about that?"

"Alarmed?" She shrugged. "No, I just figured he got sick of sitting around the house by himself and went out for some beers and a game of pool. Or to bowl a couple lines. There's three or four of his favorite hangouts right close by here."

It seemed to me there was a trace of resentment in that answer, so I asked one of the risky questions. "Is your marriage happy, Mrs. Carr?"

She raised her eyebrows and straightened in her chair, looking shocked and embarrassed, as if I had said something incredibly tasteless. After a few seconds she said stiffly, "About average, I guess."

"Is that a no?"

"No, that's an 'about average.'" She tossed her head, twitched around in her chair, sighed, and blew her nose. I waited. Finally she said, "We argued about money sometimes. I guess that makes us a lot like everybody else, doesn't it?"

"Right in the mainstream, I would say." I tried for a conspiratorial smile. "I'm sorry if I seem nosy, Mrs. Carr. Your husband is missing, we need to find him, and I'm trying to get some idea if he had any problems in his life."

"Well. I don't know if you'd call it problems exactly." She tossed her head again and recrossed her legs. "Roger was married once before. Quite a few years before, and then he was a divorced bachelor, on the road, for a long time. So he has bachelor's habits, free-spending ways. He's careless with money. Makes it hard to stay on a budget."

"I understand. Did he—did you have any cause to suspect that he might have been spending his money on other women?"

"No." She was so matter-of-fact about it that I

looked up. Most wives would hesitate, or laugh nervously, or get angry. She met my eyes and managed a shadow of a smile. "I know they say the wife's the last to know, but we, um, we get along really well in…in that way. Roger is a devoted husband, and we're a happy couple when he brings home enough of his paycheck to pay the bills."

"I see. Well. Does your husband ever use drugs, Mrs. Carr?"

"Drugs?" She looked surprised. "You mean, like marijuana and that?"

"Or cocaine. Crack. Any recreational drugs?"

"Absolutely not. He says that stuff is for losers. No, he likes to have plenty of fun after work, but his idea of a good time is big steaks and some beers, and lots of games with his buddies."

"What kind of games?"

"Oh, stock car races, all-night poker games—guy things. Pro football and basketball on TV with lots of beer and munchies. Hunting and fishing trips—he likes those outings with the fellas. But he's never pulled an escapade like this before, where he just disappeared without telling me where he's going."

"Roger's partner has a bullet hole in his head. That's quite a bit more than an escapade."

"Well, but you don't think *Roger* had anything to do with *that*. Do you?" She stood up in alarm, knocking the tape recorder off the arm of the couch. It fell sideways and got trapped between the cushion and the arm; the tape began to squeal. I jumped up and collided with her. She almost fell, and I grabbed her arm to steady her. Compared to Trudy, who is strong and solid, she felt very small and light. I let her go and rescued my tape recorder.

"I'm sorry," she said, "is it broken?"

"No, it's okay." I eased the tape past the bent spot and restarted the machine. "Can we go on? I just have a few more questions." We both sat down. "Does Roger own a gun?"

"A gun? You mean like a hunting gun? I think he kept a shotgun out at his dad's farm, for hunting pheasants and that."

"No, I mean a handgun."

"No. And if he did, I wouldn't let him keep it in the house. I'm scared of guns."

"He never took a gun along on his trips?"

"None of the drivers do. It's against the rules. Anyway, Roger could never kill anybody. You're absolutely on the wrong track if you think that."

"Why do you say that? What is it about him that makes you so sure?"

"I've been married to him five years, and he's never raised a hand to me. He's just not a violent person."

"Okay." Roger Carr was a model citizen, except for a little foolishness about money, but by some mischance his partner was dead and their rig was scattered around the countryside. None of the answers I was getting from anybody helped explain that conundrum. I gave her my card. "Will you call me if you think of anything else?" I showed her my pager number. "Any time, day or night, feel free to call this number."

Before I closed my notebook, I asked her, "Will you be going back to your sister's place in Winona? Should I have that number?" I looked up after I asked the question and surprised an expression somewhere between anger and despair on her face.

She turned and stared out of the window for a long moment before she answered, "No. I'm not going anywhere till I find out what's happened to Roger. My sister'll just have to—" she flapped her hands forlornly "—get along without me."

"If you need any help," I said, and gave her the card for Victim's Services, "seems like you've got more trouble right now than anybody should have to handle alone."

She read everything on the card, moving her lips a couple of times. Then she nodded in a businesslike way and said softly, "Thank you," and went back to staring out the window. I left her standing there, silent and small, and returned to the station, feeling inadequate. I had been as easy on her as I knew how to be, and offered all the help I had available, but she left me feeling that I should have done something more.

EIGHT

KEVIN AND LOU and Darrell were all at their desks, talking on the phone. I walked past them quietly, carrying my tape recorder. In my office, I backed up the tape to the bent spot, straightened it out carefully, and took it to Mary for transcription. I asked her to give it the highest priority, and distribute copies to me and my team as soon as she could. I went straight back to my office then, without talking to anybody, closed the door, and typed up my impressions from the interview. When I was done I read over what I'd written, shrugging with frustration. It seemed to me something was left out, but I could think of nothing to add. Finally I gave up, printed six copies of what I had, and asked Kevin to come in.

"Will you get these out to everybody on the crew? Tell them the text of the interview is coming from Mary, and we'll discuss it in the morning."

"Did she give you anything new?"

"A little suggestion that her marriage isn't perfect. Hot news, huh? Some fights about money."

"Did she seem hard up?"

"Yeah—they live in a crummy place. Hard to figure. Long-haul drivers make a pretty fair wage, don't they?"

"Pretty decent for a working stiff, I think, yeah."

"And Connie's a waitress, same as Cathy. But Wayne and Cathy, in spite of her debts, have a decent house with a big yard and two good cars. The Carrs live in a broken-down single-wide in a sleazy trailer park, they've got one automotive relic that looks unsafe to drive and an Escort that's eight years old. No children. You have to wonder.''

"Uh-huh. Unless there are a lot of kids around somewhere from other marriages, it sounds like one or two bad habits, doesn't it?''

"Yes. But she claims he doesn't do drugs, doesn't chase women. Said he loves to play with his buddies, at games that sound pretty harmless: fishing and hunting trips, card games. Huh. Anyway! You got anything on those other two drivers yet?''

"I've located the one that drove with Wayne Asleson, he's on what they call LTLs—that means less than a load, short local runs—in Raleigh. His shift's almost over, and they promised to have him call when he gets in. Roger Carr's partner is on a two-day turnaround to Moorhead, they're trying to reach him.''

"Good. Stay on it. Anything else?''

"Uh, Rosie came out of the records room a few minutes ago looking for you, said there's something about numbers in there you'd never believe. She'll catch up with you, I guess.''

I went looking for Rosie, but her cubicle was empty, so I went on to Lou's and said, "Do a search for me, will you?'' I gave him the names of the two women, Connie Carr and Cathy Niemeyer, and their current addresses and phone numbers, and said, "See if you find a gun registered to either one.''

My phone rang as I walked back into my office. I picked it up, and Darrell said, "It's at Buck's Texaco.''

"What is?''

"That trailer you told me to find.''

"You *found* it! Good job."

"State Patrol found it. You were right about getting on everybody's case."

"Works if you don't overdo it. Let's see, where's Buck's Texaco?"

"North of town. Out past the lumberyard."

"Ah, yeah. Lemme see, what's the fastest way to do this?" I thought a minute. "Okay. First, call around till you find a tow truck that can pull that trailer to St. Paul this afternoon." I gave him the address of the BCA yard. "Then call BCA and tell them we're sending it. You don't need to talk to the director; ask the person who answers the phone to put you through to the proper technician. And *then* go to work on impoundment papers for the trailer. You got all that?"

"Affirmative." Darrell's father was a career infantry sergeant, and he seems to have brought the jargon home.

"Now, I'm gonna run out and make sure we got the right trailer, so don't send anybody out till I call you."

"Understood." I went back to my PC and found the interview with Dietz. I only wanted the trailer specs and his phone number, but I didn't have time to pick out the items I needed, so I printed the whole thing. Thus do forests die. On my way out of the building I stuck my head in the chief's office. His door was closed. I asked Lulu to tell him we had found the lost trailer. She was wearing her headset and typing at breakaway speed; she glared and nodded, conveying, *I hear you, go away.*

Afternoon sun was already casting blue shadows across fields full of snow-covered corn stubble when

I turned in under the big Texaco sign. I couldn't see the trailer from the road, but I drove along the back row of parked trucks as Darrell had instructed and found it in the far northeast corner, a couple of spaces from the end. Its glossy red paint job matched the elegant tractor we had found in Schellhammer's field. Big blue-and-white logos on the sides promised speedy service from Clearwater Truck Lines. The rear end was covered with permit numbers, and a number to call if you wanted to tell somebody what you thought of the driver's performance.

I walked all the way around it, made sure the bolts on the rear doors were in place and padlocked, and checked the license plate against the report from Dietz. Everything matched, so I called John Dietz.

"We found your trailer," I said. "Locked up tight, in a truck stop. I can't see a thing wrong with it."

"Well, by golly, that's good news," he said. "How soon can I pick it up?"

"I'm sorry, Mr. Dietz," I said, "we're going to have to keep it awhile. Maybe quite a while."

"Oh, you can't," he said. "No, no, I can't let you do that. My customer needs that merchandise right away."

"I can't let you have it," I said, "until we determine that it's not involved in the murder investigation." I was striding briskly from one end of the trailer to the other as I talked, trying to keep warm; the temperature was dropping fast as the sun sank behind the grain silos on the horizon.

On the other end of the phone, though, John Dietz was heating up. "Damn it!" he yelled. "You finally give me one little piece of good news, and then you take it away. How are you going to prove something like that anyway?''

"Fingerprints, maybe blood smears, we'll have to see what else. If we don't find anything material, we'll photograph it and videotape it, and then you can have it back.''

"I thought you said it was all right!''

"It is, it looks fine.''

"Well, come on, now, you're just talking in circles! Is it all okay, or is it covered with blood and guck like the tractor?''

"Mr. Dietz,'' I said, "this trailer looks in perfect condition, not a mark on it as far as I can tell. But there are certain things we need to check to find out if it's evidence in a murder case.''

"What things? Just tell me what you're going to do with it that might take two days.''

"Or three or four. Among other things, we're going to check it for drugs.''

"*Drugs?* Now just a damn minute!'' Everything I said made him angrier. "I'm the injured party here—why are you treating me like a criminal? I run an absolutely legitimate business, ask anybody! Where do you get off suggesting I'm in the drug business?''

"I'm not suggesting—''

"This is an outrage! I'm not going to stand still for this, young fella, you may be used to dealing with know-nothings you can just push around, but I'm not going to take your insults—''

"I'm not insulting you.'' A fresh breeze blew down my neck; I zipped my coat collar to the top and moved into the shelter of a beer truck. "There's no reason to take this pers—''

"I've got customers up in Duluth that are threatening to sue me!"

Suddenly I was totally fed up with John Dietz. "I've got one of your drivers on a slab in the morgue!" I yelled, at the top of my lungs. "Which do you think is more important?"

I should have said that first, I guess; it stopped him cold. He made a little sound that was almost a whimper, and said, "Oh, dear Lord." A few more tortured noises came out of him and then he said, "Do what you have to do," just above a whisper.

"Fine." I was so disoriented by his sudden capitulation I couldn't remember what else I needed to say to him. "I'll be in touch."

He was a businessman, though; he recovered fast. "Can I at least look inside it pretty soon, make sure the load is all right?"

"Sure. In fact—" the keys, for God's sake, that was it "—you can help a lot, if you will, and prevent any damage to your trailer, if you'll bring a set of keys over to that same evidence yard on Maryland Avenue. Remember, where your tractor is? You bring the keys there, first thing in the morning, and you can see the interior when the BCA crew opens it up. But you've got to remember not to touch anything!"

"I won't." He was being a good scout now. "But listen," he started timidly and then asked in a rush, "if my customer in Duluth keeps giving me grief, can I tell him to call you?"

"Sure. I'll straighten him out." Brave talk. If I had to go through another conversation like this one, I'd probably jump off a bridge. But right now I had to get off this damned patch of frozen asphalt.

"And can you give me a date certain when I can deliver the goods?"

"No. All I can tell you is that we'll be just as quick as we possibly can." I meant to give him hope without committing us to anything. He understood me very well; he said glumly, "Uh-huh," and hung up without saying good-bye.

I called Darrell then, told him to send the tow truck right away and meet them out here with the St. Paul address and the impoundment papers.

"Kevin's looking for you, too," he said, "and Bo called."

"I'm on my way in," I said. I got in my pickup, turned the heat to max-max-max, and alternately rubbed my hands together and hugged myself till the windshield defrosted. As soon as I was back on the highway I called Bo, who sounded surprisingly relaxed.

"Just wanted you to know I'll be back to work in the morning," he said.

"Already? That was quick work. You found a baby-sitter you like?"

"I should have asked Rosie Doyle in the first place," he said. "As soon as she found out what my problem was, she said, 'Do you know how many Doyles there are, growing up in this town?' She claims her family knows every baby-sitter within fifty miles."

"So she found one for you?"

"Sure did. She called one of her brothers' wives, came back, and said, 'Caroline says this is the best one she's ever had.' So I took Nelly there, yesterday afternoon and this morning, and looks like she's right, this woman's really got a way with kids. Nelly liked her right away.''

''Well, that's great. What about Diane?''

''She's sleeping right now. I'm going to try to talk to her when she wakes up. We'll see. Anyway, I'll be back in the morning.''

''Good. There's plenty to do.''

It was dark by the time I parked the pickup. The lighted hotel towers downtown glowed amber against the black sky, and the steam from the power plant rose in shining, sulfurous white streamers. Fatigue and depression snapped at my heels as I crunched across the parking lot and dodged through Second Avenue traffic. The hardest time to be a Minnesota detective is January, when the short hours of sunlight fool the body into feeling tired by midafternoon. Also, I'd been up more than twelve hours, and I'd just frozen my butt during a stupid argument in a windy truck stop. Every molecule in my body urged me to go home and snuggle with the heater, have a couple of brewskis, and forget about crime and punishment till tomorrow. I slogged past the jail and climbed the gleaming fake-marble stairs to what suddenly felt like my own prison.

Kevin followed me into my office, saying, ''You look mean as a snake. What's up?''

''Not mean,'' I said. ''Frozen to a stump, overworked, and underappreciated.''

''Poor pitiful putz. Listen, I found Tom Deever.'' I stared at him blankly. ''Tom Deever, the former partner of Wayne Asleson? Who moved to North Carolina? Who you've been shaking shit all over me to find?''

''Of course!'' I said, emerging from my haze of

self-pity. "Good old Tom. Sit down, tell me about him."

"Well, actually he does sound like a pretty good guy. Says he's really homesick for Minnesota. I asked him if he knew what the temperature's been here all this week, and he said, 'Aw, that's just good ice-fishin' weather.'" Kevin shook his head, grinning, shuffling through a fistful of notes. "Anyway! He describes Wayne Asleson the same way Cathy Niemeyer does, sweetest guy you could ever want to know, do anything for you, quiet, peaceable, never made a fuss. He said once they were stranded three days in a blizzard in Oklahoma, all alone in a weigh station near the border, and Wayne just kept making soup, loaned him all his copies of *Mechanics Illustrated* to read, and taught him to play hearts. Deever said, 'I'll tell you this, hanging's too good for the bastard that shot him.'" Kevin looked at me and shrugged helplessly. "Wayne can't be a murder victim, he's too lovable. We're never going to find anybody with a motive."

"Okay, you win, he's not dead. How about Roger Carr's partner, anything from him?"

"Dispatcher sent him an e-mail, he got it and messaged back that he's in the middle of unloading frozen food in Moorhead, he'll call me soon as he's done. I'll talk to him later this afternoon or in the morning."

"Good. What else, now? Find out how Lou's doing on his weapons search and let me know, will you? I'm gonna go see what Rosie wanted."

I found her in her cubicle, shaking hands with an androgynous person wearing platform sandals, net stockings with rhinestones, false eyelashes, and five o'clock shadow.

"Thanks for coming in, Billie," Rosie said. "You take care of yourself out there, huh?"

"Vaya con Dios, honey," Billie said, and sidled past me into the hall, muttering, "Boy, has *this* place changed."

"You making new friends?" I asked Rosie.

"I hope so." She scooped a big pile of papers off the straight chair by her desk, and I sat down. "Bo leads an interesting life, doesn't he?"

"Interesting is certainly one way to describe it. He's coming back tomorrow. Thanks for doing all this extra work, Rosie."

"You're welcome. My baby-sitter list must have worked out for him, huh?"

"Yes, it did. Darrell said you want to tell me something strange about numbers."

"Oh. Yes. That Stacey Morse has such a freaky memory! Stacey Morse. The systems engineer? Installing New World? Did somebody hit you on the head, Jake?"

"I just froze my ass off and got in a fight. Go ahead, what about Stacey Morse?"

"Well, it's just so amazing to watch him work! Besides being awesomely smart, he's got this phenomenal memory, he seems to remember every scrap of information he's ever been exposed to." She saw me sneaking a look at my watch. "Just listen a minute, willya? Maybe this is nothing, but you gotta hear it, because it seems like it's just too crazy to be a coincidence. But I suppose it is."

"Rosie—"

"Okay, okay. We were practicing with the new software, Stacey and I were, and we were putting some current records in and making all the links be-

tween sites, and when we came to your interview with
Cathy Niemeyer, I started typing the part where she
told you about the charm bracelet Wayne gave her,
and I'm saying, 'Oh, look, isn't this sad, this guy was
so happy with his girlfriend, he had these special
dates that meant so much to him and now he's dead,'
and suddenly Stacey said, 'That's funny, those are the
same numbers that won the big jackpot in the lottery
last week!'

"So I said, 'Go on, you're not gonna tell me you
remember old winners from Powerball, nobody remembers stuff like that unless they won,' and he said,
'Well, I didn't win big, but I had the first two numbers
right, so I was paying close attention.' And then he
said, 'If I concentrate on a number combination for a
while, it will stay in my mind for some time.' Did
you ever hear anything so *freaky?* He remembers
numbers the way the rest of us remember a line of
poetry or the words to a song. You gotta get to know
this guy, Jake, he really is something else. But don't
you think it's just wild that the numbers on Cathy
Niemeyer's bracelet would win the lottery the very
week she told you about it?''

Kevin appeared in the doorway suddenly, saying,
"John Dietz is on the line. He says it's important that
he talk to you right away.''

"Oh, goddamnit," I said, "what now?" Rosie
looked at me reproachfully. I went in my office and
picked up the phone, braced, and said, "Jake Hines."

John Dietz said, very fast, "Roger's car is gone."

"His car? Gone from where?"

"From his parking space in the yard."

"He leaves his car in your yard? I don't understand."

"Not my own yard—the company yard. That's what they do, the drivers—drive an old clunker to work and leave it there when they pick up their truck to start a trip. That way they have transportation handy when they get back. Roger had an old Chrysler Imperial he said was perfect to leave because nobody would steal it, it wasn't worth anything."

"How did you happen to notice it was gone?"

"Frankie Martello, one of the other drivers. He called Laurie, my secretary, and asked her to look in the trunk of Roger's car and see if the pinch-nose pliers were there that Roger borrowed from him a few days ago. Some special pair he's got, part of a set with green plastic sleeving on the handles. Roger borrowed this tool, and now Frankie needed it to make some repair, and of course Roger's gone. But Frankie said he knew Roger kept all his tools in his trunk. So Laurie went and got the car keys off the board behind her desk where all the drivers leave their keys, and went outside and couldn't find the car. So she came back in and asked me, where did I put Roger's car? I said I never touched his car, but I went out to look for it and she's right, his car is gone."

"Any chance it could be parked in some other part of the yard?"

"No. They each have an assigned space, and that's where they have to park. I set aside this one area so they'd be out of the way, and I'm strict about it, they park where they're supposed to or I won't let them park here at all."

"Did Wayne leave a car there too?"

"Yup, an eighty-three Merc. And it's right there where he left it."

"Well...uh...so you don't know how long Roger's car's been gone?"

"No idea. Ordinarily I never set foot in that part of the yard. The drivers use it, and I don't keep anything there I need."

"Could you ask some of the other drivers, Mr. Dietz? Ask them if they remember when it was first gone or if they saw who took it. And let me know what you find out?"

"Well, yes, I can do that. I was wondering—" He stopped talking and breathed heavily into the phone.

I waited. When I couldn't stand it anymore, I said, "Wondering what?"

"Well, do you think I should ask Connie? If she took the car? I hate to bother her when she's got so much on her mind—"

"Well, she'd want to know, though, wouldn't she?"

"Yes. And it's good news, I guess," John Dietz said, "It probably means Roger is still alive. Doesn't it?" He did some of that ragged breathing that made me want to scream, and then said plaintively, "But then where is he?"

"I'll tell you what, Mr. Dietz," I said, "why don't you let me call Connie Carr?"

"Well, would you really do that? I'd certainly be grateful. I—I just don't know what to say to her."

"Sure," I said. "Could you hold on one second?" I had heard Kevin and Rosie saying goodnight in the hall. I stuck my head out and said, low and fast, "Hang tough a minute, I might have something," and went back to the phone. I asked Dietz, "Can you give me a full description of that car, now, and the license number?"

"I don't think I have the license number. Wait, maybe Laurie…oh, she's gone. My gosh, it's after five already. What a day."

"The description, then," I said, grinding my teeth.

"Well, it's black, a black 1960 Chrysler Imperial."

"Nineteen-sixty? Really?"

"Yup. One of those super models like Dick Nixon used to ride around on in parades, remember? Oh, you're too young. Well, fins, then, you know what fins are?"

"I know about fins," I said. Inside my head, a berserk renegade was holding John Dietz by the throat, demanding he shut up about fins and get me the license plate number.

But he was rattling on and on about the car, "—that massive chrome bumper and the wide grill with 'Imperial' on it in script. Very fancy car in its day. Be a collector's item now if it was dolled up a little, but Roger doesn't care about the looks, he just keeps it because it's reliable to drive and doesn't cost hardly anything for the license."

I had to promise him, twice, that I would call Connie Carr right away before he would hang up the phone. Kevin and Rosie were standing in my doorway, with Lou behind them, and when I finally hung up they said, with one voice, "What?"

"Roger's car is missing!" I told them, and then had to tell them all about Roger's old car and where he kept it. Darrell heard their chorus of questions and came down the hall, and I had to go through the whole thing again. Then Ray came up the stairs and we started over, till the chief stuck his head out his door and said, "Hell's going on?" They all started to tell him, but I yelled, "Okay, wait! Everybody quit talking a minute!'' They all turned toward me and I said quickly, ''I need to call Connie Carr to see if she took it.''

Their silence lasted till I finished dialing; then the buzz behind me started again and grew while the phone rang twice, so I swung the door shut in their faces just as Connie Carr said, in a whispery, dry-mouthed voice, ''Hello?''

I told her Roger's car was gone. She was silent for so long I said, ''Mrs. Carr? You there?''

''Yes,'' she said. ''But I don't understand.''

''You didn't take it?''

''Of course not. What would I do with another heap of junk?''

''Well,'' I said, ''the next thing we've got to do is try to find it. I've got a description of the car, but I wondered, do you know the license number?''

''Well, I don't *know* it,'' she said, ''but maybe I can find it around here somewhere. Just a minute.'' She put the phone down, came back after a few seconds and picked it up again, and said, ''Roger took care of the cars, but—I suppose it would be on an insurance bill, wouldn't it?''

''I should think so, yes,'' I said. I had always known the license number of vehicles I had owned and could not imagine having to look them up. I heard banging and shuffling and then Connie Carr came back and said, ''I'm sorry. I can't seem to find any of Roger's records right now. He must have moved them. I told you, he isn't very systematic.''

''Okay. I'm sorry to have bothered you.'' I had been pondering a polite way to phrase the next question. Nothing graceful occurred to me, so I just asked her, "Where do you think he might have gone in his car?"

"Well." She considered through another long silence before she said, "I told you, he's never done anything like this before. So I really—" Her voice broke painfully. She waited, cleared her throat, and finally managed, "I guess I really have no idea."

I told her I'd call her as soon as I had any news, and she thanked me in a raspy whisper that seemed to have all the starch wrung out of it. I hung up the phone and opened my door, half expecting my whole crew to tumble in at my feet. There was nobody in sight. "Kevin?" I said, "Rosie?" Then the chief's head came out of his door and he said, "They're all in here. Y'got the number?"

"She couldn't find it," I said.

"Gimme the description," Kevin said. "This the correct spelling of his name?" He hustled off to Dispatch and I saw him through the glass, leaning over Woody at the teletype. He came back in a few minutes, waving the paper.

"I got it," he said.

"Let's get it on the wire." Kevin wrote up the Attempt to Locate and went back in to Dispatch; Ray called the State Patrol office and asked them to relay the info to all other patrol offices in the district. Lou said, "My buddy Keith's on tonight in the sheriff's office, shall I give him a jingle on this?"

"Wouldn't hurt," I said. Dispatch would relay to all offices, but a personal call from a friend might keep the notice on top of the pile.

"Rosie," I said, "it's too late now, but will you call your list of tourism bureaus in the morning? Ask them to send one of those heads-ups they do to member motels."

"I'll put it in our own BOLOs tonight, though, huh?"

"Absolutely." When they were all gone, Frank raised his eyebrows and spread his big hands palms up. "Beats me," I said, "I just work here."

"But why the hell would a guy whose partner has just been murdered go off on a tear?"

"Maybe he left first, before it happened."

"Or he did the shooting and now he's fleeing the country in a 1960 sedan with fins? There's a great plan for you—drive the most conspicuous car you can find to sneak out of town."

"Or he's just as dead as I always thought he was, and somebody else has got his car."

"Hmm. Why do you think that?"

"It's just a feeling I have. He's a company man, he's been one for years. He might play around on his wife, but he wouldn't abandon his load."

Frank snorted. "A cheater with principles, you're saying."

"The evidence points that way."

I cleaned up my desk and drove home, still pondering the puzzle of Roger Carr's mixed-up life. He had a good job that he'd kept a long time, and a boss who plainly valued him. He'd been married five years to a pretty woman, an achievement I knew from recent personal experience was not an easy slam-dunk. But his pinched, meager possessions and the undercurrent of anger in Connie's voice when she mentioned his off-hours pursuits seemed to belong to someone different, a man who wasn't making it and didn't seem to care.

After I put the truck in the shed, I stood in the dark yard for a minute, asking myself what felt so different. Then I realized I was looking at bright stars in a clear sky. The snow had stopped, and the clouds were gone.

The phone rang as I walked in the kitchen. I picked it up and said happily, "Trudy?" expecting to tell her that the weather was clearing and we could plan some fun for the weekend. But it was a telemarketer flogging a better long-distance deal. I hung up, nuked a chicken pie, and ate it staring at my crackling propane heater, trying to imagine where I would go in a 1960 Chrysler if I had just killed my partner and wanted to celebrate by cheating on my wife.

The proposition was too ridiculous to hold my attention. I gave it up, warmed several layers of fleecy clothing on the heater while I adjusted thermostats and tucked the rug against the door, undressed and dressed again, and dashed to my cold bed. Feeling like an abandoned Boy Scout, I piled on all the quilts and slept like a stone. According to my body, the alarm sounded twenty minutes later. But the clock insisted it was six a.m.

Bo and Rosie were already in the small meeting room, talking quietly, when I walked into the investigative section. I told them I'd be with them shortly, and they nodded vaguely, looking as if they wondered who I was. I went into my office and made a hasty list of the morning's chores, came back out, and made the rounds of cubicles, urging the rest of the team to join Bo and Rosie. Even when I got them all collected, I had trouble getting a hearing. Everybody in the crew seemed to have his own agenda.

"I'd like to go look at that trailer first thing," Bo said.

"Seems to me we oughta get caught up on other work till they find the car," Ray said. "The car's the key to this whole business."

"Yeah, but listen," Lou said, "none of those four names you gave me shows up as the owner of the gun that killed Wayne Asleson. If we'd find out whose gun it is, chances are we'd have the shooter."

"How you gonna find the owner if it's not registered?" Kevin asked him.

"It's a collector's gun, there must be clubs, web pages full of owner chat, stuff like that."

Then Mary opened the door and said, "I'm sorry, but I've got a man named Buddy Hall calling from Minneapolis, says this is the second time he's returned Kevin Evjan's call and he's not gonna call again."

"Go," I said, and Kevin ran for his office.

While we waited for him to come back, I told Bo, "You're right. You should start for St. Paul as soon as we finish this meeting."

"And go through all the cartons, right? The freight company's not gonna give me flak about that, are they?"

"I already fought this out with the freight company. Do what you gotta do."

"I might want a dog."

"Can't you get the loan of one in St. Paul?"

"Ramsey County's got a couple, I think, and maybe Dakota. I'll make a couple calls before I go. I should think by now I could get a look under the bunk of that cab, too."

"Right. Do that. And call me right away, will you, if you find something?

"Ray and Darrell, you've both got a pile of break-ins to follow up on, right? Get to work on them then. If somebody finds that car, we might all have to scramble pretty fast, so try to get your desks cleaned up while we wait.

"And Lou, your point's well taken—besides following up on outstanding cases, I think you ought to surf the web this morning. The gun that killed Wayne Asleson may not be registered to anybody. But you're sure to find web pages on the net about rare and imported guns, owners of older guns. Try family collections. See if you find some chat rooms, e-mail numbers, phone numbers. It's worth a little time.

"Rosie, you still have a lot of calls left over from what we talked about last night, right?"

"Right," she said, "besides my work in the records room."

"How's that going?" Darrell asked. "We going paperless anytime soon?"

"Not soon. Eventually. Six or seven months."

"Whoa, as long as that? What all you doin', anyway?"

Rosie crossed her eyes slightly and said, in a dead-on imitation of the Taco Bell Chihuahua, "We trying to contact the bright side of The Force, man." Kevin came back during the laughter that followed. He sat down thoughtfully and folded his hands. His gravity sucked all the merriment out of the room.

"What?" I said.

"So surprising," he said. He looked around and asked, "Have you all read the transcript of Jake's interview with Connie Carr? And Jake's notes about it?'' They all nodded yes, except Bo. "Okay," he turned to me, "as I remember it, Connie Carr said there was a little problem in the marriage because her husband was a big spender and careless about money, but otherwise they were fine and trying to start a baby?''

"That's right.''

"Well, that's not exactly the picture Buddy Hall paints of him. He drove with Roger Carr for a couple of years before he got married, and for five years since. He agrees about the fidelity part, says Roger used to cruise the bars looking for women, sometimes, before he met his wife, but after he got married he was a real straight-arrow as far as sex was concerned. But Buddy says the reason he quit driving with Roger was that Roger got addicted to gambling, and it was making him crazy.''

"Really? Why would a guy's gambling be a problem for his driving partner?''

"According to Buddy it wasn't, as long as it was just for fun, a pickup poker game with other drivers or an evening at a casino when they had a layover. But gradually it got to be all Roger could think about, the only thing he did for recreation. 'If you can call it recreation when anybody takes it that serious,' is how Buddy says it.''

"I knew a guy got like that once," Lou said. "He lost his house and car and job and wife, all in one year.''

"Yeah, I guess it can go like that. Roger Carr always bet on pro basketball and football, and got very scientific about point spreads. Also, he liked to play blackjack and poker when he got near the casinos, and he bragged all the time about what a shrewd player he was. He was also very fond of the big state lotteries, and he worked up some cockamamie theory for how to win one, something about covering all the numbers around a certain number based on his horoscope, I couldn't follow it. So whenever one of the states along their route would start to build up a pretty good total, he'd be out at all the gas and meal stops, buying up fistfuls of tickets.

"The big lottery, whaddya call it, Powerball, that one really turned his crank, I guess. Buddy said Roger would be distracted and jumpy all day on the days of the drawings, waiting to call in and check the numbers. And he'd talk all day long about these big elaborate plans he had, for what he was gonna do with the money. He had trips all planned, Hawaii and New Zealand and like that, where he was gonna take Connie. Buddy says Roger got so he couldn't enjoy anything that was right in front of him, just thinking all the time about how it was gonna be after he made that big score.

"Buddy said he used to try to change the subject sometimes, talk about sports or fishing, but it wasn't any use because Roger could always find a way to get back to talking about gambling. If you brought up a sport all he wanted to say about it was which numbers he'd bet for the next game. Buddy got so sick of hearing about Roger's gambling that finally he just couldn't stand to hear another word about it. He said, 'When I found myself dreaming about jumping out of the truck while it was moving, I put in for short hauls and took the next route that came up.' "

"That's quite a story," I said. "Do you believe it?"

"Every word. He has no reason to lie, and besides,

you should have heard him. Just talking about Roger Carr, he started getting angry and jumpy. I asked him a question, and he almost bit my head off.''

"Okay,'' I said. ''It fits with Roger's wife's statement that he didn't bring enough of his paycheck home. Funny she wouldn't know it was gambling, though, isn't it? She seemed to think he spent it all playing with the boys.''

"Or maybe she suspected he was spending it on other women, and she didn't want to tell you that,'' Kevin said.

"Maybe. This is all very interesting, but I don't know yet where it leads. So for right now, I think, Ray and Darrell and Lou, best thing for you to do is go ahead on the jobs we've already discussed. And Rosie, make your calls to those tourism bureaus, and do whatever you need to do in the records room and get back to me. Bo and Kevin, let's talk about this a little more.''

When the others were gone, I said, ''Kevin, I think we need to know more about Roger Carr, how far he went with this gambling business, whether maybe he had big debts he wasn't telling his wife about.''

"That's what I was thinking,'' Bo said, ''maybe he got in bad with a shark or two and his new partner got caught in the middle by mistake.''

"Exactly. You can start with local merchants and bar owners, Kevin—in this town they all know each other's business pretty much.''

"You want me to wait and help with this?'' Bo asked.

"No. I want you to go up to St. Paul as we planned and go over that trailer. But before you go, have you got some names you can pass along to Kevin? Some people around town and in the Cities he could talk to, maybe find out if Roger was doing business with the sharks, or owed a bookie, anything like that?"

"Sure," Bo said, looking dubious. "I can do that." He hates to share sources; he's never said so, but I can tell he thinks the rest of the crew needs to practice on misdemeanors a while longer before they tackle vice on his level. Bo wants to stay on my team, though, so he took Kevin along to his office.

"And soon as Rosie gets back from the records room," I told Kevin, "she can help you make some of those calls."

When they were gone, I went in my office and started all those evasive games I play when I can't decide what to do next: I straightened my pencils in their mug, found all the loose paper clips in the room and pushed them into the gadget with the magnet, and lined up a stack of notes so they were square with the corner of my desk. Luckily, just as I was running out of anything to do but pull my nose hairs, the phone rang.

NINE

"JIMMY ASKED ME to call you, Jake," Megan Duffy said. "To give you the results from the blood work on the truck."

"Really? You have DNA results already?"

"Yes. Jimmy said you had a John Doe you were trying to identify, so go for STR."

"I remember he said that," I said. I didn't see any point in letting the air out of her tires by telling her our victim had been identified. "I just didn't realize how much faster this new method is. Are you testing the same items as before? Blue eyes or brown, that kind of stuff?"

"We don't care about anything like that, Jake."

"You don't? What are you looking for, then?"

"Well—you know that DNA is, like, an encyclopedia of the human genome, right? All the information is there, everything you need to know to create a human body."

"Right. And it's all different for each person, I understand that."

"Well, no, there's a lot of duplication actually. We all have eyes, noses, hearts and livers. What forensic DNA testing does is take snippets from places on the double helix that have been identified as being unique for each individual. But we don't know, yet, if we're looking at eye color or the shapes of their tushies. We won't know that till the human genome mapping project is complete."

"And you don't care?"

"Nope. We just test thirteen places where we know each human being is unique. That's all the ID you need."

"Be damned. And this STR, it's just as reliable as the old way?"

"Better. You can pretty well bet the farm on STR results. It's gonna be the universal method as soon as somebody finds a way to bring the price down."

"It came on-line fast, didn't it? I just heard about it; I don't even know what the initials mean."

"Short Tandem Repeats. Don't make me explain any more, or we'll never get to the results."

"Okay. So what have you got for me?"

"All the blood in the truck matches the victim, except for that little double row of drops on the roof. And the blood on the railing of the overpass is from the victim, too. The blood on the roof matches the blood on the curbstone of the overpass, but we don't know whose it is. He's not in our database."

"He? You know the sex?"

"Yeah, STR is gender-specific."

"Okay. But if you can't find him in your database he hasn't been, uh, convicted—?"

"Hasn't been convicted of a sex crime. Those are the only ones we're storing now."

"Oh, that's right. Hmm. Not much use in this case."

"Not much use in most cases. Soon as everybody stops fighting about it, we'll have DNA records from Felony One convicts on up."

"Uh-huh. But for now I'll just have to find my own bad guy."

"Yup. Jimmy is very happy about these results, of

course, because they tend to support his thesis that the double-row spatter pattern came from a wound on the shooter's hand.''

"Yes, that's right. They do. Which dovetails nicely with some of the other evidence, and makes no sense at all with the rest of it.''

"Isn't that always the way? See ya, Jake.''

"Thanks, Megan.'' I hung up and tapped a pencil eraser on the desk for a while. Then I looked up Cathy Niemeyer's number and called her.

She answered in that quiet, reasonable tone that grieving people often adopt to disguise their need to scream. She said she was doing all right, thanks. Victim's Services had been very helpful. Wayne's mother and sister were arriving tomorrow to help her sort out his things, and they would stay for his funeral, which would be in Mantorville as soon as his body was released.

"The most surprising thing,'' she said, ''Wayne left a will.''

"You didn't know about it?''

"No. We never talked about it. But a lawyer called yesterday and asked if he could come to see me. He brought it with him. Wayne left me—'' Her voice broke. When she could talk again, she said, hoarsely, "He left me everything he owned. So now I have three cars,'' she managed a little barking laugh, ''and this house. Looks like I'll be able to keep the house. It's almost paid for, and the bank said I can extend the loan on the rest.''

"Is that what you want to do? Keep the house and live in Mantorville?''

"Yes. It feels like home to me now. People in this

town have been really nice to me since Wayne got killed.''

"I'm glad it's working out then. Look, I apologize for bothering you again, but there's one more question that I forgot to ask. Did Wayne ever gamble?''

"Gamble?'' She sounded puzzled. "You mean, like, play cards and that?''

"Or bet on Bingo, the state lottery, anything like that?''

"Oh. No, he never gambled for money. I never saw him do that. Some of his friends used to come over Saturday nights if he was home, and play rummy or hearts. But they just played for high score, they never bet anything. If they played poker, they used matches.''

"So you're quite certain that Wayne wouldn't have been betting on Powerball?''

"On Powerball? That big lottery thing? No. He wasn't interested in anything like that.''

"Okay. Thanks, Cathy.'' I put the phone down and stared out the window. Bright sunshine was clearing off roofs; I watched a big section of icy snow slide off the top of the library. I got up and walked down the hall to Rosie Doyle's cubicle. She was standing, picking records out of stacks of paper on her desk and knocking the ends together on her desk, making a pile to take with her.

"I was just coming to see you,'' she said, "to tell you I talked to the directors of both the innkeepers' associations—Rutherford and the Twin Cities. They've got a hot line they use to warn each other about clients who skip on bills and break up rooms and so forth. They call each other in alphabetical order and just keep going till they get to Z. They promised to pass our license number around to their hotelmen.''

"Good. You headed for the records room?''

"Yeah. Gonna go sit at the feet of the cyber guru for a while."

"You still want to get rid of that job?"

"What, and let somebody else hear Stacey Morse's math jokes first? In your dreams, Jake."

"Well, okay, if you're sure. Can you spare me five minutes before you go?"

"Sure. What's up?"

I sat down in the little chair by her desk and looked up at her. "Don't laugh."

She laughed delightedly, pulled out her chair, and sat down. "God, I can't wait to hear this. What?"

"What's the deal on Powerball? Why is everybody so excited about it all the time?"

She stared. "You never played the lottery? Where do you live, on the moon?"

"I know I don't have any luck, so why waste the money?"

"You don't have any luck?" She chuckled. "How can you say that, you who get to live all winter in Rutherford, Minnesota, and work with this wonderful crew?" She broke up completely then. I waited, admiring her dental work. "Seriously," she finally said, "you really don't think you have any luck? Why?"

"It's just something I know. I'm not asking about Powerball for myself. It's just…that coincidence with Wayne's good numbers keeps making me twitch."

"I know, isn't it crazy? Well, playing the lottery, Jake, I guess it's that the prizes get so big so fast. Only costs a buck a try, and sometimes you end up having a chance on millions. And it's so easy, right there at the places you're going to anyway, almost any gas station or convenience store.''

''And there's no big brain work, that's part of the attraction too, isn't it? Just pick six numbers—''

''Yes. One number for Powerball and five more on the other side of the ticket. And you're right, any idiot can play; they give you the ticket, and if you're not sure how to mark it, they'll help you.''

''It's the choice of numbers that intrigues me. Why should any set of numbers be any better than another? Do you have yours chosen before you go to play?''

''Usually. But if I think random chance would be better, I can always let the computer pick them for me.''

''Really? You'd do that? Play with the machine's numbers?''

''Sure, if that's the mood I'm in.''

''How strange.'' I looked at her, so assertive, so bright, and imagined her indignation if I demanded she play my numbers next week. ''Okay. Now I have the ticket, now what do I do when I win?''

''When you win?'' She chuckled merrily again. I was obviously more amusing than I had realized. ''Well, I'm not so experienced with that part.''

''What, you mean you never won?''

''Well, I never won any of the bigger prizes. There's all kinds of little prizes along the way. Like if you guess the Powerball number and one other number correct, you win four dollars. I've won that several times. And Powerball plus two other numbers, that's seven bucks, I've won that, uh, twice I guess.''

''But you've never won the big prize?''

''Well, no,'' she said, sounding as if my dumb

questions weren't so funny anymore, "not so far. Would I be working here if I had?"

"Really? You'd quit your job if you had money enough? I thought you liked being a cop."

"Oh, *I* don't know, Jake, it's just never come up. Not even close."

"How long you been playing?"

"How long's it been running? Since 1992, I think."

"And you put money in it every week—?"

"Well, not every week. Whenever I fill my tank, I usually buy a chance in the next drawing."

"That's pretty close to once a week, though, isn't it?"

"I guess." She was getting defensive. "What's your point?"

"Why do you keep playing it, if you never win?"

"Oh, Jesus." She snorted and flounced. "You don't understand how this works!"

"I guess not," I said. "Explain it to me."

"The law of averages! See, the law of averages says that sooner or later, my turn's gonna come up. So every time I buy a ticket and I don't win, I'm that much closer to the time when I *will* win." She threw her hair around some more and asked me, "Are you trying to catch flies, Jake, or why is your mouth open like that?"

"You're usually such a logical person," I said.

"Yeah, well. Logical, hardworking, law-abiding. That's what we are, the Doyles. Some days that feels okay. Other days it seems like all I do is shovel shit, you know what I'm saying? You get to feeling like you deserve better. So I play the lottery, so someday something nice might happen that I haven't *earned*."

"Okay." I was dumbfounded by this kink in her personality, but wary of making her angry. "Just one person wins, each time?"

"No, no, there can be several winners. Usually two or three, anyway. Because there's a bunch of states in on this, see, it's not just in Minnesota."

"All right. You think you could do something for me? There must be a headquarters, isn't there, a place where somebody manages this game?"

"Sure. In Minnesota it's in Roseville."

"Call them. Find out whether everybody who won on Wayne's numbers last week has collected the money, will you? And see if you can find out who they are. Use your badge number, make it an official call."

"Absolutely. Oh, this'll be fun, I'll—" Noise erupted in the hall suddenly. I stepped out and collided with Darrell.

"Oh, Jake, here you are, good. We've found that second driver's car."

"You have? Where?"

"You're not gonna believe this," he said. "It's at his own house."

"At his—who's watching it?"

"Vince Greeley. You wanna talk to him? Schultzy said she'd patch him through."

"Yes. No, wait, I don't want to make all that noise on the radio, ask her to get him on the phone and put it through to my office." I walked along the hall to my office and waited by the phone. When it rang I said, "Vince?"

"Hey Jake. How they hangin'?"

"Fine. What do you see there?"

"Guess I found the black Chrysler you're lookin' for, buddy." He read the license plate to me.

"That's the one. Is it parked in front, or—"

"It's under the overhang, as far as it can get, nosed up against an old Lincoln that's taking up about a quarter of a mile in the back there."

"Is there a tan Escort parked around there anywhere?"

"Uh, nope, don't see one."

"Anything moving in the house?"

"No lights, no action, no sound."

"You okay there for ten minutes?"

"Maybe fifteen even. After that I gotta go peepee."

"We'll be right there."

"Get Kevin and meet me by the front door," I told Darrell, grabbing my briefcase and running for the back stairs. I signed for an unmarked car, picked a set of keys off the rack outside the parking garage, and was idling the motor and fiddling with the air blowers when the other two huffed out the door, still buttoning their coats.

I didn't want to use a siren, but even so I got to Granny Goose much faster than before because I knew the way and didn't have to futz around peering down dead-end streets. Once inside the gate, I crept over the speed bumps discreetly and rolled past the rear of the sun-faded Chrysler Imperial protruding from Connie's carport like a buffalo trying to occupy a phone booth. I made a U-turn at the end of Bo-Peep Lane, came back, and pulled in behind Vince's squad in a vacant lot two doors beyond Carr's house. Vince got out quietly and came and leaned in my open window. Our white breath mingled in the frosty air.

"Any movement?"

He shook his head. Profound stillness surrounded the dingy mobile home and its two old cars.

"Well, I guess—" I said finally, and we all got out of the car. "Better spread out," I said. Kevin and Darrell crossed the road with Kevin in the lead. Vince walked three steps ahead of me on my side. We all unbuttoned coats and stuffed scarves in pockets, making sure we had easy access to our weapons.

When we reached the Carr single-wide, I took the lead up the narrow gravel walk to the door. With the other three standing behind me along the path, hands ready at their sides, I knocked and waited. Nothing happened, not a sound. I knocked and waited again.

"Okay," I said, "let's do it." We all took out our Glocks and armed them, wincing at the noise the slides made. I tried the door with my left hand. The handle turned easily. I pushed and the door swung open. I flattened against one side of the doorway, Vince against the other. We peered around the narrow space. Nothing moved, so I pivoted around the narrow doorjamb and stood with my back against the wall. Vince moved to stand against the open door, and Kevin and Darrell followed us in.

Nothing moved. I could hear Darrell breathing beside me. The refrigerator turned on, and we all jumped. After it purred a few seconds, I moved into the tiny kitchen and listened. Nothing. Vince moved past me into the bathroom. He came out in three seconds, shaking his head.

The door to the bedroom was closed. Kevin and Darrell flattened against the bulkhead on either side, and I kicked it open. Fragments flew from the splintered jamb, and the air was filled with fragments of fiberboard as they stepped sideways through the doorway and flattened against the walls. We all stared into the dusty gloom, till our eyes adjusted enough to see the newspaper on the bed, and, below the paper, a pair of legs, dressed in jeans and dark socks.

I aimed my Glock at the middle of the newspaper and nodded to Kevin. He moved quietly along the wall, leaned, closed his fingers on the corner of the newspaper nearest him, and snatched it quickly away.

A sturdy man with heavy shoulders lay on his back, with his arms at his sides. He was fully dressed except for his shoes, which stood neatly, one behind the other, against the wall. His sandy hair was cut short, receding a little at the hairline, and the skin of his face was pink with sunburn. His eyes were closed; he looked asleep till you noticed the tiny, black-rimmed hole in his forehead. As my eyes adjusted fully, I saw that the comforter beneath him was soaked with blood.

Darrell inhaled, suddenly, and we all became aware we were holding our breath and began sucking air, feeling our heart rates decelerate. One by one, we holstered our weapons, cleared our throats, pulled on gloves, and moved toward the bed. Except Vince, who said, "I'm gonna call in, ask for backup," and went out to his car.

"He's cold," I said, groping behind one ear, finding no pulse.

"Stiff already," Kevin said, his fingers on the dead man's hands.

"Look at his left hand," I said.

Kevin held the left hand up and said, "Some kind of a scar here," and then looked at me excitedly and asked, "Is this—"

"Sure is," I said. Two healing scabs from thin cuts

ran across the skin between his thumb and forefinger.
"The wound he got when he gripped his Walther
wrong. When he shot Wayne Asleson," I said. "I'm
almost sure of it."

"Well, yippy-kay-aye," Kevin said, "now if we
just knew who shot *him* we could knock off for the
day, huh?"

"Is it Roger Carr?" Darrell asked me. "Do you
know what he looks like?"

"Well now," I said, "isn't that a good question?"
To my chagrin, I realized I'd been taking his identity
for granted. I tried to remember the physical description I'd copied from Dietz's records. Then a different
memory tugged at me; I walked to the front of the
house and found the studio portrait that had been on
the table by Connie's chair the day I interviewed her.

"She said it was their wedding picture," I said,
bringing it back. The three of us looked, and all said
together, "Yeah."

I took the picture back, found a pen and spiral notebook in my briefcase, came back to the bed, and
started writing: "Thursday, January 6—" I looked at
my watch and asked them, "Can this be right, nine-
forty-eight?"

"Yup," Darrell said, "It seems later, doesn't it?"

"For sure. Kevin, you saw the entry wound on
Wayne Asleson. Doesn't this look a lot like it?"

"Yeah. Kinda. All shrunk up and small and crusty.
But this one's got black powder all around it, see?"
He pointed. "And don't you think there's kind of a
pointy bruise around it too?"

"Uh, yeah. What did Stuart call that? A stellate
pattern. Which means the gun was a little closer,
right? Maybe even right up against the head. But it

could be the same gun, don't you think? The bullet's probably in the mattress. Let's see if the casing's around here someplace.''

"Or the gun," Kevin said, "wouldn't that be fine?''

We spent ten minutes, the three of us, grunting and sweating and bumping asses, searching the tiny house as carefully as we could without touching the body. We found out Connie Carr was a neat housekeeper with few possessions. We found threadbare sheets and towels and a few groceries, a few paperback books, and a cheap camera, but no bullet casing.

"Might be under the body," I said, "and we'll find it when Pokey gets here.''

"You know what, though," Kevin said, squatting on the other side of the bed with his eyes just above the mattress, "I see his wallet. Can I take it out of there?''

"Lemme see." I moved to his side of the bed and leaned. The wallet lay just above the rear jeans pocket, with the plastic pockets shining in the dim light from the window.

"Yeah. It's not really on the body. Let's have a look." Kevin reached two gloved fingers delicately under the dead man's lower back and fished out the wallet.

"Careful. Is there blood on it? We don't want to smear—''

"Huh-uh. Blood didn't soak down that far. Here you go." He dropped it into my cupped hands, a dark blue nylon wallet with a Velcro closure. The plastic pockets held a driver's license with a trailer and tanker endorsement, social security and insurance and teamster's union cards, memberships in the Elks

Lodge and a gun club, and half a dozen credit and bank cards. Connie's picture was in the top pocket. The money compartment held fifty-seven dollars.

"Well, he wasn't robbed." I found an evidence bag in my briefcase and dropped it in. "What else, now, before I call everybody?"

"Everything's neat here," Darrell said, "no signs of a fight."

"He must have been reading the paper and fell asleep," Kevin said, "and somebody came along and shot him."

"Through the paper? Does it have a hole?" I picked it off the floor and looked. "No hole."

"I thought I saw a little bit of forehead above," Kevin said.

"That was very well done, by the way," I said.

He smiled ironically and said, "Little skills we didn't even know we had. Yanking newspapers off of stiffs."

"He could have been waiting for you with a weapon. And I advise you never to duck a compliment, you aren't gonna get that many in this line of work. Anything else? Okay, I'm gonna start the calls. Darrell, go out and help Vince string some crime scene tape around this place, will you? Or we're gonna have people crawling all over this place in about a minute. And Kevin, probably you better walk up to the office and find the manager. See if anybody there knows where Connie is, while you're at it." I pulled my cell phone out of the briefcase, turned my back on Roger Carr's body, and began hitting speed-dial numbers.

I called Dispatch first, to report the body we had found here and get an ICR number. I felt certain we

were looking at a further development in the Asleson
case, but since we were a long way from proving it,
we'd have to give it a new file number. When I'd
given Schultzy enough details to put the incident in
the day's BOLOs, I asked her to switch me to Frank's
office. Lulu said he was in a meeting. I was halfway
through leaving a message when he came on the
phone and said, "Jake? What's up?"

"We've found the missing driver, Frank. He's right
here in town, at his house. He's dead, though; he's
been shot."

"The hell," he said. "How's it look?"

"Like he might have been shot with the same
gun," I said, "but that's highly tentative. I'll get
enough details to you in a couple hours so you can
put it on the evening blat. In fact maybe you oughta
call the TV station right now and promise them full
details in a couple hours if they'll hold off comin' out
here right now."

"Worth a try," he said. "I'll do it. Anything else
you need?"

"I'll yell if I do. I better start calling everybody
else."

Pokey's assistant put me through to him. He was
working on one of his legion of teenage acne patients,
said he'd be done in ten minutes and would come as
soon as he was finished.

BCA was answered on the second ring by somebody named Clarice, who said they were just about
back to normal, "whatever that is." She checked the
schedule while I held on, and came back to say she
thought a van was just about ready to leave Red
Wing. "Hang on while I page them," she said, "and

we'll see if they can detour down to you on the way back.''

"I caught 'em," she said when she came back on. "Zumwalt says he thinks they've got enough gear on board for one more stiff. He's such a mouth. Anyway they should be there in about an hour."

Kevin opened the outside door while Clarice was still talking, and began motioning frantically for me to close the bedroom door. It wouldn't close much, since we'd just reduced it to splinters, but I swung shut what there was of it and stood in front of it.

"The manager is here," he said. "This is Mrs. Peavey."

Angela Peavey both did and did not want to come in; she two-stepped in and out, horrified and excited, curious and appalled, desperate to get first crack at anything newsworthy but anxious to keep any sordid aspects of this crime from rubbing off on her or her place.

"Honestly, isn't this just the end?" she said. "I certainly wish I'd known the Carrs were this kind of people before I ever rented to them." She seemed to equate sudden death to nuisance behavior, like spitting in public or being drunk at breakfast.

While she dithered in the doorway, Clarice said in my ear, "Gimme that address again?" and I said, on sudden inspiration, "Mrs. Peavey, I'll bet you know the best way to tell strangers how to find this place, don't you?"

"Well, I guess, I do it about twenty times a day," she said, and took the phone.

"Honey," she said, "which way are you comin' from?" She listened a few seconds and then gave brisk, one-two-three directions from the Fifty-fifth

Street exit. Kevin watched her, smiling and shaking his head, enchanted to find this capable professional hiding under the gabby ditz.

As soon as she got off the phone, she said, ''Listen, you guys, as long as you're here...'' as though we had just dropped by to sell raffle tickets. She had a long-standing campaign going, to persuade the city council to install a stoplight at the quiet corner in front of her place, and she wanted us to put in a word with ''the powers that be.''

''Doesn't look as if it's exactly gridlocked with traffic,'' Kevin said, squinting down the empty, snow-clogged street along the creek.

''So what?'' Angie said. ''It would do wonders for the neighborhood. Seems to me you guys ought to give a little more thought to us taxpaying citizens, instead of looking after criminals all the time.'' Enchanted by this dazzling leap of logic, Kevin beamed down at her, plainly prepared to talk to Angela Peavey all morning.

''Kevin,'' I said, ''why don't you walk Mrs. Peavey back to her office and see if she has any emergency numbers there where we might find Connie Carr? Bring back a spare key for this place, too, if she's got one.'' They strolled away, with Mrs. Peavey chatting happily, so I leaned out the door and added, ''As quickly as possible.''

Angela Peavey looked up into Kevin's beaming face and said, ''He's kind of a crab, isn't he?''

I called the county attorney's office. One of Milo's temp secs said he was in court. I gave her the address of the crime scene and asked her to include my cell phone number on the message, in case whoever came to view the crime scene got lost.

"In Rutherford?" She giggled delightedly. Young women were finding me irresistibly comical today.

Pokey may have cheated his patient a little on the last few pimples; he wheeled into Granny Goose while I was still talking to the CA's office. His Jeep performed a spectacular flying leap over the first speed bump, since he had ignored all the signs demanding that he slow down. Only his ragtop kept him from braining himself. His tires squealed alarmingly during the sharp turn into Bo-Peep Lane, and he slid to a stop in front of Carr's house with the nose of the Jeep nudging the yellow tape.

"Crimenently," he said, hopping out with his leather bag, "is one really Goth place here, huh? What other treats they got, land mines under little cute goosies?"

"I think maybe they wanted you to slow down."

He snorted and stomped past me into the tiny living room. "What's in here, dead tourists that couldn't make last turn?"

"Roger Carr. The driving partner of that truck driver we found in the snowbank Sunday night."

"Oh, yah? This one died in bed, though, huh? You think? How come eyes closed?" He moved toward the bed, pulling on gloves, firing questions without waiting for any answers. But he did ask good questions, I thought, watching him bend over the body.

Darrell walked in and said, "Okay, tape's all strung. What's next?"

"Go and borrow Vince's Streamlight, will you? Bring it in here and point it wherever Pokey says. He's gonna need more light."

Kevin, coming back from the office, had to negotiate smilingly through the growing ring of gawkers circling the yellow tape. "Mrs. Peavey doesn't have any other numbers for Connie Carr. She wants to know, do we have to put it in the paper that Roger Carr died here?"

"Did you tell her this man was shot in the head? Even she must know that's not a communicable disease."

"I strongly advise against discussing gunshots with Mrs. Peavey, Jake."

"Okay. Did you try the House of Pancakes for Connie Carr?"

"Yes. They haven't seen her this week."

Pokey called from the bedroom, "Jake?" We walked back there, and he said, "Wanna roll 'im. Here," he said, scrunching up flat against the bed, "slide by here." He had Darrell posted on the other side of the bed with the light. I brushed past him, pulling on gloves, and when Kevin had his gloves on and put his hands on the dead man's feet, I leaned across the body and gripped the right shoulder. He was heavier than I expected, a solid, muscular man. We rolled him onto his left side and then a little past, so that his whole back was exposed. Most of the back of his head was spread across the bed; the viscous string of brain tissue, bone fragments, and blood hung out the back of the head, this time, and was dark red, turning black. Pokey pulled the bloody shirt up and pulled the pants down a little. The whole back was dark red. He pushed the pants legs up. The backs of the legs had the same liverish blush as the back.

"Settles one question, anyway," Pokey said. "Looks like he died right here in this bed. Didn't go riding around and then get thrown off no bridge like his partner, hah?"

"Take a look at his left hand," I said. "You ever see a wound like that before?"

Darrell turned his light on the hand, and we watched while Pokey squinted at it. "Nope," he said finally, "don't think so."

"It's a railroad track scar from a handgun slide," I said, "I'm pretty sure." I showed him how it worked. "I'm very glad to see it, because it's gonna prove this guy killed Wayne Asleson."

"This one killed frozen guy?" His foxy face pursed as if he'd just swallowed a pickle. "Is very convenient, huh?"

"What do you say about this entry wound? Kevin and I thought it looked very much like the one you found Sunday night. Like it might have been made by the same gun." I watched while he showed Darrell how to direct the light on Roger's face, and stood looking.

"Coulda been," he said finally, "or by million other guns of same caliber. You find casing for bullet? What, not here? Funny. Better hope BCA finds bullet in mattress, then. Probably not gonna prove helluva lot after blowin' this fella's head apart, though."

"Any thoughts on when he died?"

He pursed his lips. "What's temperature gadget say? On wall there?"

I looked. "Seventy-three."

"Uh-huh. He registered seventy-five in anus. So…body lost twenty-four degrees in twelve hours like book says, or fella's been dead two days, got to room temperature and stayed there. But—lividity complete, rigor mortis—" he felt the stiff jaw again "—pretty close. So twelve to twenty-four hours. Probably."

"Why do I ask?" I said.

"For fun. To watch old Ukrainian do math." He was packing his tools. "Any more wise-ass cop questions?"

"I'll call you as soon as they come up."

"Good. Gonna go try death-defying leap out Gramma Goosie's front gate." He closed his bag and went out, leaving the door open, and I heard him say to someone on the walk, "Is wonderful place here, hah? Sure keeps tires limbered up."

Milo walked into the small space and said, "You really want this door open?"

"No," I said.

He closed it and immediately said, "Jeez, though, this place would stink a goat off a gut wagon, wouldn't it?"

"Then leave it open, Milo," I said, "but it's eighteen degrees outside." I always forget how fast I can get sick of him when he's got his anxious whine tuned up. It was true, though, that Roger Carr wasn't getting any sweeter, and with the repeated entry of so many people whose stress levels rose in the presence of death, the air in that restricted space was turning decidedly rank.

I turned down the thermostat and motioned Darrell and Kevin outside. We stood on the cold gravel walk with our heads together.

"All these people standing around here might as well have their time put to good use," I said. "Darrell, here's a notebook and pen. Kevin, start working your way along the yellow line, see if you can find any near neighbors. Get them to tell you what they heard around this place yesterday, last night. Who heard loud fights, or gunshots, and when did they hear them? Darrell, write down everything they tell him.''

"Chat 'em up," Kevin said, "Gotcha." Turning Kevin Evjan loose on a crowd of people is really taking unfair advantage. He has a handsome, trustworthy face and bottomless patience; he loves talking to people, and they open to him like a flower to the sun. I have seen him wade into hostile, even combative, environments, stand around a few minutes, looking friendly and kind, and soon have people crowded around him, competing to tell him what he wants to know.

I went back inside and found Milo standing where I'd left him in the middle of the tiny living room, looking as grumpy as a tourist in a traffic jam. "Okay," he said, looking at his watch, "I'm working against the clock today. What have you got here, Jake?"

"We got a dead body, right there on the bed," I said, thinking, He can't even act like a pompous ass and do it right. At least his predecessor had been very good at that. And Milo used to have moments of ironic honesty, before this job made him so edgy and mean. The impulse to throw a lamp at his head was so strong in me that I turned away to hide my anger. "Excuse me, I gotta make a couple of calls." He moved past me, looking offended, and went and stood in the bedroom door with his hands in his pockets, fanning himself with the unbuttoned front panels of his car coat.

I called the department, got Ray on the phone, told him what we had at Granny Goose, and said, "Will you call Cathy Niemeyer? Somebody should tell her about this before she hears it on the news, and she knows you.''

''Sure I will,'' he said, not sounding reluctant at all. ''Uh—you want me to tell her what killed him?''

''Um, you can tell her a gunshot very similar to the one that killed Wayne. Just between you and me, he's got a railroad track scar on his left hand, so I think he's the man who shot Wayne. But we haven't proved anything yet, so keep that to yourself. Just tell her we wanted her to know what was happening.''

''I'll do it.''

''All right. Now switch me to Lou's phone.'' When Lou answered, I said, quickly before he could protest, ''Lou, I'm busy here and I need you to do me a favor. Call John Dietz at Clearwater Trucking and tell him—'' I went over it all again. ''Dietz is pretty distressed, Lou, so do the best you can for him, will you? Tell him we'll give him more details as soon as we have them. Uh—'' I looked at Milo Nilssen's back, which unlike most people's backs can look every bit as forlorn as his front. I could feel him thinking that he never got the help he was entitled to, which was true. I said, ''Then, Ray, tell the chief I said Roger Carr appears to have died of a gunshot wound, twelve to twenty-four hours ago, BCA is taking charge of the case this afternoon, there's no weapon on the premises, and I'll give him more in a couple of hours.''

To Milo's sad back I said, ''You get all that, Milo?''

''I heard you. You got any suspects for this second shooting?''

''Nope. Doesn't look like suicide. That's as far as we've gone.''

''Uh-huh. But the second shooter appears to have

had the same gun and a remarkably similar shooting style, huh? Interesting.'' He finally turned around and quit flapping his coat. "Well. You'll be in touch when you're ready to charge somebody for this unseemly carnage, right?"

I nodded, watching him hunt through his pockets for the gloves he had left on the chair arm when he came in. I felt that awful sadness that seems to follow him like a cloud, and said, "Is somebody being mean to you, Milo?" ignoring the fact that I'd just been mean to him myself.

For a minute I thought he really might cry. He was caught off guard by the question and torn between his longing to unload and his fear of dropping his defenses. Finally he managed the ghost of a grin and said, "I never had any idea, you know? I used to think I did all the work and Ed took all the glory. Now that he's gone—" He shook his head wistfully.

"Right. For a showboating inconsiderate cheapskate, he wasn't so bad, if you leave out how much he exploited his help and cheated on his wife."

He laughed out loud, suddenly looking ten years younger. "Doris knew a few tricks, too," he said, "if you remember. You know something, Jake?" He suddenly stood tall and buttoned his coat. "I gotta get some decent help. I just can't do this any longer, baby-sitting this starter set of lawyers they've shoved onto me. I gotta quit trying to make everything come out all right by working night and day. It's making me crazy, and all I'm getting out of it is blamed for other people's mistakes."

"There you go," I said. "Tell the commissioners to get real, or you're going to stuff it, and where would they be without you?"

"Better off, maybe. I suspect several commissioners of harboring the thought. But at least they wouldn't be driving me nuts any more."

"Way to go, Milo. You can only do what you can do."

"That's deep," he said. "Who said that?"

"John Wayne, probably. You gonna be all right?"

"Yup. I got my gloves," he said, suddenly finding them on the chair arm, "and I got a plan. Thanks, Jake." To my astonishment, he walked over and shook my hand before he left. I stared after him, hoping he hadn't seen me flinch away. For one terrifying moment I had thought he was going to hug me.

The BCA van arrived then, with Megan Duffy and Ted Zumwalt aboard. We all helped them lug bags into the little house, which quickly became too hot again, and beyond crowded. I turned down the thermostat some more and followed Megan into Connie Carr's increasingly chaotic bedroom.

"This man," I said, "has a scar on his left hand—see it?—that I hope is going to match that blood spatter pattern you cut out of the cab of the truck the other day. Remember that?"

"How could I forget it?" she said, "You ever try to cut fabric out of one of those babies? Shee! Talk about built to last!"

"Okay. I want you to bring this to Jimmy Chang's attention as soon as you get the body to St. Paul. Will you? If he's so hot to make his reputation on spatter patterns, let's see him start by proving this is the man who killed Wayne Asleson."

"Hey," she said, pointing a light into Roger Carr's eyes, "DNA tests are gonna prove that for you, if all this blood matches the spatter pattern. So who killed this guy? Do you know?''

''No. But I'm hoping you're gonna help me decide if he was shot with the same gun.'' I told them about the casing we hadn't found and the bullet I believed was in the mattress, and they agreed to look for both as soon as they got the body loaded.

''This is a pretty straightforward crime scene,'' Zumwalt said, blazing away with his flash camera, ''not gonna take us long, huh, Megan? No miscellaneous body parts, no scattered entrails, no messages written on the walls with feces—''

''Is there a way to get him to stop?'' I asked Megan.

She giggled. ''Well, it has been a pretty bizarre week,'' she said, ''he's entitled to rave on a little. Let's see, you're not gonna do prints here, are you?'' she asked him.

''Nah. Wait'll we get him back to the lab,'' Ted said. ''I'm pretty sick of bending over this bed, aren't you?''

''Jake, can your guys do the rest of the print work, dust the furniture, and so on?''

''Sure. You'll take all the bedding along, right?''

''Yes. I don't think we need to take the whole mattress, we'll just take samples of the bloody part. We can dig for the bullet when we do that. And Ted, now, keep an eye out for that casing when we take out the bedding.''

I helped them bag the body and get it on the folding gurney. The TV van had pulled up behind the BCA van, and the cameraman was nicely set up just outside the Carr's doorway. He got some good footage as Ted and I maneuvered, grunting, out through the cramped space. Kevin's disaster groupies got pretty excited at sight of the body; Darrell had to show some of his muscle to keep the amateur photographers behind the yellow line.

Megan was fussy about how the bedding had to be folded and stored in the van so the pieces didn't contaminate each other. "Come on, Duffy, it's all from the same body," Zumwalt said, but she held one small, blunt-fingered hand aloft, looking stern, and he sighed and did as she asked, lamenting softly, "I'm just putty in this woman's hands."

When they got to the mattress, I held the bag while they dug. Blood had soaked almost all the way to the underside, so the sampling went on and on. We were almost to the bottom cover when we found the bullet, crumpled and bloody.

"Looks like a piece missing," I said. "Not gonna be much use."

"You'd be surprised what shows up under the microscope," Megan said, "and we might find the rest of it inside the head. Also, that casing could still turn up in all this fabric."

She promised to let me know when the autopsy was scheduled, and I helped them tote bags to the van.

After they drove away, we shortened the crime scene tape and pulled it closer to the house, to allow cars to drive by in the road. Kevin helped me put a sign on the front door that read, "Crime Scene. Please check with the Rutherford Police Department." Angela Peavey had come back, hugging her coat around her in the early winter twilight, and stood glaring at the sign and the tape, trying to talk me into taking these unwelcome signs of trouble off her premises.

"I can't do that yet," I told her. "We don't know

where Mrs. Carr is, for one thing. Also, we have to come back here tomorrow and dust for prints, and search this place again when there aren't so many people in it." I still thought we might find the casing there.

"As soon as you've done all that, will you get this trash out of here? Please. Because it's just gonna *kill* my business, you know. People don't like to see trouble." I was getting tired and very hungry, so I just turned and stared at her, hoping she might realize how self-centered and stupid she sounded. She glared back at me briefly, said, "You don't give a damn about any of that, do you?" and walked away, muttering to herself.

Kevin, beside me putting the staple gun back in the sign kit, said softly, "You're kind of a crab, aren't you, Jake?"

Darrell was trying to lock the door with the keys Kevin had brought back from the office. "Hey, Kev," he said, "is it the round key, or the obligated one?"

TEN

"THE FIRST THING WE NEED to do," I told my crew Friday morning, "is review this crazy week and make sure we're all on the same page. After that we'll divide up the new chores. Uh, wait a minute, the chief said maybe he could sit in on this. Kevin, would you tell him we're ready to start?"

Kevin walked out the open door and right back in with McCafferty, who said, "Sorry to be late," and took a seat at the foot of the table.

"Okay, here goes. I believe we found Wayne Asleson's shooter yesterday. Unfortunately, the suspect is dead, so we don't get to ask him any questions."

"But you're sure, now?" Lou asked. "We can prove Roger Carr shot his partner?"

"He's got a railroad track scar on his left hand," I said. "They're testing the blood and measuring the scar at BCA. If the DNA from the dead man matches the DNA from that spatter pattern on the roof of the truck, and the tracks on his hand are the right distance apart, we'll know who killed Wayne Asleson."

"Well, now," Lou said, "isn't that convenient."

"That's what Pokey said. That bothers you too, huh?"

"Yeah, kinda."

"If the evidence supports that conclusion, though, we gotta go for it. Don't worry about running out of puzzles, because we've got a better one, now, than before: if Roger Carr killed Wayne Asleson, who the hell killed Roger Carr?''

"He was found in his own house, and his wife is missing," Frank said. "What's wrong with the spouse as a suspect?''

"Ordinarily nothing. But this killing doesn't make much sense as a domestic dispute. In the first place there were no signs of a fight; the house was neat. Also, he's been missing since Sunday, when his partner got killed and his rig disappeared. The scar on his hand appears to date from about that time, and if the blood work supports the rest of the evidence, it's reasonable to suppose he killed his partner. Whatever his reason for doing that, his wife couldn't have been involved in it; she'd never even met his partner, and she was in Winona taking care of her sister when Wayne was being shot.''

"Besides," Lou said, leafing through reports, "didn't I read in here somewhere that the wallet that was found with the body had fifty-seven dollars in it? What wife's gonna off her husband and then leave fifty-seven dollars in his wallet?''

"Good point. Have we established where Wayne Asleson was shot?'' Frank asked.

"No. Somewhere between I-Thirty-five and the Twenty-ninth Street overpass on Burton Hills Drive. But we still don't know why they left the Interstate. Their boss claims they'd never do that voluntarily. They have an assigned route, and they stick to it.''

"It would help," Ray said, "if we had some idea why Roger Carr killed Wayne Asleson.''

"Wouldn't it? Which brings us to you, Bo. How'd your day go, yesterday? You find anything in that trailer?''

"Nothing. I took my Valtox kit up there and tested a couple dozen cartons in the morning. In the afternoon one of the sheriff's deputies from Mendota Heights brought his dope-sniffer dog over. We took that puppy all over that trailer, and all he did was yawn."

"What does Dietz say about the load? He met you there, didn't he?"

"Came with all the records and stayed all day. He swears the trailer contains exactly what it's supposed to contain, CD players and amplifiers for a store in Duluth."

"Okay, and the cab of the truck, did you ever get around to that?"

"First thing in the morning. Because I was sure I'd find an extra compartment under that bunk that would explain everything." He shook his head sadly. "There's nothing under the bunk but flooring. It's an honest piece of work. By the way, that cab was built right over here in Winona, Dietz told me yesterday. It's never been to Mexico."

"Well. I've been wanting to eliminate some possibilities, and you just did. Good work." Bo didn't look gratified. "Cheer up, drugs aren't the only vice there is. Let's talk about Roger Carr's gambling addiction."

Bo raised his eyebrows. "Gambling isn't a vice anymore."

"It may not be illegal, but—"

"Better believe it. Hell, the state runs most of it. And the tribes."

"Sure, but some things don't change. In olden times, when gambling was a vice, what kind of shit would you expect to find piling up around a man who couldn't stop gambling?''

He held up a hand and ticked off on his fingers. ''Unpaid bills, household items hocked, angry friends who want their loans returned. Eventually, divorce and a loan shark on his tail.''

''Excellent. Why don't you spend today looking for signs of some of those things in Roger Carr's life? Check hock shops, loan sharks, collection agencies— ask Dietz if anybody's tried to garnish his wages, huh?''

''I can do that, sure.''

''You next, Kevin,'' I said. ''What did you get out of the crowd around the crime scene yesterday?''

''Shep and Celia Squires live next door,'' Kevin said. ''They didn't hear anything unusual night before last. They watch TV every night, they like cop shows and action movies—also she wears hearing aids, I noticed. I don't think one loud noise next door would bother them much, unless it happened after midnight. They didn't know the Carrs at all well. They say Connie said hi sometimes, but he was almost never there.

''The lot on the other side of Carr's house is vacant just now, and the one beyond that is occupied by a couple of young men that nobody seemed to want to talk about. Looks like they all think they're a gay couple, but they don't want to say so for fear of sounding bigoted. Anyway, they work odd hours and nobody talks to them. I got their work addresses from Mrs. Peavey, in case you want me to follow up with them. There isn't any house on the other side of the Squires, that's the corner.

''Angela Peavey made a couple of snide remarks about Connie not being at all friendly. Another woman in the park said, 'The Carrs aren't mixers.' Nobody knows how they got along with each other. They didn't have loud fights, everybody agreed on that.''

"In other words," I said, "you didn't get diddly."

"Hey," he said, defensively, "I can't get diddly if diddly ain't there."

The chief raised his right hand like a kid in school and said, "I don't want to slow you down here, but—"

"Go ahead," I said, "we're floundering anyway."

"Well—up until now you've been assuming the two men disappeared from their rig at the same time, right?"

"Yes. But of course if Roger killed Wayne, he must have stayed with the rig a little longer. And he may or may not be the one who abandoned the trailer in the truck stop and drove the tractor into Schellhammer's field. Now that we've found Roger, and we know he's been shot, it's worth thinking about the possibility that he may have had a helper."

"Okay, but here's my question: who's the last one talked to them?"

"As far as we know, Connie Carr. She says Roger called her from someplace in Iowa, midafternoon Sunday. Also, at three o'clock Sunday afternoon, they sent an e-mail to the dispatch office of Clearwater Trucking."

"Saying what?"

"Uh—" I scrabbled through my notes. "Well. Good question. I don't have the wording of that message, I guess. What John Dietz said was, 'I got to work this morning—' that would have been Monday '—and found my night dispatcher very concerned because he'd just checked his list and found one rig, Wayne's rig, that hadn't checked in since three o'clock yesterday.' Which would have been Sunday. The system at Clearwater Trucking was, they checked in every five hundred miles. Or eight hours. Whichever came first.''

"So probably just a routine all's well."

"Probably. But why don't we find out? Make that your first task, Lou: call Dietz's office, get him to send you copies of all the e-mail traffic on that vehicle since they left Nogales.''

"You got it."

"Now, Kevin, you saw both bodies. I want you to tell everybody here what you said yesterday about the entry wounds, and what the coroner had to say about them.''

"Um. Let's see, I guess I said the entry wounds looked much the same, both smaller than you'd expect, maybe half the size of a nine-millimeter bullet, dry and crusted as if they'd only bled a small amount, but the difference was that the second wound was ringed with black powder and had a star-shaped bruise around it.''

"From which you concluded—?"

"Well, the doctors said at the autopsy that the first bullet was fired from close range, but not point-blank range. About six to eight inches away from the head. From things they said while they were deciding that, I figured the second shot came from even closer to the victim, maybe with the gun right against the head. Because there was powder residue around the wound, and a star-shaped bruise from leftover gas blowing out of the barrel.''

"Good. But when I told Pokey we thought the

same gun shot both men, do you remember what he said?"

"Some kind of a put-down about that gun or a million others like it."

"Right. Good old Pokey, he does enjoy his little jokes. So that's what we want to know, did the same gun kill both men, or not? If yes, then Roger Carr's shooting must be in some way connected to the shooting of Wayne Asleson. But if no, if two different weapons were involved, we could just be picking up the pieces after two different fights."

"Well, we got both bullets," Kevin said.

"True. BCA dug the first bullet out of the door post of the truck, and we found the second one out there in the mattress yesterday. They're both badly beat up, but Megan seemed to think they might show enough lands and grooves, under a microscope, to at least show they *could* have come from the same gun. It would be a lot easier to prove that they *did*, if we found the casing of the second bullet. So, Darrell: your first job today is, go back out to Connie Carr's house, with a good big Streamlight with fresh batteries, and search every inch of that place. While you're at it, of course," I said, smiling at him, "my feelings won't be hurt if you find the gun itself."

"How much time have I got?"

"As much as you need. Stay at it till you're sure you've looked at everything. Ollie Green and Nick Kranz will be out there sometime this morning, to dust the whole place for prints. They may bring a few items back to fume in the tank. All you have to do for them is keep out of their way and don't touch anything without gloves on."

"Gotcha."

"Okay. It would be nice if we had Connie Carr here so we could get her prints the easy way. Otherwise we'll have to try to get some off an item we know is hers. Maybe she has a locker at work. That's the most troubling thing hanging fire right now: where is Connie Carr? I sure hope she's not the next body we find." I kept remembering how light and fragile her arm had felt when I held her up.

"She's never shown up at her place, huh?" Frank asked.

"No. I had squads check the house a couple of times an hour all night. I've called her several times. Nobody at her workplace has seen her. I'd like to turn the search for Connie Carr over to you, Rosie: put out an Attempt to Locate on her car and on her person. Her physical description is in the report I wrote of her interview, and the license number is the one for the Escort at the beginning of that report. Keep calling her. And you might try asking the people she works with if they know any names or phone numbers of friends or relations."

"Right, right." Rosie scribbled.

"What about the autopsy on this Carr?" Frank asked.

"They're gonna let me know as soon as they schedule it," I told him. "Have you got enough now to keep the news people happy?"

"I think so. Be good if one of you would loan a full set of these records to Lulu so she could make me a copy, in case they throw me a question I can't answer."

"I'll do it, Chief," Rosie said.

"By the way," Ray said, "is this right, the Roger Carr shooting's got a new ICR number?"

"Well, yes," I said. "I can't treat it as an extension of Wayne's case till we prove the two are connected. But we're going to have a helluva time deciding which new reports go where, because they're so closely related. In fact, you know what I think? Just copy everything you add to either file, and add it to the other one at the same time. We can always throw out some paper after the whole mess sorts itself out."

Rosie looked at Frank and smiled. "Paper piles up fast in a homicide, doesn't it?"

"Sure does," he said. He stood up and held the door open. She walked through it, and he followed her down the hall. "Is this Stacey Morse gonna fix that problem? Really, you think so?"

"Count on it," I heard her saying as they walked away. "He's going to make all this paper go away, and—"

"Rosie Doyle creates a profile," Kevin murmured.

"She took on that pileashit job as a favor to me," I said. "So please don't begrudge her if she finds a way to make a few points with it. Next question, Kevin: anything new come in overnight that we have to look after?"

"Oh, sure." He shuffled through the dispatch reports that he'd brought in with him. "Car heist at Mohawk Mall. Purse-snatching downtown. Two break-ins: apartment on Southeast Twenty-third Street, house out northwest in the Castle Heights section."

"Can you and Ray take care of those between you?"

"Sure." He slid a couple of report forms across the table to Ray.

"Okay. Lou, you've got all your usual stuff, right?"

"Yup. Pile of stuff on my desk."

"Okay. I'm gonna try to find out if there's still a desk and phone under that pile of trash in my office. Keep in touch, guys."

I remembered seeing an old metal typewriter table buried under boxes of audio tapes in the supply room, so I went down there, made space on a shelf for the boxes, and rolled the table into my office. Parked by my desk, with its metal wings raised, it had just enough surface for four wire baskets. Quickly, so I wouldn't get discouraged, I began grabbing paper items off my desk and sorting them into the baskets, one basket each for messages, reports, and letters. The fourth got the miscellaneous brochures, reports, letters marked "box holder," all the paper trash that piles up on my desk as soon as my back is turned.

When my desk was clear, I got a cup of coffee, called BCA, and asked for Trudy.

"Hey, babe," she said, "the sun is shining."

"That's what I called to say! It's twenty-six degrees here, and rising. Definite warming trend for the weekend. Let's make a plan."

"Let's open up the whole house, muck it out, do laundry."

"That's tomorrow. What about Sunday?"

"Decide tomorrow. Maybe we'll just want to stand in the yard watching icicles melt off the roof."

"Oh, whee, I forgot about that game." She giggled. "You sound up. As if you got some sleep."

"I stretched out on the cot in the women's john for a little nap about seven o'clock last night. We never got a call all night, and I woke up at six-thirty this morning.''

"Wow. You must be ready to go three rounds with a bear.''

"At least. I was seriously dehydrated, but after I had a shower and about half a gallon of juice and coffee, I burst into song.''

"Beautiful. Come home to Mirium tonight and sing for me.''

"I can't wait. Early, I hope. Depends what happens. How are you doing? I understand you sent us another body last night.''

"Yup. It's like they say on TV, opportunity abounds.''

"Cute. I'm gonna start wading through report forms and hope for the best.''

"Me too. See ya.'' I hung up and sat grinning at the phone, thinking that if Trudy came home early and still had plenty of energy, and if the weather kept on warming up, maybe dinner could be a Friday Night Special, one of those feasts where the celebrants wear fewer clothes with each course, and dessert is each other. I wrote on my notepad, "Buy wine,'' and waded into the message basket.

Milo's secretary asked, in a reverential tone, if she might say who was calling. I expected her to come back on and take another message, but Milo opened his line and said, "Jake? Thanks for calling me back.''

"Howsgoin', Milo?''

"I just wanted to tell you I came back here to my office yesterday and called three county commissioners and demanded a meeting right away, and they all came in. I told them I wasn't going into court one more time with a pile of shit like the brief that Berrigan kid laid on me yesterday. I said I was fed up with being worked to death and humiliated besides, and if they didn't get me some emergency funds so I could put a decent staff together and get caught up on all the old cases clogging my schedule, they could take this job and shove it." He laughed out loud, a couple of happy barks, and added, "I actually said that! Just like the song!"

"I'm proud of you, Milo. So are you out on your ass?"

"Au contraire. They gave me ten thousand out of the contingency fund to use as I see fit right away, and we're meeting next week to discuss a new budget. I've already fired Mickey Berrigan, and the most useless of the girls from the secretarial pool. I was going to get rid of the other one too, but she's suddenly being so good to me I might marry her instead."

"Careful, Milo. Remember what the Greeks said about hubris."

"Is that the stuff that comes wrapped in grape leaves? Don't worry," he said, "I've still gotta face Hang-'em-All Hanley this afternoon and ask for a second continuance on the guys who held up Murphy's Bar." The senior judge of the district court, not content with maximum sentences for defendants, also enjoys making the attorneys on both sides of the case look like jackasses.

"I just wanted to thank you for being there for me when I needed you," Milo said, inducing a gag reflex on my part that ended the conversation abruptly. Wherever the hell "there" was, I knew I wasn't going there for Milo Nilssen. It was pleasant to think, though, that for a couple of hours he might get comfortable enough to stop looking at his watch and shooting his cuffs.

I was picking the last pink slip out of the message basket when the phone rang. Les Miller said, "Jake, I think there's some mistake in the license number you put out on this Attempt to Locate." Les is the best field training officer in the department. When he talks, we all listen.

"You talking about the request for Connie Carr?"

"Well, yeah. You got any other ones out? This is the only one I saw."

"Uh... Actually Rosie put that out."

"I know. But when I called her, she said you had the original information, so she switched me over to you."

"Hang on." I located the license number of Connie Carr's Escort, and read it off to him.

"Hmm. That's what we've got here."

"What's the problem, Les?"

"Well. I was just showing my trainee here how to look up the owner of a car using the license numbers. But when we put it in the laptop, it came back registered to Patricia Vickers. Your report says you're trying to locate Connie Carr."

Rosie Doyle appeared in my doorway, making frantic signs for attention. I said, "Hold on, Les, I'll check it again," punched hold, and said, "What?"

"I transferred that call in here to you, because I wanted you to hear it from Les Miller with your own ears. He's saying that license number is registered to Patricia Vickers, right?"

"That's right."

"Tell him the number is right. Tell him to keep

looking for Connie Carr in an Escort with that license number, and hang up."

"Rosie—"

She made claws of her hands and held them up, one on each side of her head. Poised there like some furious freckled dinosaur, she hissed, "Will you just once for Christ's sake do what I ask you?"

Watching her carefully, I got back on the phone and told Les Miller to keep looking for Connie Carr in an Escort with the license number I had given him. Rosie Doyle listened from the doorway, bouncing anxiously. When I put the phone down, she said, "I called Roseville yesterday like you asked me."

I could not remember asking her to call Roseville ever. "And—?"

"There were three winners on the day Wayne Asleson's numbers came up."

"Oh. *That* call."

"Yeah. *That* Roseville. Two of the three winners have already come in and completed the paperwork to claim their winnings; their checks will be sent to them in a couple of weeks. The third one is coming in sometime today."

"Well, so—?"

"So her name is Patricia Vickers."

"What? *What?* What are you saying?"

"I don't know what I'm saying! I mean I know what I'm saying, but I don't know what it *means.* How can this be?"

"I don't know. Rosie, get me the number of that manager in Roseville right now." She ran to her office. I called Bo and said, "Come in my office. Bring Lou with you."

When they walked in together, I said, "Something

damned odd is going on. Just stick around here a minute.'' Rosie came back with the number. I dialed it, asking, ''What's his name?''

''Mizner. David Mizner.''

Mizner remembered his conversation with Rosie Doyle very well. He thought the strange coincidence between their winning numbers and our case was sure a funny thing. He didn't know what time Patricia Vickers was coming. ''She asked me if some time in the late morning or early afternoon would be convenient for processing her claim, and I said that would be fine.''

''We just found another coincidence,'' I told him, ''so we think her claim might be suspect. If it isn't, we should be able to clear up the confusion as soon as we talk to her. We're coming up there right now. If she arrives before us, can you arrange to slow everything down? We'd like to meet her without her knowing she's waiting for us.''

''Oh, sure.'' Mizner chuckled. ''For a third of twenty-eight million, people don't make much of a fuss about a little wait.''

''What's happening?'' Lou said when I hung up.

''I'm not sure. But whatever it is, it's gonna happen fast. You two guys, go down and check out two cars and meet us at the front door. Leave your phones on voice mail, wear your weapons, be sure you've got good batteries in your beepers.''

''Shall we tell the desk—''

''I'll do it. Go! Rosie, get a tape recorder and plenty of extra tape and meet me by the front door as soon as you can.'' I checked all of us out with the desk, put the case files for Wayne and Roger in my briefcase, and crammed my phone and camera in on top of them. On the way out, I ducked into the supply room for a couple of rolls of film, and ran down the wide front stairs, zipping them into an inside pocket. Rosie was right behind me.

"You know the address, Rosie? Get in with Bo, then, you lead." Bo's vehicle was splashed all over with salty mud; his windshield wipers were turned on high, throwing filthy glass cleaner off the clearing semicircles on the glass. Rosie ducked behind the spray and jumped in. Lou was right behind Bo with all his windows open, dumping parking-garage air.

"Leave 'em open a while, the air feels good today," I said. Rain gutters were awash with snowmelt on all the buildings downtown. Pedestrians were hopping warily across the intersections, dodging the slush thrown up by cars.

"Nothing like a good old blizzard to make thirty-six feel like a heat wave," Lou said. Heavy breathing be damned, he still drove like a cop, and he was enjoying being out on the street, noticing everything around him.

"Did Bo have to take the dirtiest car we own?" I asked him. "We don't have time to fool around."

"We took the last two cars in the garage. Where are we going?"

"Roseville."

"So, what, north on Fifty-two—?"

"Till you get to Ninety-four. Take that west to Thirty-five East and follow that north. Rosie's got directions from there."

"What are we doin', by the way?"

I told him as we rolled past snow-pillowed fields blazing with reflected sunshine, Minnesota winter countryside at its postcard best. While I talked, I loaded my camera, put fresh batteries in my beeper, and checked my weapon. Bo drove fast and steady, and Lou stayed right on his tail, not crowding but never dropping behind. When I saw Rosie pointing at an exit sign, I said, "Here we go." Lou moved into the lane behind Bo and did a close tail through the exit and along the busy streets beyond; we passed a Comfort Inn, and I saw a long building ahead of us, white with blue trim and dark glass. "That's it," I said, and we pulled in under the three flapping flags.

We parked side by side and walked together silently, coats unbuttoned, holster flaps tucked out of the way. Mizner was waiting for us in the lobby. The claimant hadn't arrived, he said. He offered coffee and an office upstairs to wait in. I refused both those favors but asked if he had a newspaper I could borrow. We took four chairs at intervals around the room, with me nearest the door, and began to do what police do better than anybody: wait.

At twelve-thirty a pale blue Chevy Caprice parked in the lot near our cars. A blond young woman in very high heels got out, said something to the driver, and closed her door. She wore dark glasses and carried a sling purse over the shoulder of her neatly tailored dark suit. The driver got out the other side and locked the car carefully, a pale young man with nervous gestures, wearing wrinkled slacks and a tattered Minnesota Vikings jacket. Something about the way he touched her arm as they walked together toward the building told me they didn't know each other well.

Rosie whispered, "Is it—?"

"Can't tell," I said, "wait." I sheltered behind my newspaper as she came through the door. After her heels had tapped on by, I lowered the paper and watched her walk past Rosie and Bo. When she was almost back to where Lou was leafing through a magazine, she turned her head to look up at the clock on the wall. I saw her profile then, and was sure.

I walked up behind her quickly and bumped her hard. The dark glasses slid down on her nose, and the wig was knocked a little sideways. "Sorry!" I said. When she turned, I looked down into the brown eyes behind the glasses and said, "Well, hi there, Connie."

The nervous young man clenched his fists and stepped toward me, but Lou and Bo were there on either side of him. He looked around at all of us and said, "I didn't have anything to do with the killing."

ELEVEN

"HELP ME OUT HERE," Frank said, "I'm a little mixed up."

"Who isn't?" I said. "Just remember this: Connie Carr's the bad guy. Or the last one standing, anyway."

"You're convinced of that, now? She killed her husband?"

"Yes."

"For the money."

"Always the best reason."

"And he killed his partner—"

"For the same money. Well, not exactly." I stifled a yawn. It was only three o'clock, but I felt as if I'd been running a marathon all day. "It's kind of complicated. You wanna come in my office and listen while she tells it?"

"Yes. Gimme two minutes to tell Lulu so she can cover my tracks."

Rutherford doesn't have one of those fancy boxes with trick mikes and two-way glass like you see on TV. The jail has half a dozen open cubicles where we question juvenile miscreants and small-time dopeheads, but for serious stuff I take suspects in my office and close the door. Rosie had already brought Connie in there. They were sitting side by side in front of my desk. I went in and asked Connie, "Is there anything you need before we start this? Coffee?

Water?'' She said no to coffee, yes to water, and watched silently while Rosie brought it.

She had regained her composure quickly, I thought. In Roseville, finding herself suddenly surrounded by the four of us, she had stretched her hands out like an imploring child, babbling, "Oh, no...not now...you mustn't—'' For a couple of minutes, she simply could not accept that she was being stopped when she was so close to the money. When David Mizner demanded to see the winning ticket and her identification, she sank suddenly into a chair, put her head in her hands, and sobbed heartbrokenly.

Her boyfriend continued to sputter denials like, "Listen, I just drove her up here in my car.'' He wouldn't shut up, so Bo and Lou took him into another room and explained how uncomfortable life could be for a suspect in a murder case. In a few minutes he was anxious to help, but he only knew about his little corner of the game.

Left with Connie, I had begun with reasonable requests to see the contents of her purse, progressing quickly to threats when she remained curled up on herself, weeping. When nothing I said got her to even raise her head, Rosie and I fast-walked her into Mizner's office, stripped her purse off her by force, and cuffed her. She had all the usual documents—social security, driver's license, and insurance card—to prove she was Constance Carr, and a second set, equally current and valid-looking, that showed she was Patricia Vickers. The photographs on the driver's licenses resembled each other closely, except that Patricia Vickers had blond hair.

Mizner and I composed a document, which he typed and I signed, that said I was taking his third claimant into custody and was taking possession of all her documentation as well. We added a sentence, for good measure, saying I would keep him informed as to the disposition of the case. Neither one of us had ever been confronted with a situation like this one, so we were composing legalities as we went along.

"If you find a way to establish the proper claimant for that ticket," Mizner said, "we'll work with you on it."

While Lou and Rosie got Connie and her boyfriend settled in the backseats of the two department cars, Bo and I stood on the slushy asphalt between cars while he told me what he had learned from the nervous young man.

His name was Russell Spilky. He lived a couple of blocks from Granny Goose's Mobile Home Garden, in an apartment above a popular neighborhood bar. He had known Connie Carr casually for some time, from the bar, where they both often met friends after work. Two nights ago she had appeared there suddenly by herself, "looking kind of wired." After a little chatter by the pinball machine, she had played the jukebox and asked him to dance. Within an hour, they were in bed together up in his apartment. She had been there ever since. Bo said Russell seemed quite dazzled to find himself suddenly cast as the neighborhood stud.

She had woven a fabulous tissue of lies around the two of them in the past forty-eight hours. First she told him about "this unbelievable piece of luck," winning the big prize in the Powerball lottery just when she needed it most, when her marriage, she said, was "failing miserably." Fed up with her husband

and hoping to find "somebody decent" to share her good news with, she had come to the bar, "and there you were," she said to him, again and again. It was like an explosion, Russell said; he'd never seen anything like the way they suddenly "clicked."

She needed a little help, though, for a while; she had to keep her car hidden in his garage so her abusive husband wouldn't find her. And she, too, had to stay out of sight, till it was time to go to Roseville to claim her winnings. Otherwise, he explained solemnly to Lou and Bo, they would be "overwhelmed by the media," a possibility that plainly thrilled him. Once, when he went out for food, she asked him to bring back an atlas, and they had spent happy hours, between bouts of lovemaking, debating the relative merits of various island hideaways.

It was only after they were in the car, headed for the payoff, that she told him she had shot her husband. She really had no choice, she explained quickly; the man had been abusing her for years, and that night he would have killed her if she hadn't stopped him. But "policemen never believe the wife," she said, so as soon as they had processed her claim and left the number of the new account she had opened in Montreal, they should drive to Canada. Why go back, she asked him, and face all those complications?

According to Russell, she never did get around to explaining to him why she was claiming the prize in somebody else's name.

"Leave the details to me," she had advised him, and he had been too besotted not to oblige.

Bo and Rosie took Russell in their car, and I rode home in the backseat with Connie, while Lou drove. We sat side by side for upward of a hundred miles,

and never spoke a word. When we got back to Rutherford, Lou took Russell over to the jail and had him
held for questioning in a homicide. Bo walked Connie
through fingerprinting and found a female deputy to
take her through the strip search and mug shots and
get her into the orange Hampstead County uniform.
While they completed the booking process, I ran
around the station making a lot of work for people.

At quarter to four the chief walked into my office,
took a straight chair into the corner behind my desk,
and sat down facing Connie. He didn't say anything,
and nobody introduced him. I dropped a fresh roll of
tape into the recorder and turned it on, spoke the ICR
number, time, and date, and named everybody present. The phone rang.

Schultzy said, "I got it for you, Jake." I copied
fast and said, "Thanks."

"Before we go any further, Connie," I said when
I hung up, "it is my duty to inform you that you have
the right to remain silent, and that anything you say
may be used against you in a court of law—" She
listened quietly as I completed the Miranda warning,
waived her right to silence, and said she would take
a court-appointed attorney "later."

"Let's get this over with first, huh?" she said.

"Okay. Patricia Vickers is your sister's name, isn't
it?"

"Right."

"Your sick sister in Winona. Except actually she
isn't sick anymore, is she? Because she died last summer."

"Well," Connie said, "yes."

"But you didn't exactly report that to everybody,
did you?"

"She died at home," Connie said. "I can't help it if everybody didn't get word."

"Oh, well, it's a little more complicated than that, isn't it? Social Security and the Welfare Department were never notified about her death, and somebody's been drawing her disability check and food stamps ever since."

"My mother and I had plenty of extra expenses helping her at the end! It's only right we get a little of it back!"

"Uh-huh. So then, since you kept her social security number and driver's license all current at the same address and phone number, it was handy when you needed a new identity to use to claim your husband's winning ticket, huh?"

I saw the little light flare in her eyes, and then she looked away and began that characteristic twitching people do in a chair when they're about to lay a big stinking whopper on you, and I knew I'd figured it right. Watching her careful eyes come back up to meet mine, I was tempted to let her play with it a while longer, since she had turned out to be such a colorful and talented liar, but there was a lot of work to do yet today, and I had a favor I wanted to do for Cathy Niemeyer, if I could. So I said, "Except it wasn't your husband's ticket either, was it? Wayne Asleson bought that ticket, didn't he, Connie?"

"How would I know?"

"Why else would Roger kill him?" I watched her a minute. "Or did you kill him?"

"Of course not. I was never anywhere near their truck."

"Well, now, Connie, that isn't exactly true either, is it? Some time or other you must have been in the cab of that truck, because we've already matched one of the fingerprints we got from you today with one that we found inside that cab.'' I could feel the chief's eyes on the back of my head. He knew very well that unidentified fingerprints wouldn't have been entered in the AFIS database, and since we don't have electronic scanning in place yet, there was no way I could have got Connie's prints to St. Paul so soon. What I had was Trudy's assurance, after I described the core, delta, and minutiae from one of Connie's prints on the phone, that it sounded like a good match to the unidentified forefinger print they'd found in the cab. I felt certain the scanning equipment was going to back me up when we got to it.

In the end my mini-whopper didn't matter, because just then my phone rang again and Darrell said, "Jake? I found the gun."

"Aw, Darrell, that's just about the sweetest thing you ever said to me." We both laughed. "Where was it?"

"Under that silly-looking Bo-Peep thing in the planter at the end of the street. Shee! You know, I was standing out in front, getting ready to leave, after I looked all day and never found anything, and all of a sudden I remembered Pokey coming in here the other day saying something about how he bet they had land mines under the goosies. Remember that? So I walked over there and looked under that wooden cutout figure, and there was a spot under one leg where it looked like the ground had been dug up a little, so I got a screwdriver and poked around. It wasn't buried very deep, I hit it on the second probe."

"It's a Walther?"

"Sure is. Kind of a neat little thing."

"Bring it in and get your gold star."

I punched off, sat back, and smiled at Connie Carr. She'd been listening; her face showed she knew it was over. "He wouldn't stay away," she whispered bitterly. "Crazy fool." She seemed to shrink, and for a few seconds she looked old.

"I begged him," she said finally, in a normal voice. "I said just be patient a little longer, and we'll have it all. But he had to spoil everything."

She told us the whole thing straight through, then, in just a few minutes. She didn't need a lot of prompting. She had a deep need to tell somebody about the heavy load she had been carrying, ever since her husband, "her crazy husband," had called her last Sunday afternoon in the middle of that terrible storm to tell her he had just shot his partner in a fit of jealous rage.

"Where was he?"

"On the public phone in the parking lot at the welcome center, just inside the Iowa-Minnesota border. The storm got so heavy right there that they couldn't see the road, so they pulled in there to wait for it to lighten up a little. As soon as they parked, Roger said, 'Hey, last night was the Powerball drawing, let's check the net and see if we won.' Wayne was back in the bunk changing clothes, getting ready to take a nap, so Roger got on the Internet and checked his tickets against the winners and came up empty. He read the numbers to Wayne, and Wayne said, 'What? Can't be.' He jumped up in the passenger's seat, just as he was, with no shirt and one shoe off, to look at the numbers. Then he started laughing and yelling, 'I won! My God, those are my numbers, I won!' "

Connie turned her hands up in a helpless gesture.

"Roger told me, 'I looked at him over there laughing and crowing, that dumb shit that didn't even know how to put circles around the numbers until I showed him, and there he'd gone and won, on his first ten-dollar bet. After all the money I'd put into that lottery. It just wasn't right, I couldn't stand it. I reached under my shirt and got my gun and shot him in the head before I even thought what I was doing.' "

"He'd had this gun along the whole trip? Did Wayne know about it?"

"No."

"How could he have a gun in that small space and his partner not know?"

"He'd gone to a lot of trouble, got a special little flat shoulder holster that wouldn't show under his shirt. And of course they kept their jackets on most of the time. He was careful because it was strictly against the rules. But he'd heard all these bad things, about how dangerous the desert around Nogales was, full of drug traffickers and immigrants hiding from the border patrol.... To tell you the truth, Roger was getting kind of...not quite right in the head."

"In what way?"

"He was completely out of control about gambling. He knew I was getting fed up with it, so he kept trying to find somebody else to blame, and after a while he began to believe his own stories. He got a lot of those magazines that say the government's out to take away our freedom, it's all a conspiracy. Other days it was the big corporations that were robbing the citizens blind. He was starting to see enemies everywhere.

"When he came back from his dad's farm with that gun, just before this trip, I told him it was the dumbest thing he could possibly do when he was starting with a new partner. But he had this fantasy that they'd get held up or something out in the desert, and he was going to save the day with that little souvenir pistol of his dad's and be a hero to everybody."

"I'm surprised it still worked after all those years."

"I guess his father kept his guns cleaned and oiled whether he used them or not. They talked a lot about the bullets being old, but it turned out they worked fine too." She shrugged.

"For sure. Okay, so Roger's rolling along in the truck with his gun hidden from his new partner, he's learning a brand-new route, and in the middle of all that he talks his new partner into playing the lottery? That sounds really crazy to me."

"Oh, but that was just SOP for Roger; one of the most infuriating things about his addiction was that he got so he was just determined to have everybody around him playing the same games he was playing. That's why his previous partner bailed out on him, you know."

"I did hear that."

"Yes. He didn't want to gamble, and he was sick of arguing about it. I couldn't stand it anymore myself; I told him if he mentioned one more game of chance in front of me, I was leaving. Period. So he shut up about it at home."

"But they'd been out of the state for over a week. How'd they get the tickets for that Saturday night?"

"Ah, you don't play either. They bought an advance draw, in a truck stop near Albert Lea, on their way out of the state that first night they drove together. You pay for ten drawings in advance, pick your numbers once, and play them twice a week for five weeks."

"Wow. Roger must have been some salesman."

"On that one subject he was."

"I suppose it helped that Wayne already had those six lucky numbers in his head."

"I guess. Something about his girlfriend's birthday, I don't know."

"Okay. Next thing. Roger shot Wayne in the welcome center, and nobody noticed?"

"It was terrible weather, there weren't any tourists around. There was one other truck, he said, at the other side of the parking lot when they got there, but the snow got so thick Roger didn't even notice when it left. He said for a while he could hardly see the front of the cab."

"What did he do, then?"

"I think what he did was get out of the truck and walk around it for a while, crying. He was scared out of his wits. Eventually he pulled himself together enough to find some change and make a call to me. He could hardly talk; I couldn't understand him at first. He kept saying, 'The windshield's all covered with blood, what'm I gonna do?'" She rolled her eyes up. "The easiest part of all, is what he was hung up on. When he calmed down enough to listen to me, I said, 'Have you got the ticket?' and would you believe it, he hadn't even thought about that? He just killed Wayne because he got so mad. Till I asked about it, he never even thought about trying to cash the ticket."

Connie had thought of it right away. She sent him back through the snow to see if he could find it. It wasn't in Wayne's clothes bag or his drawer, and Roger could not bear to touch the body of the man he had just murdered. He found more quarters and tramped back through the snow to the phone. His anger was coming back, now; he was anxious to find something to blame her for. "Will you shut up about the goddamn ticket?" he yelled, "I'm in a jam here, and I need some help." That was when Connie knew she had to figure everything out herself.

"I told him to go back and move Wayne's body back into the bunk and cover it up, and wash the blood off the windshield and the window. He had plenty of glass cleaner and towels. I knew he couldn't get the blood off the door or the seat or any of that, but he was already in Minnesota, he wasn't likely to get stopped. I said, 'Switch onto I-Ninety at Albert Lea, and come over here. I'll meet you in the parking lot at the farm implement store north of the airport.' I knew they'd be closed Sunday night."

By the time he arrived, he was totally spooked from riding with a dead body, and beginning to get the shakes. She had brought him a half-pint of brandy, and she let him sit in the front seat swigging it while she got in the back. She wrapped Wayne's jacket and shirt around herself to keep the blood off her clothes, and began searching his pockets. The Powerball ticket was in his wallet.

"He hadn't signed it," she said. "Most people don't; they figure they'll take care of that if they win something. As soon as I found that unsigned ticket, I told Roger to get his head out of his ass and help me get rid of all this mess."

They stopped in the middle of the overpass, turned on the emergency blinkers, and threw Wayne's body over the railing.

"That was the hardest part of the whole thing," she said. "Roger was so strong, ordinarily, he could have pulled that body out of the bunk by himself, but by the time we got to the overpass he had the shakes so bad he could hardly even help me. He was better, though, once we got that body out of the truck.''

She had already realized that the way to win was to slow down the search. That's why she kept Wayne's wallet and keys, everything from his pockets that would have identified him.

''And is that why you split up the truck?''

''Partly. Also I wanted to get the bloody part as far off the road as possible, and Roger said he could maneuver better without the load.''

She had followed in her car to the truck stop, where they ditched the trailer. She rolled Wayne's bloody jacket and shirt into a bundle, took it along with her in the car, and threw it out a few miles along, at the top of a windy hill. After that she followed Roger again, to the track back of Schellhammer's woods where they left the tractor.

''It was just bad luck that you found it so fast,'' she said. ''It could have been a lot longer.'' After Roger had parked the truck and walked out to where she waited by the road, she drove them both to Eagan, where they picked out a motel for his hiding place; it was near the airport but small and off the main highways. ''He agreed to stay out of sight and be quiet till I got everything lined up,'' Connie said. ''I should have known he wouldn't.''

They had agreed he should get no phone calls, but he found a public phone nearby and began calling her every few hours. ''I told him I had to go to Winona and get all Patty's documents. And I had to go out to a public phone to call the lottery office, so there wouldn't be any record on our phone. I had to get a wig so I could look like the picture on Patty's driver's license. High heels so I'd look two inches taller. I mean I had a lot to do. He knew that, but still every time he got me on the phone, he started yelling why wasn't I ever home. It was driving him bananas that I had the lottery ticket and he wasn't there to watch me.

"By the second day he got obsessed about his car. He had to have wheels, he said, he felt trapped, I had to go to the trucking company yard and get his car and bring it to him. He was getting nuttier by the minute. Still, I thought if I could keep him quiet a couple more days, I could finish the paperwork and we'd go." Her eyes made a sneaky little trip around the edge of the ceiling and then she said, "Or I could go. Was what I was starting to think."

"You decided to leave him there, huh? Take the money and run?"

"It was obvious he was gonna blow wide open before long. I thought, why let him spoil it for both of us? If I could keep him out of sight a little longer— but then the crazy fool went and got his own car."

"Is that what happened? He took it himself?"

"Uh-huh. Went over there in the middle of the night Tuesday, got the extra key he kept under the fender, and drove it away. Just pure luck nobody saw him. For a while nobody even noticed it was gone, I guess, but then they noticed and called you, and you called me and told me it was gone. I knew right then I was gonna have more trouble with Roger.

"Even then, I didn't give up," she said, as though she expected me to applaud her persistence. "I thought I might be able to get everything done and get out of here before you found him. But then the idiot came home.''

''He just turned up at the house?''

''While I was at the beauty shop being fitted for the wig I'd ordered. I came home and saw that big old rear end of the Chrysler sticking out of my carport, I almost dropped my teeth.''

We were coming to the hard part. I asked her gently, ''Was he asleep when you came in the house?''

''Mmm-hmm.'' She raised her hands, clasped them together behind her neck, and began to rock her head gently in her cradling arms.

''Where'd you find the gun?''

''It was right beside him on the bed. That's the kind of a fruitcake he was turning into, the kind that keeps a loaded gun right out in plain sight. Handy, so he could threaten his wife with it probably, as soon as she came home. But he laid down to read the paper like he always did, and just like he always did when he read the paper in bed, he fell asleep.''

''So you picked up the gun—''

''I didn't even stop to think. I was frantic with worry, he had driven me to the point where I didn't know what I was doing anymore—''

She was already going for the diminished capacity defense. ''Did you take the safety off?'' She looked at me blankly. ''The little lever on the slide that covers the red dot.'' She had no idea what I was talking about. ''Never mind,'' I said, ''go ahead.'' I'd been hoping to get a confirming detail, but had only risked distracting her. I held my breath till she went on.

''I didn't even take the paper off his face. I just

picked up the gun and put it against his head and pulled the trigger, hoping the darn thing would go off. I don't know anything about guns, but I guess I must have done it right.'' She rocked her head a little more. ''It sounded very loud. I expected people to come running from everywhere. But nobody came and Roger never moved, so after a long time standing there I put the gun in my purse and put on my coat and left. On the way out of the park I stopped and dug a little hole under Bo-Peep with a bottle opener I had on my key chain, and stuck the gun in there. I couldn't make much of a hole in the dirt but I heaped some extra snow on top of it. But of course the stupid weather had to warm up then, and everything started to melt.

''I've never had any luck at all, from the start to the finish of this,'' she complained bitterly. ''I worked so darn hard and did the very best I could, but I never had any luck.''

The chief got up abruptly, said, ''See you a minute?'' and walked into the hall.

I followed him as far as the water fountain, where he turned and said, ''Woman's work is never done, huh?''

''Right. And husbands are no damn good. There is one positive thing coming out of all this—her statement makes it crystal clear that the ticket was Wayne Asleson's. I believe we're gonna be able to get a nice pile of money for Cathy Niemeyer.''

''Good. And you've got enough physical evidence to make this story stick, right?''

''Like glue. And the gun's gonna give us the rest.''

''Good. Isn't this the damnedest thing? She didn't

even know enough to look and see if the safety was off, but she killed her husband as neat as you please."

"It's wonderful. Kevin's gonna shit purple when he hears the Carrs did all this destruction with two lucky shots in a row."

He laughed. "Damn good police work anyway, tell all your crew I said so."

"I will. Thanks." I went back to my office and told Connie we'd have a transcript of today's interview ready for her to sign Monday. Rosie put the cuffs back on her and walked her over to Women's Detention, and I took the tape out to be transcribed by the weekend support group. I rang my house and found Trudy already home and cooking lasagna. "What kind of wine shall I bring?" I asked her.

We were debating the relative merits of Chianti and merlot when Bo appeared in my doorway. "Gotta go," I said, and hung up.

Bo said, "I'm sorry to interrupt."

"You're not. We're done."

"I just got a call from Diane."

"Oh, shit. What?"

"She's in jail. In Austin. She's crying, asking for help. It might be a break, really."

"Go," I said. "You can finish up reports later."

"Sure. But I'm due to pick up Nelly in half an hour."

"One of us can do that. Can't we? Is she afraid of strangers?"

"I've taught her not to get in a car with somebody she doesn't know. She'd be okay with you—she's seen you a couple of times, and she likes you, I thought maybe—are you done talking to that Carr woman?"

"Yes. I don't know anything about kids, Bo, but I'll get Nelly and take her to my house if that'll help."

"God, it would. Rosie knows the new day care address. Thanks, Jake."

"It's okay. You got my home number? Go then. Good luck."

I called Trudy back and told her the evening's plans had changed a little. She told me to call on the way home if I found out what the kid liked to eat. I caught Rosie cleaning up her desk; she said, as she was looking up the baby-sitter's address, "You gonna be okay with this little girl, Jake, or you want some help?"

"I think I'll be okay," I said. "She's too short to kick me in the crotch."

"Just keep your gloves on," Rosie said. "The teeth can be pretty devastating."

The house was only a few blocks from Granny Goose, actually, on a short block between the railroad tracks and the creek, in a row of modest one-family houses with large fenced yards.

There were three small heads looking out the front window. One of them was Nelly. The door was opened, as I walked up to it, by a boy about five. He watched me carefully a moment and then yelled something I couldn't understand. A gray-haired woman straightened from buttoning a child's coat and came toward me. I had my badge out, ready to explain who I was, but as she looked up at me quizzically, I saw that she had one green eye and one brown one.

"Maxine?" I touched her hand, unbelieving, and then the years melted away. "Maxine," I said, "It's really you, isn't it? Oh, Maxine." My arms went all the way around her now.

EPILOGUE

"I'M SORRY I keep crying," she said. "I can't seem to stop."

"You cry all you want to," I said, blowing my nose. "We never had time to, that day, did we?"

"They took you away so sudden! Not even a minute to say good-bye. That woman was there, with two policemen, saying, 'Get his things.' Remember? She said, 'This boy's not staying in this house another day.' As if we all had the *mange* or something. I mean she was *right*, but—"

"She wasn't right. She was a battle-ax. I remember you packing my clothes and saying, 'Well wait, have I got all his socks?' "

"And I wanted so much to put *Treasure Island* in too, but it was a library book," she said. "We were only halfway through reading it, and you liked it so much. Afterward I kept thinking that was the worst part: that they wouldn't let you stay until I could finish reading that book to you. Did you ever read the rest of it?"

"I don't remember. The worst for me was the seeds."

"Seeds?"

"That we ordered from the catalog, remember? During a big storm, a lot like this one we just had, only later in the winter, sometime in March, wasn't it? The house was cold, so you and I and Patsy sat on the couch with a quilt over us, and picked out seeds to order from the Burpee's catalog. You said I could plant two rows, whatever I wanted. I chose string beans and bachelor's buttons." We laughed together then, holding hands. We were sitting at the kitchen table, where we always sat in Maxine's house, and it seemed to me I could never get enough of holding her hands. Nelly was eating a cookie and watching us with great curiosity.

"That was the last week you were with me," Maxine said. "I do remember the catalog now. We were sitting on the couch in our coats and overshoes with a quilt over us, because the power company turned off the gas."

"I guess that's right. All I remember is the beautiful pictures of flowers. Why did they turn the gas off?"

"Because Lucas got drunk with the money I gave him to pay the bill. Why did I ever give him the money? I knew better. But he said, 'Oh, you don't trust me,' and I gave in and let him take the cash." She shook her head. "He really couldn't help himself, Jakey."

"I know. He was always good to me."

"To me, too. Well, if you leave out stealing and lying." We laughed again together, roaring with laughter while the tears ran down our cheeks. One of Maxine's special skills had always been making catastrophes into jokes. She'd had plenty of practice, with Lucas for a husband.

"Listen, Maxine," I said finally, "I have to explain to Nelly what's going on here, and then I have to take her home and feed her. But we're going to get together this weekend, right? We're going to see a lot of each other from now on."

"Oh, I hope so, Jakey. You're not gonna disappear on me, are you? I kind of feel like this is all a dream."

"Absolutely not a dream. Real as this." I knocked on the table. "I'm gonna call you tomorrow morning and make a date for Sunday, is that all right?"

"It certainly is. It's more than all right. It's supercalifragilistic —" She laughed, shaking her head, and said, "I always get stuck."

"Expialidocious," I said. "Now, where's this pretty girl's coat?"

Nelly was a little dubious about being buckled into a strange red pickup and going to a house she'd never seen, but she didn't make a fuss. She just wanted to be sure of the facts.

"You know my Daddy at work, huh?" she asked me, as I shortened the straps.

"That's right. We worked together all day today."

"But then he had to go get Mommy?" She listened carefully, to be sure I answered all the questions the same as I had before.

"Yeah, he did. She got sick in another town where she went to do some shopping. So he had to go and help her."

"Mommy gets sick a lot." She wasn't complaining, just reporting the news.

"That's too bad. Anyway, your dad will probably come get you after supper. Which reminds me, I'm supposed to ask you what you like to eat?"

"Hot dogs."

"Anything else?"

She hesitated, risked the tentative edge of a smile, and said, "Ice cream?"

"Hot dogs and ice cream, that's what I like too.

Hang on here while I ask the cook if she needs anything for this feast.''

Bo called a little after nine. Nelly, who'd been lured away from watching the door by an old Lassie movie on TV, was asleep on the couch.

"You mind if I come get her?'' he asked. "She gets scared if she wakes up away from home.'' He looked exhausted when he came in, but he said, "Diane's at Fountain Lake Treatment Center in Albert Lea for the weekend. She signed commitment papers for Mower County, starting Monday.''

"Is she okay? She's not beat up?''

"No. Just too depressed to think straight. They've got a suicide watch on her.'' He said, to Trudy and me equally, "I owe you a big one.''

Trudy said, "We enjoyed talking to Nelly. She's very well informed. And Jake got all the hot dogs and ice cream he wanted, for once.''

Bo touched her elbow and said, "You're a nice lady.'' In one practiced gesture, he lifted his sleeping daughter off the couch, blanket and all, and carried her to the car. Without really waking, she felt him there and snuggled contentedly into his arms.

I stood in the doorway, watching him drive away. After he made the turn onto the highway, I locked the door and went over and leaned against the sink. Trudy was making coffee for morning.

"Thanks for being nice about the sudden change in plans,'' I said.

"You're welcome. Tell me about Maxine, now; I've been waiting all night to hear.''

"She looked much older at first. But after a few minutes she seemed the same as always.''

"Did she know you?''

"Well, not right away. I was nine years old when she saw me last. But as soon as I started to talk, she said, 'Jake? Is it really you, my darling boy-o?'" I laughed. "That's what she used to call me. Hard to believe! Somewhere behind this big nose she recognized that scrubby little kid." I laughed again.

"You're really happy to see her, aren't you?" She began handing me pans to put away on the high shelf.

"She's the best foster mother I ever had. By a mile. While I lived with her, I felt as if I belonged someplace. Things were pretty grim sometimes, at their house, but...even when the heat had been turned off, or we didn't have anything to eat but oatmeal, Maxine would start some game or read to us, and make it all right."

"Put that one on top of the roaster. What do you mean, us? Who else lived there?"

"Her daughter Patsy. She was a couple years older than I was. She was blind. That's why Maxine became a foster mother, so she could stay home and take care of Patsy. This round one doesn't seem to fit."

"It goes inside the bigger round one. If you were doing so well with Maxine, why did you have to leave?"

"My caseworker found out Luke was drinking up the aid money and letting us all go hungry. She asked me and I said, 'No, lookit, I'm getting fat,' and tried to puff myself up, but that asshole Lucas had hung a couple of bad checks in bars. So he went to jail, and I got scooped up and put with somebody more 'appropriate.' "

"Ah, that terrible word." She touched my arm. "What else could she do, though?"

"Nothing. It was one of those times when all the answers are wrong."

"Well—" she plugged in the coffee pot and set the timer "—now that you've found Maxine, will she come to dinner? Is that the best way to start?"

"What I'd like to do is ask her out here Sunday, maybe about noon. Could we do that? So she could stay all afternoon. The weather's gonna warm up, we can make the house pretty comfortable, don't you think?" Trudy had brought our night clothes out of the cold bedroom and was laying them over the radiator to warm. "We could show her the barn and everything, and you could get to know each other. She's anxious to meet you." I put a chunk in the woodstove and turned the damper to almost closed. "I told her I live with the most beautiful woman in southeast Minnesota."

"You did, huh?" She handed me warm long johns. "You really know how to get your way about Sundays, don't you, darling boy-o?"

Kathleen Anne Barrett

Milwaukee Summers Can Be DEADLY

A BETH HARTLEY MYSTERY

**Ex-attorney turned legal researcher
Beth Hartley knows that history often
repeats itself—especially when it comes to
untimely death. The murder of a prominent
CPA sends a buzz through the historical city
of Milwaukee, and the desperate pleas of a
sixteen-year-old boy, the son of the dead man,
draw Beth into the case.**

**Beth's talent for finding the missing links leads
her to a solution as tragic as it is shocking, and
reveals why this Milwaukee summer could
turn out to be quite deadly for her.**

"...you'll be at the edge of your seat..."
—*Rendezvous*

Available August 2001 at your favorite retail outlet.

WORLDWIDE LIBRARY®

WKAB393

J.R. Ripley

Skulls of Sedona

Struggling musician and amateur sleuth Tony Kozol heads for the Crystal Magic of the Skulls Conference in Sedona, Arizona, to play guitar at the request of an old college friend, a New Age music guru. But when his buddy is found sitting at his piano—dead from the crushing weight of the piano lid—Tony finds himself investigating a murder.

A Tony Kozol Mystery

"Wacky characters, liquid prose, frequent humor, and a decidedly light plot place this in the fun, breeze-to-read category."
—*Library Journal*

Available July 2001 at your favorite retail outlet.

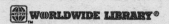

WJR390

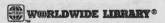